Jan Carew was born in the historic town of Dunfermline, in the Kingdom of Fife. She has a deep love of Scotland, both the Highlands where she spent childhood holidays with her relatives, and Edinburgh where she read English at University. Both settings appear in "FLOWERS OF THE FOREST".

France is her other passion; a year at the Sorbonne turned her into a life-long Francophile. She is a frequent visitor to Paris and Brittany, where she has many friends.

Jan is the author of twenty published books, both fiction and non-fiction. She hopes to publish future historical novels with a Scottish background. Her home is in South Wales where her husband is a lecturer at Cardiff University. They have one daughter who lives near London.

FLOWERS OF THE FOREST

JAN CAREW

FLOWERS OF THE FOREST

Pegasus

A CIP catalogue record for this title is
available from the British Library.

ISBN 978 1 90349 027 3

Pegasus is an imprint of
Pegasus Elliot MacKenzie Publishers Ltd.
www.pegasuspublishers.com

First Published in 2007

Pegasus
Sheraton House Castle Park
Cambridge England

Printed & Bound in Great Britain

For
Derek and Caitríona

PART I

EDINBURGH – JUNE – 1745

Chapter One

"There's the witch! Over yonder, with her draughts and her potions ready to poison decent folk. Something has to be done about it!"

The small wizened man named Wilson had a fanatical gleam in his eyes as he pointed furtively at a corner of the Grassmarket where a middle-aged woman was calmly setting up her stall. The market would be busy today and "Highland Janet", as the locals called her, wanted to be ready in good time for the customers that the bright June weather would bring into Edinburgh. She was known as a "wise woman" and her skilled knowledge of the medicinal value of herbs had earned her quite a reputation in the town. Unfortunately, it had also made her some bitter enemies.

James McNab, the apothecary, was one of them. A crafty man who never jumped till he was sure of his footing, he had been waiting for some time for an opportunity to discredit "Yon Highland bitch". A dour Lowlander, he had no time for anyone who came from beyond the Highland Line, and his resentment was fuelled by professional jealousy. The more Janet's cures were sought, the more he festered in fury, seeing his own reputation as a potion-giver reduced to the level of a quack.

Now he listened with secret glee to the hysterical outpourings of the little man with a face like a walnut. McNab decided there was no harm in stirring things up a little. With a hypocritical expression of sympathy, he gently encouraged the wee man to give further details of his complaint against Highland Janet.

"She killed my brother – that I'm sure of!" The words were viciously spat out. "She gave him medicine to take which was nothing more than poison. I ken more than she thinks and I ken that the juice that comes out o' foxglove leaves is deadly. Why else did we aye keep away from that flower when we were

13

bairns? Because we kent it could kill us, that's why!"

"Digitalis," murmured McNab, unable to resist the opportunity of displaying his pharmaceutical knowledge. "A powerful toxin, indeed. What was it ailed your brother?"

A weak heart apparently had been the victim's complaint and it was a final attack of heart failure that had carried him off in spite of, or according to Wilson's bitter belief, because of Janet's ministrations.

McNab saw a wonderful opportunity beckoning. The market was becoming busier by the minute. Groups of chattering girls were gathering round pedlars with trays of trinkets and ribbons and the Musselburgh fisherwomen in striped aprons pushed through the crowds with creels of silvery fish balanced on their heads. In a crowd, McNab reflected, anything could happen. Especially an Edinburgh crowd which was prone to the eruption of violence like a match to dry tinder, given the right kind of stimulus. The Edinburgh mob was a fearsome animal, as McNab well knew. He had been part of it himself nine years before, not out of design but carried away with it like a cork on a torrent, up the High Street and then down the West Bow until they reached the Grassmarket. He could still recall the feverish excitement, the blood lust that ended in a victorious yell of triumph as the helpless, night-gowned figure of Captain Porteous kicked and dangled from a barber's pole. The authorities had tried to reprieve the officer for his shooting of civilians. Well, there was another kind of justice that night, and James McNab had been witness to it. The very memory still made him shiver, partly from fear and partly with some dark kind of pleasure.

He looked speculatively at the little man who wanted so badly to hurt Janet but was too afraid to point at her openly in case, as rumour whispered, she had "the evil eye". Certainly many folk credited Janet with having the Second Sight, a particularly Highland gift. McNab pondered deeply and felt that the time was as right as it could be for him to finally settle accounts with that Highland slut.

If Janet did have the Second Sight, it seemed to have deserted her today. She felt totally at peace with herself and the world as she set out her little bottles and boxes with care. She took great pride in her medical skill, and the knowledge passed on to her by generations of "wise women" in her family. It puzzled her sometimes that people were so wont to associate herbal cures with magic. What could be more natural than to learn, as she and her forebears had, from the animals, which knew with unerring instinct the plant to cure them of a wound or a fever? It was by watching them that knowledge had come.

Janet's kindly brown eyes lit up with pleasure as she saw the girl making her way over to her. Maire Drummond was her mistress now, though in her childhood she had been more like Janet's daughter. Maire was orphaned early in life and there was a bond between the two women that was far deeper than usual between mistress and servant.

A skinny wee lass Maire had been in those days, and Janet couldn't bear to leave her in Edinburgh after her mistress, Maire's mother, had died. Her own desire had been to return to the Highlands as quickly as possible. She stayed for the bairn's sake and enjoyed watching Maire grow up into a beautiful young woman.

Janet noticed with pride how heads turned to look after Maire in the crowd. Though not tall, the girl walked very erect, her head held high with copper-coloured hair catching the sun. It was arranged simply with curls falling on to her shoulders and setting off to perfection the apple green gown with its wide hoop. Red high-heeled shoes and a fan completed her outfit as a young lady-about-town, though no powder or patches masked the healthy skin, glowing unfashionably from the sun. Maire's eyes widened when she saw Janet behind her array of bottles, winking brown, green and amber like polished jewels. Janet was very meticulous; every bottle was carefully labelled, made up to her own secret recipe.

The girl was about to speak when another voice intruded. It was a male voice with a Highland lilt to it, a voice she did not know.

"Och, Janet, is it your intention to put poor quacks like myself out of business?"

A young man joined them, with a warm smile which lit up his normally solemn countenance. It was a pleasant face with one arresting feature Maire could not help noticing – very piercing, intelligent grey eyes. His clothes were not fashionable like the young gallants who sometimes escorted her to a dance at the Assembly Rooms. They were in fact a little shabby but he looked like a man who would not notice such things. Janet started to laugh and the two exchanged a few remarks in Gaelic, which left Maire feeling a little left out. She could understand some of the language – Janet had taught her – but this exchange was too fast for her. She twirled the fan on her wrist in idle irritation and the young man, immediately aware of her reaction, apologised at once with great sincerity.

"I beg your pardon. I interrupted your conversation with Janet. Do forgive me."

It was impossible not to. Janet introduced the two young people to one another and Maire was intrigued to learn that Iain Macdonald was training to be a surgeon. That explained the poor apparel; students were notoriously hard-up and Highland ones most of all. They had to live for half the year on a sack of oats brought from home, which had to be replenished before they actually starved. It turned out that both Iain and Janet came from the Loch Mhor area, as had Maire's mother. Maire was even more interested to learn this. She often dreamed of going on a visit there to see her Highland relatives.

She became aware of the young man's eyes fixed on her often as he spoke. Male admiration was nothing new to Maire; she found it flattering but no more than that. She had never yet seen a man she was truly interested in – certainly not this down-at-heel medical student. In order to give Iain Macdonald no hint of encouragement – for Maire was not a flirt – she took her leave, telling Janet she wished to go round the market on her own. It was no empty excuse. Maire had not been to a market like this before.

Within five minutes, she completely forgot about the impecunious young man with the intense grey eyes and plunged into the heaving, arguing, bargain-hunting crowd that now filled the Grassmarket. She bought a pretty necklace of coloured pebbles in a soft yellowish green, which the pedlar swore would protect her from drowning; he said they came from Iona and this gave them their holy source of power. Maire was unconvinced, but the beads went well with her dress so she happily parted with her money. She was choosing ribbons at another stall, wondering why the shopkeeper was doing such a brisk trade in white ribbon, when a commotion broke out at the other side of the market.

It sounded like an altercation of some kind and at first Maire paid no heed to the angry shouts. Probably someone had caught a pickpocket; there were plenty of them in crowds like this. She turned back to the ribbons, fluttering from the stall like satin butterflies.

Then her heart leapt into her throat as a woman's scream scythed through the market hubbub. Maire knew that voice. It was Janet – she must be in some kind of trouble. Men's voices were raised, drowning out the scream and now Maire could hear how brutal and threatening they were. One word kept reaching her ears in the melee of shouting: "Witch! Kill the witch! Drown her in the loch – drowning's as guid as burning any day. Aye, and a damn sight quicker."

Panic seized Maire. She had to reach Janet and stop this madness – for that's what it was. How it began, she could not imagine. Janet was the gentlest soul on earth; she wouldn't hurt a fly. Tears stung Maire's eyes as she tried to push her way desperately through the crowds which seemed suddenly to be blocking her like an enemy. It was impossible; she could make very little progress against the amorphous, yielding and then suddenly resistant human wall. Her breath started to come in rasping sobs; she had never been so frightened. Janet represented the only security she had ever really known.

Part of the crowd broke away from the rest and could now be seen dragging a struggling woman slowly but inexorably in the direction of the Nor' Loch. This dark green and slimy stretch of water nestled at the foot of the Castle rock. Maire picked up her wide skirts and ran after the murderous gang who were now at the edge of the Grassmarket.

The day seemed to have gone suddenly dark though the sun still shone. Maire's gaze was fixed on the faces of the ringleaders who held Janet in a tight grip. One was a little brown-faced man and the other tall and pale, with a sneer of such bitterness that Maire quailed. What could she do against so many? She couldn't even reach them through the crowd. A cry broke from her as she looked vainly round for help. There was none to be seen. By the time the authorities heard of this incident, she thought grimly, it would be long over.

In despair, she pushed once more at the crowd wall to try to reach the ugly group in front. But what was this? Something was happening ahead. She could hear cries of surprised anger.

The witch-hunters were in disarray, stumbling and falling over each other as a heap of golden balls ran and bobbed under their feet. Someone had overturned a stall of oranges, which the stall holder had taken all morning to arrange in a shining and tempting pyramid, and the owner was screaming with fury. A lucky accident, Maire thought as she finally caught up with them, and then she stopped and stared. It was not chance that had stopped the rioters after all. Iain Macdonald stood there blocking their way and looking as if it would take a mountain to move him. He hurled a last orange into the sullen group and fixed them with a glare of devastating contempt.

"What in the devil's name do you think you are doing?" he began, his grey eyes glinting dangerously. There was a power about him which belied his shabby clothes; a kind of authority born of inner conviction. Maire felt it, and saw how some of the shamefaced group were beginning to shuffle uneasily and avoid meeting Iain's gaze. Her hopes rose.

"Aye, it is the devil right enough," came a mutinous reply from one of the group, a small man with beady eyes burning with hate in a wrinkled, tanned face. "She poisoned my brother and she should die for the murdering witch she is."

A small chorus of approval followed this statement but quickly died away when Iain spoke again. Not with such fierce anger this time, however. His next words fell with steely precision and remorseless logic.

"Your brother died of a simple heart attack, Wilson, for he always had that weakness. Everybody knew that. As for putting a poor woman to death for witchcraft, you seem to have forgotten that there was a law passed in 1736 forbidding such superstitious murder. You could well find yourselves swinging at the end of a rope!"

There was silence for a moment, then someone sneered, "An English law, made in London!" but with no real expectation of support. One by one, the mob drifted away, unwilling to argue further. What had seemed like an amusing diversion to break the day's monotony had lost all its savour. Maire watched them slink off, her heart thudding with glad relief.

Chapter Two

In an amazingly short time, the gang of witch-hunters melted away into the market. It was as if the entire horrifying incident had never happened. Except, Maire saw with a flash of anger, there was a cut on Janet's cheek caused by a sharp stone. Iain carefully staunched the blood with his handkerchief and made sure the wound was clean. Janet made no complaint but she was very white and shook a little; it was clear to Maire that she ought to return home as soon as possible.

"I am most grateful to you, Mr Macdonald," said Maire with great sincerity. "There is no knowing what those brutes would have done had you not intervened. I don't know how to thank you."

The young man felt uncomfortable. He did not wish for effusive thanks; he had only done what any decent man would do. Also, he wished that Maire would not look at him with her large, blue eyes soft and warm with gratitude. It was somehow unnerving. Iain was not very used to the society of young women; there was always too much work to be done if he was to achieve his goal of becoming a surgeon.

He hastily offered to escort the two women to a place where they could take a carriage home to Cramond. That at least covered his embarrassment. They walked together until they reached the High Street, Maire supporting Janet with a hand on her arm. Iain covertly noticed the warm affection with which the girl treated the servant woman, and wondered a little at it. It was unusual to say the least, but it made him like her the more. He realised with some alarm that he was experiencing stronger emotional reactions than he was used to, in the company of this girl. He wasn't at all sure he liked it. Iain had always prided himself on his self-control and the way he felt attracted to Maire was somewhat disturbing. He kept his eyes firmly ahead.

An ugly scene, which was yet another reminder of man's

cruelty to his own kind, prevented their progress any further. A crowd had gathered to see a public flogging of what looked at a distance like a couple of dingy scarecrows. Tattered and emaciated, the two men were already tied up ready for the lashing; a sad little group of two women and a few children hovered as near as they dared, in obvious distress. It was clear that they all belonged together, for they were easily distinguished from other bystanders by the black dust that impregnated every part of their skin and clothes. Their eyes showed weirdly white against this mask, causing ordinary citizens to recoil in revulsion. It was the normal reaction to the people referred to usually as "the black yins" and Maire instinctively drew back also. She had never seen these people before and she was a little afraid. They looked scarcely human.

Iain steered the two women skilfully away from the crowd and down a side street. His lips were set tight and his face had become hard. He had noticed Maire's aversion to those poor creatures and it made him angry. But why should he expect anything else of a pretty creature like her? She was only a social butterfly, and knew nothing of the real, harsh world.

"Who – who are they? And why are the men being punished?" She looked up at him as he strode along, faster than he meant to and making it difficult for the two women to keep up. Iain softened as he saw her obvious concern. Perhaps he had been too hard on her.

"Coal miners," he said. "That is why they are covered with grime and soot. They belong body and soul to the mine owners, to the extent that even if a mine is sold, the workers change hands with it, together with their families. Why should they be punished? Probably, they tried to run away and they were caught. They're lucky only to receive a flogging. It could have been death."

Maire was silent for a moment, digesting this information.

"But that means they are no better than slaves!" she said in horror. Iain warmed to her once more. She was more sensitive than he had given her credit for. He wasn't sure that he was glad of it, however. It was becoming harder all the time to dismiss her from his mind.

"Yes," he said. "Hereditary slaves. Each generation is born

21

into bondage. A terrible system, is it not?"

The journey home to Cramond seemed very quick to Maire because she had much to ponder over. She knew she lived in a cruel world. It was just that this particular aspect had not been explained to her before and it appalled her. All in all, it had been a dreadful day so far. Poor Janet!

Maire looked anxiously at her old friend. She seemed well enough now. The colour was back in her cheeks and the ugly wound showed only dried blood.

Iain had promised to visit them tomorrow to check the injury. It was kind of him but Janet did not really consider it necessary. After all, she had no small healing skills of her own. She wondered whether Iain Macdonald might not have other reasons for wanting to visit Cramond. His admiration for Maire had not escaped her vigilant eye, but she had no reason to suppose that her young mistress was in the least interested. She had enough problems of her own, poor lass, managing to survive in that hostile household that passed for a home.

Maire's spirits fell as the carriage arrived at Cramond village. She was always happiest out of her uncle's house. It was an imposing residence of two storeys set in its own large gardens. The tiled hall led to a comfortable reception room with soft woollen rugs on the wooden floor gleaming with wax polish. There were heavy velvet curtains and draperies in a rich burgundy which gave the room a warm, if womb-like, feeling. Sometimes Maire felt stifled by it all. It was a luxurious house to live in; Maire absolutely hated it.

Her guardian and uncle, Hector Grant, was a successful wine merchant who thought of nothing but making money. He had never been fond of Maire and did not even have the grace to pretend. Worse, however, was his housekeeper (and, Maire was sure, his mistress) Wilhelmina Burt. A blowsy, vulgar bully of a woman, she was a perfect match for Hector Grant for her greed even rivalled his own. Janet had caught her once in the act of appropriating some jewellery that had belonged to Maire's mother and was to be given to the girl when she was old enough. The housekeeper had tried to bluster her way out of the situation but Janet in her quiet way managed to shame her into putting the jewels back. Wilhelmina Burt never forgave the servant for this and took her revenge at every opportunity. If a spoon went missing or a plate was broken, she always accused Janet first. The Highland woman gritted her teeth and put up with this victimisation for Maire's sake. The girl needed a friend and Janet was determined to stay as long as Maire was there.

Besides, someone had to watch over her since she was beginning to arouse the interest of Grant's son, an unsavoury young man who was no stranger to the taverns and brothels of Edinburgh. Janet didn't't like the way Alec had begun to eye Maire recently. Not for the first time, Janet wondered why her former mistress, Maire's mother, had not left matters better arranged to protect her daughter's future. She had owned the house and it was always a mystery to Janet how Hector Grant had become the undisputed proprietor. She suspected murky dealing, but as a servant she had no power to do anything about it.

Fortunately, the housekeeper was busy that day preparing for a large dinner party in the evening. The extra work made her even more bad-tempered than usual but had the desirable effect of keeping her out of their way. Janet went to rest while Maire decided how to spend the rest of the day. She remembered that she had promised to visit an old school friend in Edinburgh, Sheena Ferguson, some time soon. It seemed a good idea to call on her that afternoon and take tea with the Fergusons. She longed to tell Sheena about the terrible events at the market. It would be a great relief to share it with someone who cared.

Wilhelmina Burt complained when Maire wanted to use the carriage and horses, but was too preoccupied to stop her. Maire was quite able to stand up to her now she was a young woman. The times were gone when the housekeeper bullied, and even beat her. She was no longer a child and the harsh treatment, which could have cowed Maire, had instead bred in her a sturdy independence of spirit. She was in fact much tougher and more resilient than Iain Macdonald imagined.

Four o'clock was striking at St Giles Church when Maire arrived at the Fergusons' home. She was always sure of a welcome there, even if she was unexpected. It was with dismay therefore that she saw a most peculiar expression flit across Mrs. Ferguson's face when she was admitted. Even her old friend Sheena looked taken aback. Her smile seemed a little forced and her dark eyes were wary. Not at all like her usual frank, open manner. Maire realised that she should not have come, and was sorry. The Fergusons had company, which was rare for them. Three ladies sat on the couch, and two others on chairs, chatting and sewing busily. There was an atmosphere of festivity – excitement even. Reels of white satin ribbon wormed their way from the ladies' knees to cascade in a tangle at their feet. The needles flashed in and out as the sewers worked as if their lives depended on it.

Maire was curious. What on earth was going on? They seemed to be making little white rosettes with the looped ribbon. Wasn't that the emblem of the Stuarts – the white rose? It was white cockades like these that adorned the bonnets of Jacobites who fought for King James in the '15 Rebellion.

Her eyes met those of her friend, Sheena, who had quite recovered her composure and, remembering her manners, invited Maire to sit and take tea with them. While they were sipping the expensive beverage, the sound of men's voices drifted out of the room next door. There was a communicating door which was open and Maire was intrigued to see an odd ritual being carried out. The men were drinking wine and each passed his glass over a bowl of water which held, Maire noticed with interest, several white roses floating on it. She was puzzled for a moment, then realised the significance of the gesture. The gentlemen were drinking the King's health, but it was not King George II they were toasting. They were raising their glasses to the "King-over-the-Water". Maire realised that she had unwittingly walked into a Jacobite meeting! No wonder the Fergusons had hesitated to ask her in. An odd snatch of conversation reached her from the other room. They seemed to be drinking to a "little gentleman in black velvet". Maire was interested to know who that could be; perhaps it was some kind of code.

She smiled reassuringly at Sheena and was glad to see that her friend understood the message she was giving, that she knew what was going on, but that Sheena need not fear betrayal. It was quite clear to anyone with half an eye that these people were not loyal subjects of the Hanoverian regime. All must be Tories, some were no doubt Catholics, but these considerations did not weigh with Maire. Brought up in the expediently Whig

Presbyterian household of Hector Grant, she saw no reason to respect his values and way of life above any other. Rather the reverse. She had a shrewd idea that Hector would always support the winning side in any situation. He knew which side his bread was buttered and he had no principles except money. It was in fact, Maire decided, rather refreshing to meet people who were willing to put themselves at risk for an ideal.

The tiny teacups were handed over to Mrs. Ferguson to be refilled, every lady remembering the number on her silver spoon so she would receive the same cup back again.

"Is Neil present?" asked Maire and was disturbed to see the stricken look on her friend's face. She hoped sincerely that there was nothing wrong with Sheena's brother. Neil Ferguson often escorted her to various soirées in the town; they were good friends. He was an easy-going, uncomplicated young man.

"Neil has left home to be a soldier." Sheena spoke the words slowly as if each one pained her to have to utter it. "My father says he will never speak to him again. He has disowned Neil because he claims that no son of his should fight for an army which is against the rightful king. My brother has become an enemy, Maire. Please do not mention his name again."

Close to tears, Sheena went to the spinet in the corner and began to play. Both girls were musical though Maire preferred singing. She listened to the tinkling notes with pleasure but sadness too. So the Ferguson family was already divided over the Jacobite issue. How many families would this happen to? Also, Sheena's use of the word "enemy" almost shocked Maire. It was so unlike her friend's usual vocabulary and quite outside both girls' experience. The word had ugly connotations to it; it summoned up visions of violent death that accorded ill with this peaceful sunny afternoon in Edinburgh.

The men were still in earnest conference next door. Odd phrases drifted across to Maire, interspersed with Sheena's songs, which had become openly Jacobite in sentiment: "Preparations", "French assistance" and "the Young Gentleman" were easily heard through the open door. Maire was glad to see her friend becoming more cheerful as she sang and the words of the final song resounded in Maire's mind as she carefully made her way down the narrow stone stairs into the High Street:

Then look for no peace,
For the wars will never cease
Till the King shall enjoy his own again!

Chapter Three

It had been a strange afternoon. Maire pondered deeply on the remarks she had overheard at the Fergusons'. She was young and inexperienced in matters of politics but she was no fool. What she had heard sounded to her suspiciously close to treason. This thought, like the word "enemy", struck Maire with a jolt; the day suddenly seemed less warm. A chill took hold of her and she shivered with a strange prescience, an unwanted premonition of violence and death. She had never known such a feeling of impending doom and for a brief second or two, it frightened her. Then the moment passed. Maire pulled herself together crossly. What was the matter with her? This was Janet's role, not hers. *She* was not gifted with the Second Sight – thank goodness! It wasn't like her to give way to superstitious fancies. She told herself firmly that the temporary, icy sensation was due to the high, storeyed tenements in whose gloomy shadow she walked.

She was quite glad to happen on a street brawl at the top of the High Street; it cleared her mind at once of any last shreds of nameless fear. It looked to her like a very unequal contest, however. A plump, self-important man dressed in the prosperous clothes of a merchant was laying about him with a silver-topped cane. The blows were aimed at the skinny shoulders of an undernourished street urchin whom Maire recognised, to her surprise. It was Colly, one of the Edinburgh caddies, the army of young lads who delivered letters all round the city and very efficiently too. Maire knew him quite well and had used his services more than once. The vindictive swish of the cane through the air angered Maire. She hated that kind of cruelty and could not resist interfering on Colly's behalf.

"Will you please stop this instant!" she ordered peremptorily, causing the portly merchant to almost have an apoplectic fit.

"Madam!" he sneered with false politeness, recovering from

27

his surprise. "I will thank you to keep out of my affairs. The matter is between me and this thieving wee rascal. I'll teach him a lesson he'll no' forget in a hurry. Lose my letter, would ye?" And he once more started to rain blows on the hapless caddie who was by now beaten down to the ground.

Maire lost her temper. "You great bully!" she cried, and caught hold of his flailing arm. "Whatever the boy has done, I am sure it was not meant. If anything has gone missing, you will be amply recompensed by the Caddies' Organisation. They have an untarnished reputation in their business dealings – which is more, sir, than can be said for you!" This was perfectly true; the caddies were known to be scrupulously honest.

Maire's speech drew a little cheer from some bystanders who began to take the boy's part.

"Aye, leave wee Colly alone!" boomed a large, aproned woman with sinewy arms akimbo. The merchant took one look at those arms ending in hands like spades and decided that on this occasion, perhaps discretion was the better part of valour. He left the scene hurriedly with what was left of his dignity, crude catcalls sending him on his way.

Maire helped Colly to his feet, tightening her lips as she looked at the scarlet weals across his back. His shirt was in tatters because of the scuffle. She slipped a coin into his hand. "Go home and get yourself something to eat. You'll feel the better for it."

The gratitude on the lad's face brought a lump to her throat; he scarcely knew kindness – that was clear. "Mistress Maire," he said hoarsely, "If there is ever anything I can do for you –" Words failed him and he was gone, like the will-o'-the-wisp he was. Caddies had a way of darting through the Edinburgh streets faster and more efficiently than anyone. They knew every close and wynd in the city.

This encounter left Maire in a militant mood when she arrived home. A face like thunder greeted her; the housekeeper was clearly annoyed that she had so much extra work to do for the dinner that evening.

"So my lady has deigned to favour us with her presence," was her sarcastic greeting to Maire. "I wonder if ye would come and help in the kitchen – as long as ye don't mind soilin' yer dainty hands."

It was on the tip of Maire's tongue to give a retort but she decided against it. There was no point in wilfully antagonising Wilhelmina. She could do that easily enough without even trying. The two women maintained an uneasy truce, which at times flared into open hostility. The housekeeper could not forgive Maire for being no longer under her thumb. She treated the girl as insolently as she dared, allowing for the fact that she was herself only a glorified servant. Her dubious relationship with Hector Grant lent a brazen edge to her impudence and she regarded Maire as a kind of poor relation who was there on sufferance. Maire detested the woman; the moment she began to grow up was the day she finally defied Miss Burt who was about to thrash her for some minor misdemeanour. Maire seized the cane from her and snapped it in her face. To the young girl's amazed delight, there were no repercussions from her guardian. Wilhelmina had overstepped her authority for some time and like all bullies, she was a coward at heart. She now confined her ill will to nasty remarks, and picking on Janet whenever possible.

Maire was glad she did agree to go to the kitchen. The heat from the fire filled the room and the pork and beef joints, sizzling on their spits, were turning slowly and efficiently because of the hard labour of Glen, an old collie Maire was fond of. Round and round he trotted in the treadmill hung against the kitchen wall, driving the spits round by means of a cord and pulley contraption. Maire hated that treadmill but it was the housekeeper's pride and joy. One look at Glen showed the girl that the dog was parched with thirst and exhausted with intense heat. His pink tongue was lolling out and his sides heaved with effort. One lugubrious eye looked down at her with a flicker of hope. Maire ordered the sweating cook to set the dog free; the roasts were ready in any case. No sooner had this been done and Glen was gratefully lapping a great bowl of water when Wilhelmina came bustling in. A satisfied gleam in her small, black eyes did not escape Maire though the housekeeper's expression was one of outrage. Wilhelmina was always pleased to find some fault with her to carry to Hector Grant. She opened her mouth to berate Maire but the girl forestalled her; she had not lived here for so long without learning some guile.

"The roasts were ready so I stopped them turning," said Maire. "You know how my uncle hates his meat overdone." She added sweetly, "Would you like me to decorate the marchpane for you?"

Wilhelmina gulped. She was in a dilemma. On the one hand, she longed to report Maire for interfering and "ruining" the dinner. On the other hand, she knew how deft the girl was at cake decoration; she could turn this dessert into a work of art with her arrangement of nuts and cherries. And Hector liked to keep a good table. Her pride as a housekeeper won over her innate malice.

"All right," she said ungraciously. "But get that filthy cur out o' the kitchen if he's finished his work."

"I have no doubt," said Maire dryly, "that Glen will be only too pleased to get back to his kennel." She turned away from the abominable woman and began to set cherries on the marchpane. It had been made by Janet the day before and the stiffened egg white had set crisp and snowy; no doubt Janet had not been thanked either for her labours.

The dinner party went off without a hitch. The panelled dining-room glowed in the light of many candles, which were reflected in the mirrored surface of the table. Most of the guests were business acquaintances of her uncle, except for Mr. Ramsay who had visited their house for years. He was a middle-aged lawyer and always had a kind word for Maire. She felt he was more her friend than anyone in the Grant household, with the exception of Janet. There were times when Maire wondered about the connection between her grasping uncle and this courteous man with the honest eyes. She caught an odd look passing between them sometimes; a look of silent menace as if Grant was sending an unspoken threat across the table. As for Mr. Ramsay, Maire had the feeling that he was afraid of something. But of what? How could Grant have any kind of hold over this respected lawyer? It puzzled Maire.

She found herself sitting next to Ramsay at dinner and discreetly asked him a question which had been at the back of her mind all day. She wanted to know who the "Little Gentleman in Black Velvet" was. His reaction astounded her. His ruddy cheeks paled and his eyes showed for a second, an unmistakable look of panic. Maire was sorry she had asked. In a moment, he recovered his composure and, dropping his voice, explained that the old Jacobite toast referred to the death of William of Orange who, when King of England, had fallen from his horse. It was said that the animal stumbled over a mole hill. Now Maire understood. What she failed to see was why the reference to this old saying should so upset Mr. Ramsay. He explained it however.

"It's as well not to talk of these matters in certain company," he said quietly. "And this is one of them. You live in a Whig household, lassie, and don't forget it. Your uncle and his friends would as soon hang a Jacobite as drink with one. So wherever you heard that toast, I hope you'll forget all about it."

Maire assured him that she would and they spoke amicably for the rest of the evening. He was interested in her welfare and seemed to care whether she was happy. Something told her he had a shrewd idea how things really were, but Maire made light of any difficulties she might have with Wilhelmina and her guardian. He gave her a look which was sad and warm at the same time.

"If I can ever be of service to you, Maire, I hope you will not hesitate to ask. I would like you to feel you can count on me as a friend. Don't forget – you may need one some day!" He said this very deliberately and Maire had a strange feeling she could not put her finger on, that he knew something he was not telling her.

She was glad when the evening came to an end and the guests took their leave. It had been a very eventful day and Maire felt she would fall asleep as soon as her head touched the pillow. She prepared for bed and looked for the little key with which she always locked her door. It was a habit she had; it made her feel more secure. The key was nowhere to be found, which was annoying. Maire was too tired to search for it any more; it wasn't important.

As she slipped into bed, she thought how her uncle seemed to have softened in his attitude towards her lately. He had been quite polite to her tonight. Maire wondered with youthful cynicism what her uncle wanted from her. She devoutly hoped it was nothing to do with her cousin Alec, but the thought had crossed her mind more than once. Hector Grant did seem to be pushing them into each other's company lately, encouraging them to talk and so forth. He had even remonstrated roughly with his uncouth son for using crude expressions in Maire's hearing. It was out of character and the girl was both suspicious and amused at the same time. Something, she felt, was definitely in the wind.

Snuggling down beneath the sheets, Maire drifted off to sleep quite quickly. It had been an exhausting day. She woke with a start to find Alec bending over her. He was obviously very drunk and the smell of ale seemed to fill the room. His voice was thick and indistinct as she realised with horrified anger that he was attempting to climb into her bed.

"Lemme in, Maire," he mumbled. "You're a pretty lass. I've aye wanted you. Ye don't have to worry aboot us being cousins, ye ken. There's no consan – consan –" He failed to get his tongue around the word.

"Consanguinity?" Her voice was icy. She was thoroughly wide awake now and shaking with fury and fright. She knew what he meant. There was little blood relationship between them; Alec was only a second cousin.

"You need have no fear on that score," said Maire coldly, giving him a hefty push off the bed. "I would as soon mate with a hobgoblin as you. Now take your drunken carcass out of here before I call my uncle."

Alec sniggered nastily. "Ye'll have no help from that quarter, my wee hen. It's my father who wants the match. And he aye gets what he wants. Ye should ken that by this time." He hiccupped loudly. "Why do ye think your key went missing tonight? Because Wilhelmina has it, that's why! Now stop your nonsense and let me into your bed. Stop playing the shy virgin wi' me. Ye needn't worry – it'll all be made legal in good time."

In a sudden surge of sobriety, he leapt and managed to launch himself on top of her, pinning her down and covering her face with wet, slobbering kisses. The stale smell of ale made her head spin. Maire was utterly revolted and also now a little afraid. She could hardly move. Only her hand reached out, clawing for something – anything – to use as a weapon. She touched the handle of the warming-pan with which Janet – faithful Janet –

smoothed her sheets every night, even in June. It was almost too heavy for her to lift with one hand in that awkward position but desperation lent her strength. She brought it down on Alec's head with a gong-like thud. He slumped to the side of her and Maire, with no compunction, pushed him off the bed on to the floor. He lay in an untidy heap on the carpet. For a moment, Maire was afraid she might have killed him but a loud snore set her mind at rest. He was only stunned. When he did come to, she had no intention it would be in her room. She flew for Janet, who slept nearby and was already awake with the commotion. Together, they tugged the inert Alec out on to the landing and left him there for the servants to find. It wouldn't be the first time his steps had faltered after a late night at one of his haunts like the Sulphur Club. Let it be thought he'd had a drunken fall.

Maire felt strongly that she could no longer bear to stay in this house, beautiful though it was. She had never really felt at home there and now she felt surrounded by enemies. Hector Grant had plans for her – that was clear. Why, she could not guess, for to her knowledge she had no property or expectations of any. However, to stay in Cramond would be to play the part of a fly in a spider's web. There was only one thing to do.

Janet was strangely taken aback when Maire told her of her decision. They would both leave for Loch Mhor as soon as possible. Maire had been invited often and she knew that her Aunt Isobel would welcome her help in looking after young Jamie. Besides, Maire longed to see them all; they were a link with her dead mother. She had always meant to undertake the journey; no time could be better than now.

The older woman could not help but see the sense of it. Maire had to leave this place if she was not to come to harm. That woman Burt was evil, and as for the foul machinations of Hector Grant and his degenerate offspring – Janet clenched her fists with anger. They must certainly leave, and it would be wonderful to see her home again! She missed the mountains and lochs of her native land with a sharp yearning. Why then did she hesitate?

Janet said nothing to Maire but a cold prickle of gooseflesh warned her of dark clouds looming. For a few seconds, there was a red mist before her eyes and a roaring in her ears. It was all going to happen, just as before. Nothing could prevent it. She only hoped with all the fervour of her Highland blood that she and Maire would not find themselves travelling straight into the eye of the storm.

Chapter Four

The journey to Loch Mhor took the better part of a week, and that was because it was summer. During the long Highland winter, many of the roads were impassable and the rivers too swollen to cross safely by ford or bridge.

As the terrain became wilder and rougher, it was impossible to proceed any further by carriage and the travellers had to take to horseback. Maire found the expedition very exciting; she had never been out of Edinburgh and as the soft green velvet slopes of the Pentlands fell far behind them, she gazed in awe at the towering majesty of the Highland mountains. She had never seen scenery like this, and though it was not then fashionable to appreciate the austere and rugged beauty which surrounded them, the call of the hills found an answering echo in Maire's heart. She felt as if she belonged here.

Also, it was good to be far away from Hector Grant and his hateful son. Maire felt she could breathe more freely and took deep gulps of the clear mountain air. Her guardian of course had been furious at her leaving but there was no way he could prevent it. Maire had the right to visit her relatives after all; he could hardly keep her locked up.

To Maire's surprise, they had an unexpected escort on the journey. When Janet told Iain Macdonald of their plans, he at once offered to accompany them, saying he was due for a visit home in any case. Dr Galbraith, the surgeon who tutored him, was away on a visit to Leyden University.

"And in any case," Iain added with a wicked twinkle, "my sack of oats is empty and I'm starving!" Maire interpreted his mischievous glance correctly and felt embarrassed that he should guess so accurately how poor she had first thought him. In fact, Iain's mother owned a small farm.

There were many times when the women were glad of his company. It was not safe for anyone to travel alone because of the vast numbers of vagabonds, known as "sorners", who preyed on vulnerable travellers. Also, Iain drove a hard bargain at the coaching inns, preventing the two women from being exploited and made to pay over the odds for their transport.

They were now mounted on Highland garrons, sturdy little mountain ponies which never lost their footing. They rode round shining Loch Rannoch and picked their way through the foothills of the Grampians until at last the vast range of the Monadhliath Mountains stretched before them. Maire gasped to see them, feeling tiny and insignificant as an insect before such fierce grandeur. It was almost threatening. At last, they came to the shores of Loch Mhor. It was an unusual shape and zigzagged like a jagged mirror through the bulrushes.

On the other side of the water lay the house, substantial without being imposing. Some of it was built of granite, which sparkled in the sunlight. They chose to go the long way round the gleaming fork of water because of the baggage, which would have been awkward to ferry across in the little boat which lay moored among the reeds.

Maire was conscious of a flutter of nerves as she approached the house. How would she be received, coming as she did, totally without warning? Letters took so long to arrive; there had been no time to send one. Then she remembered the warm letters from her Aunt Isobel. Surely she would be welcome here.

A servant came to meet them as they approached and led them to the stables. Maire wondered why. Then she saw a man who had an air of authority about him, giving instructions to a young stable-lad about a horse.

" – and dinna forget to rub him down well. I want none of your lazy ways here or it'll be a horsewhip you'll feel on your back!"

The voice was harsh and Maire took an instant dislike to the owner of it. Surely this could not be her uncle? She sincerely hoped not! She was aware of his cold stare of curiosity and pulled herself up to her full height. Before she could speak, however, Iain Macdonald did it for her.

"Would you let the Laird and his lady know that they have visitors? This is their niece from Edinburgh – Miss Maire

Drummond." He seemed to enjoy saying these words and it certainly knocked some of the insolence out of the man's face. Iain turned to Maire and Janet.

"This is your uncle's tacksman, Sandy Macdonald. He helps the Laird run the estate." The words were quietly said but the message was clear: the man was only a servant.

The tacksman turned to the stableboy. "Gavin, you'd best go and tell them inside. You can see to this beast later." He turned away rudely.

Soon another servant came to escort them to the door and led them in. Their footsteps echoed on the flagstones as they walked through the entrance hall. It was a large room, spartan in comparison with the Edinburgh houses Maire knew. There were no rich upholstery or velvet curtains here, only a few rather faded tapestries hanging on the bare walls. Yet the room had a kind of austere grandeur.

Maire's nervousness grew as they approached the drawing-room. Would she be welcome?

Her fears were groundless. As soon as she and Janet were shown into the drawing room, Maire found herself face to face with a woman who was strangely familiar. She realised she was looking at an older, more faded and washed-out version of herself. Aunt Isobel could not have been more delighted to see her dead sister's child. Maire liked her immediately, and found her gentle and unassuming.

Her Uncle Ewan also made her welcome with a quaint courtesy which Maire found charmingly different from the sophisticated – and at times insincere – town manners of Edinburgh. The Laird was a thin, shallow-chested man with the stoop of a scholar rather than the leader of men she had expected. He had sustained a wounded leg in the '15 Rebellion and it had caused him to limp ever since. Maire soon learned that Ewan was happiest in his library with his books; he ran the estate from there through his tacksman.

"You must come and meet Jamie," said Aunt Isobel, animated at the thought of having Maire as a companion and helper. She enjoyed indifferent health and there were times when the boy tired her. Maire willingly came, but not before she noticed to her surprise that Iain Macdonald had slipped away. He had not even said goodbye, let alone allowed them to thank him. Maire found it odd and a little ungracious. However, no doubt he had his reasons.

She put Iain Macdonald quite out of her mind when she met her cousin. Jamie was nine years old and very active. His earnest, freckled face with hair the same colour as Maire's looked at her appraisingly with the disconcertingly frank gaze of childhood. Maire hoped she came up to expectations. Apparently, she did.

"Can you fish?" asked Jamie without preamble. He added generously, "I'll show you how to catch a trout without a hook. You put your hand in the water like this –"

They became friends immediately, and frequent companions, to her Aunt Isobel's great delight. Jamie took Maire round his favourite haunts. He showed her where you could sometimes see a golden eagle circling high above its eyrie, where the shy deer ran on the hills, where you could see ptarmigan and plover and where the best peat could be found for the fire. He also rowed her across the narrow inlet to the other shore, bursting with pride at Maire's casual acceptance of his nautical skill. In fact, she was gripping the side of the little boat so tightly that her knuckles showed white, but the confident smile never left her face. Jamie adored her; he had been lonely without realising it, before she came. As for Maire, she felt she belonged to a family for the first time in her life. She looked on the boy as the young brother she had never had. Every morning she woke up, it was as if the shimmering waters of Loch Mhor and the now familiar shapes of the hills greeted her like old friends.

Not everyone, however, was as happy as she was. It did not take Maire long to realise that there was bitter discontent and hardship among the crofters on the Laird's estate. Always observant, Maire was appalled at the conditions some of the poorer tenants had to endure. The small cottages were little better than huts. Known as "bothies", they were pathetic, makeshift attempts at refuge from the elements. Made of sod, heather and stone, they could not even withstand a heavy shower of rain, let alone the snow of a bitter Highland winter. Maire shivered just to look at them.

The methods of agriculture too seemed, even to her town-bred eyes, to be somewhat primitive. At one end of the estate there was an unpromising stretch of land, not very big and pitted with stones. The ground looked as hard as iron and she wondered how the little wooden ploughs could ever break through it. Worse still, the field was divided into narrow strips or "rigs" so each person could only plough and cultivate his tiny patch. Hardly an efficient way of obtaining a decent harvest! When Maire asked the Laird about this, she was told it had always been the custom for each tenant to receive enough land "as will sow a boll of oats" and that the strips were allocated by lot each year. The tacksman, who leased the land from the Laird, was in charge of this "run-rig" system.

Maire remembered her dislike of him on their first meeting in the stables. Sandy Macdonald was a bully if ever she'd seen one. Not with the furtive sneakiness of Hector Grant who could always be outfaced if one had the courage; this man had a cold, rapacious look which, together with his aquiline features, reminded Maire of a bird of prey. A hawk rather than an eagle, she told herself. He was clever, though. She noticed the way he manipulated her uncle who, being an honourable man himself, obviously could not see through his tacksman's duplicity.

This was brought home to her one day when she came unexpectedly on a heated argument in the hall. A woman with a strong, brooding face and heavy features stood her ground opposite the tacksman. Maire knew the woman as Morag-of-the-hill. She was one of the five tenants who tilled the land leased from Sandy Macdonald on behalf of the Laird.

Maire had met Morag the previous week while she was working on her patch, sweat beading her brow. Most of the land looked very poor. Maire noticed, however, that this patch had been cleared of stones and that Morag was working what looked like seaweed into her soil. "To feed the crops," Morag explained to Maire, whose genuine interest endeared her to the older woman.

Now Morag stood with her legs apart, arms folded in defiance as she glared at Sandy Macdonald.

"What kind of justice is it, to put up my rent without reason? A poor widow like myself with a son to keep? We'll see what the Laird has to say about this!"

"Aye, that we will!" The tacksman shrugged with cold contempt. "You know the rules well enough, woman. You owe a portion of what you produce to your chief. He is the land-owner and if you manage to produce more, then he is entitled to more also."

Morag exploded. "The only way I've increased my yield is by breaking my back lifting stones and feeding the ground with the green weed I've carried myself from the loch. Sack after sack till I thought my back would break. Aye, and my son Allan's too. And now you reward me with a higher rent!"

"What is all this?"

The Laird had arrived unnoticed and all at once the atmosphere changed. Maire had been tempted to intervene on Morag's behalf but now something made her cautious. She knew little yet of Highland ways. Maybe she should listen and learn.

The tacksman's manner changed completely in his master's presence. Gone was the surly manner and bullying voice. He explained in reasonable tones how Morag wanted to resist paying her dues in spite of increased productivity. It was a very smooth performance, Maire had to admit. The tacksman presented his case so cleverly that it was difficult to pick holes in it. He didn't actually lie, just made Morag seem in the wrong. The woman had plenty of courage but was defective in cunning. The tacksman won his case and was praised by the Laird for his careful husbandry. It made Maire grind her teeth. It also made her think less of Uncle Ewan. He was a man of limited vision, in her opinion. Not willing to be involved in any of the day-to-day details of running the estate, he could not even see injustice under his nose.

Like many idealists, the Laird often had a far-away look in his eyes. Especially these days. Also, there was an undercurrent of excitement in the house which Maire detected but was not part of. It was as if everyone was waiting for something to happen. She heard fragments of conversation which would break off as she arrived and which she could make no sense of, in spite of her increased fluency in Gaelic.

One day, she was sent for by Ewan and she knew as soon as she entered the room that he had something important to tell her.

Isobel was there also, sewing quietly, but Maire intuitively felt that her aunt's mind was not on the tapestry.

"I have news for you, Maire," said Uncle Ewan. "We are expecting visitors. From France. They are important to us and I hope you will help your aunt to have everything ready to welcome them." He paused and waited for his niece's response. Maire did not know where the words came from but to her amazement she heard her voice saying them.

"Of course, Uncle. I shall be glad to help. These visitors – is one of them by any chance 'the Young Gentleman'?"

Chapter Five

The silence that followed was almost tangible. You could have cut it with a sword. The look on Uncle Ewan's face was quite comical. It was clearly the last remark he had expected from his niece. He turned to his wife with a baffled expression which seemed to say, "How much does she know?" Aunt Isobel shrugged helplessly. If I had let off a cannon, Maire thought, I could not have created a bigger stir.

The Laird cleared his throat. "No, Maire, we are not expecting him – as yet. These are his friends who are preparing the way for him. But what do you know of these matters? I know Hector Grant is not of our way of thinking. So where have you heard talk of 'the Young Gentleman'? I'd be obliged if you would tell me."

Maire began to enjoy herself now. They had thought her totally ignorant of all their plans – as indeed she was. Her sense of fun took a mischievous delight in showing Uncle Ewan that she knew at least something of what was afoot.

"I cannot tell you where I heard it because I would be betraying a confidence. However, I *can* tell you that there are people in Edinburgh who are of like minds, and await his coming with a similar eagerness."

This time, she saw with relief, she had said the right thing. At hearing this, the Laird and his wife beamed with happiness and the atmosphere in the room became suddenly festive. Uncle Ewan poured three glasses of wine and held up his own in a toast.

"To our visitors," he pronounced deliberately, "and to the more important one later, whose coming we have awaited for thirty long years."

The words resounded with all the solemnity of a vow. Maire realised that she was on the brink of a momentous event, the repercussions of which she could not even guess. Perhaps it was better so.

The next week was spent in feverish activity. When her uncle spoke of "preparations" he did not simply mean having beds ready and adequate food laid in. It was Maire's first experience of how seriously Highlanders took their hospitality and she was amazed by it. The prodigality of it all took her breath away. Normally, they ate simple meals, but now the kitchen was laden with all kinds of plenty for the coming feast to welcome the two visitors from France. Maire only hoped they were hungry!

There was a side of venison to be roasted, several hares to be jugged, various fowls including chickens and grouse to be plucked, salmon and carp for boiling, and a large game pie with a pastry crust. This was made by Aunt Isobel with the cook helping. Maire and Janet willingly joined in and were greatly appreciated for their culinary skills, especially in desserts at which the Highlanders were not so practised. At least, Aunt Isobel appreciated them. Maire was not so sure of the approbation of the other servants. She was aware of a frostiness emanating from a kitchen maid called Fiona, a slight, pale girl with eyes as green as a cat's and, Maire suspected, the nature to go with it. She had tried to be friends with her for it was never Maire's way to be uppity with servants; she knew what it was to be treated with arrogance herself. It was no good. Her tentative approaches to Fiona met with a distant politeness, and Maire felt uneasily that there were times when those strange, pale eyes gleamed with more than a hint of malice before they were quickly averted. Maire shrugged it off as unimportant. She could do without Fiona's goodwill.

It was the day the guests were expected and the kitchen was a cauldron of heaving activity. The perspiring cook was turning the venison again on its spit; Maire saw thankfully that here, there was no treadmill. She was herself engaged in whipping up a frothy syllabub with cream and wine. Expense apparently was no object. Janet, of course, had made a marchpane and was carefully decorating it as a *pièce de résistance* for the centre of the table.

Aunt Isobel arrived and shooed Maire out of the kitchen, telling her it was time to go and dress. The visitors had arrived safely and were with the Laird. Everything was in order and other guests expected soon. Maire would look a fine sight, with a shiny face and her hair in sweaty tendrils round her neck! Her Aunt was clearly proud of Maire and wanted to show off her niece that evening. This touched the girl, who was not used to anyone caring about her, except, of course, Janet. It was Janet who helped her to dress and transformed her tousled mop into a lustrous copper knot on the top of her head with ringlets falling down to her neck. Maire chose her dress with care. She knew there would be dancing tonight and since she loved to dance, she chose a swirling gown of cream silk with coffee coloured lace at the neck and wrists. She knew it would look well on the floor and she always felt happy in it. Janet smiled as she saw her young mistress twirl and perform a few steps of the minuet before a mirror. It was a long time since she had seen Maire so happy. Coming home to Loch Mhor had been a good idea after all.

***

The ceilidh was well under way when Maire came down. The entrance-hall had been transformed into a ballroom with music and laughter resounding from the rafters. She arrived in the middle of a hectic Highland reel and had to thread her way carefully through the whirling, hooting circles of dancers. She looked about for Uncle Ewan or Aunt Isobel but could not see them. The pipes swelled to a climax and the red and green and blue of the tartans danced dizzily before her eyes. She looked vainly for a place to sit down out of the melee until the dance should be over. A hand reached out to her arm and guided her to a chair in the corner. Maire looked gratefully for the owner of the hand and, to her surprise, found herself looking into the intense grey eyes of Iain Macdonald.

For some reason, she had not expected to see him here tonight. And yet – why should he not be here with all the other members of the estate? He was a member of the clan, after all. She thanked Iain for having delivered them safely and was about to tell him how happy she was at Loch Mhor when her uncle interrupted them. With scant politeness, the Laird swept her away to his table to introduce her to the two newcomers. Maire found his lack of courtesy to Iain surprising; it wasn't like her uncle to be rude or ungracious. She fancied too that a coolness existed between the two men, and wondered at it.

Not for long however. As soon as she set eyes on one of the visitors, Maire experienced the oddest feeling. It wasn't the strange sensation of déjà vu which one sometimes has on occasion, a familiarity which can't be explained. It was just that, for a frozen second, as the young man from France turned laughingly towards her to be introduced, the world seemed to stand still. Maire knew with blinding certainty that her destiny and his would be inextricably mingled. The moment passed so swiftly that she wondered if she imagined it.

His name, her uncle told her, was Alasdair Macdonald. He was the son of the Laird's best friend, who, exiled after the '15 Rebellion, had lived in France until his death at the court of "King James" at St Germain. Alasdair was an officer in King Louis' army and was here for reasons which were not explained. He looked, Maire thought, like a man with an important mission on his mind.

His handsome features showed a touch of arrogance in the tilt of his chin. It wasn't personal vanity; more an unquestioning belief in himself. He had a soldier's military bearing and a frank, confident way with him which, Maire noticed with slight acidity, brought the ladies flocking round. She herself preferred men who were slightly less sure of themselves. She was not all that favourably impressed by Alasdair Macdonald.

His friend, on the other hand, was very amiable. A small wiry man, Davie Hamilton was quietly spoken, and sincere. Older than Alasdair, he made a perfect foil for his more volatile companion.

Maire was determined to enjoy the evening. Her heart was lighter than it had ever been, she was miles away from the cold house in Cramond and she felt like a child that had been let out of school. She danced until her feet were tired. It was during a stately (and mercifully, slow) minuet with Uncle Ewan that she learned a little more of the newcomers. Wine loosened the Laird's tongue and he saw no reason not to tell his niece that Davie was in fact a wanted man.

45

"You'd never guess he made one of the most daring escapes I've ever heard of," said her uncle with clear admiration. "He was arrested years ago as a Jacobite spy and condemned to be transported to Virginia as a felon."

"How did he get away?" Maire was genuinely fascinated to know.

"The prisoners were fed rubbish, mostly offal. Davie used a pig's bladder to make an air cushion. He managed to slip overboard and keep afloat till he reached the shore. The penal boat sailed without him."

Maire was so impressed with this story that she almost missed the intricate steps of the dance. She looked across at Davie Hamilton. He looked such a quiet, unassuming man. No-one would guess he'd had such exciting adventures.

She was also touched and pleased that her uncle trusted her enough to tell her about Davie's position. She felt completely accepted as one of them now.

The conversation at the table became less discreet as the evening wore on. The Laird was excitedly describing the exact whereabouts of some very important place and Alasdair and Davie were listening intently, heads bent towards him, when Maire fancied she heard the words "French gold". She could not be sure. As she fanned herself furiously in an attempt to cool down her flushed cheeks, she saw a figure standing quietly beside them. It was Gavin, the young stable hand who took care of the horses. She had not seen him come; he had a habit of moving quietly.

"Excuse me, sir." The groom's voice was respectful enough but Maire always felt it betrayed a hidden cocksureness she did not care for. "What do you wish me to do with the gentlemen's horses?"

The Laird looked blank. He wasn't used to taking care of such household details.

"What do you think, man?" he answered testily. "Rub them down and give them food and water. I suppose they are the same as any other beasts?" He turned away dismissively but Maire noticed a faint curl on Gavin's lip as he murmured a meek apology for interrupting. What was it about that young man? The only person he seemed to have a relationship with was Fiona.

She had seen them together whispering and cuddling outside the kitchen. Maire thought they were well matched.

After dinner, there was Gaelic singing and this was for her the high point of the evening. She knew many of the Scottish folk songs but these were a revelation. They touched her heart with a yearning sadness which brought tears to her eyes. She longed to participate and finally plucked up courage to do so. There was one song she had always loved more than any other; Janet had taught her the Gaelic words. It was the old lament for Flodden when the flower of Scottish manhood was cut down. The same song is now famous in the Lalland tongue:

> *I've heard them lilting*
> *At our ewe-milking,*
> *Lasses a-lilting*
> *Before dawn of day.*
> *Now they are moaning*
> *On ilka green loaning:*
> *The Flowers of the Forest*
> *Are a' wede away.*

Maire sang it as she never had before, with total lack of self-consciousness. She felt at one with the song. It was a moving experience for her and for everyone who heard that hauntingly beautiful dirge for the dead so long ago. The last notes died away into silence.

It was broken by Uncle Ewan who praised her singing but objected to her choice of song. "This is a night to be merry, not to be thinking of sad thoughts and lost battles!" He broke the spell by calling on the fiddlers for a last reel.

Maire slipped away during this and went to the kitchen to see if she could find some water to splash her face. It was also an excuse to be alone for a moment, to collect her thoughts and emotions. She found Janet there, sitting at the kitchen table with her hands clenched before her and her eyes fixed at some point in front of her. Maire did not speak; she knew Janet would not hear her. A "*taibhsear*" did not ask to see visions of the future; they came unbidden. It was not so much a gift as a curse. At last, Janet sighed and the glazed look left her eyes. Maire saw with alarm that a tear was rolling slowly down her friend's face.

"What is it, Janet? What did you see?"

The older woman shook her head. "It is coming," she said. "Just as before. It started with your song and I had to leave. I thought I could escape it but you canna escape what is written. You canna run away from fate. I saw – much blood on the heather. I saw broken claymores and torn plaids. I saw fire and I heard the screams of wounded and dying men. And not only men –" She stopped as if she could not go on.

Maire thought quickly. She could not bear to see Janet in such anguish.

"But my dear friend," she said, slipping an arm round her. "Who is to say that you saw the future? It could have been the past, could it not? There were broken swords and much bloodshed at Flodden field and that was the battle I sang of, remember. Perhaps you saw a vision of the past, Janet! Do you not think so?"

The girl's voice was pleading and Janet did not have the heart to disagree. Besides, maybe the lass was right. Janet hoped with all the strength that was in her, that she was.

Chapter Six

Next day, after breakfast, Uncle Ewan invited Maire to accompany him on a walk with Alasdair Macdonald. The young man was keen to see the places his father had known so well in his youth. Jamie wanted to come too but was told he must attend to his lessons. This caused a certain amount of sulking which was only dispelled by Maire's promise to fish with him that afternoon.

She had an opportunity to observe Alasdair more closely now as he talked animatedly with her Uncle. The proud tilt of the head was still there but there was a wistful look in his fine hazel eyes as he listened eagerly to all the details of his father's early life here. Suddenly, Maire saw with a flash of insight how life must have been for the young boy, brought up in a foreign land with an exiled father. Bilingual in French and English, Alasdair could also speak Gaelic, though with a French accent. He must have dreamed often of seeing Scotland for himself. Certainly, he could hardly see the Highlands to better advantage than on this fine morning in late June. It was early as yet and a heat haze still clung to the purple hills like wisps of gossamer. On the lower slopes, a few sheep grazed and the black cattle lowed at intervals to announce the coming of morning. Loch Mhor sparkled diamond-sharp in the clear air.

Maire breathed deeply and luxuriously, enjoying the heady smells of pine and honeysuckle and dog-rose. It was, she thought with amused delight, quite a contrast from the odours which cynical townsfolk called the "flowers of Edinburgh" – that inimitable mixture of burnt fat, rotting vegetables and excrement, which polluted the city air at ten o'clock every night, winging their way down from upper storeys to lie in the streets till the next morning. A good reason for living out of town in Cramond!

Her smile of pleasure was seen by Alasdair and he noticed,

not for the first time, what a pretty girl she was. Not that she interested him; his taste was for more sophisticated women, preferably married. He could not afford serious entanglements. There was much to achieve this next few months and his whole life had been spent looking forward to it. The French army of King Louis was a very good training ground but Alasdair knew that the real fighting lay ahead. That was in a way what he had been born for; his father had seen to it that his Jacobite ancestry was not wasted.

A sharp exclamation from the Laird made both young people stop short. He had just remembered an important order to his tacksman and felt it could not wait. Would they forgive him if he returned to the house at once and sent for Sandy? They did not really have much choice. An uncomfortable silence fell upon the two of them as they watched Maire's uncle hastily wending his way back towards the loch. They both knew that it was hardly customary for a young woman to be left unchaperoned like this; Uncle Ewan would receive the sharp end of his wife's tongue no doubt, when she found out.

"Perhaps," said Alasdair uncertainly, "we had better go back at once."

Maire frowned. It always annoyed her to be treated like a piece of china or some rare merchandise that must be carefully supervised lest it lose its value. She was quite capable of taking care of herself.

"I shall show you the rest of this part of the estate. It becomes quite wild at the top of this slope." Her voice was defiant. Alasdair heard the hint of challenge in it and, in spite of himself, his spirit rose to meet it. There was more to this girl than he had first thought. His pulses quickened a little as he followed her to the top of the bank. The undergrowth was thick here, and the moist, earthy smell of bracken was released where their feet trampled the leaves. He felt a sudden exhilaration that he could not explain. The girl sparked off some reaction in him; he found it stimulating because it was unusual. Women up to now had held few surprises for Alasdair; he was in danger of becoming world-weary at twenty-four.

The burst of energy made him run down the slope towards the beginning of a wood of birch trees. He turned to give his hand to the girl to help her but something in her face arrested him. She was looking fixedly at something in the foliage near him; something she could see but he could not. Alasdair felt that particular kind of alertness he knew before a battle; he smelt danger here.

"A wild cat. In the bushes. She has a litter. Do not make a sudden move. Come towards me slowly. She is ready to spring."

Maire's voice was low, steady and calm. Nothing in its tone would alarm an animal in a defensive position. Alasdair clung to that voice and its clear directions as he climbed back up the slope, his heart hammering and a scream only just contained in his throat. No-one could know about his one unconquerable fear. He hid it well enough. A soldier steady under fire and an acknowledged leader of men could not admit to this shameful and inexplicable weakness. Not really inexplicable, though. Alasdair had been told by his nurse that he was nearly suffocated in his cradle by a cat. He'd never been able to stand the creatures since; he could even tell when one was in the same room with him.

He fought the panic well as he reached Maire but he saw her eyes widen in surprise and compassion as she looked into his. She understood what he was feeling; strangely, he did not care. He felt instinctively that he could trust her with this intimate knowledge.

"I – I don't like cats," Alasdair said briefly. "I never have. I'd rather face a field of cannon."

Maire felt a wave of sympathy for this man she hardly knew, a desire to protect him that was totally unreasonable. It was as if this fleeting moment of vulnerability had stripped the social mask from each of them and for an unforgettable second, their souls touched. Almost without knowing what he was doing, Alasdair drew Maire to him and kissed her. It began innocently enough as a gentle kiss of thanks for saving him, almost a courtesy kiss. Neither was prepared for the sweeping passion the kiss began to kindle within them. It was like being shaken by a tempest. Alasdair found himself showering kisses on Maire's face and throat, murmuring endearments in her ear that for once he actually meant. He reverted to French, which was natural to him in this situation; it was, after all, known as the language of

51

love. To his surprise, she answered him in the same tongue.

"You speak French?" His voice was low, musical, full of delight.

"*Mais oui, Monsieur*!"

Nothing could be more perfect. Alasdair felt he had found his ideal woman, a personage he had doubted the existence of up till now. The timing could have been better, that was all. He was like an actor waiting in the wings for the most important cue of his life. And the drama he had rehearsed was destined to be played out on a world stage – at any rate, the whole of Europe would be watching. He could, he thought ironically, have picked a better time to fall in love.

They went back to the house together, each moved by what had just happened. They didn't speak: words were superfluous. Maire felt she wanted to catch the day to herself and hold it for always. Her perceptions seemed mysteriously heightened; the colours around her were more vivid, the sounds of the summer afternoon enveloped her with a sharp awareness she had never known before. Every detail was etched as it were, for ever; a bee flew up from the roses outside the house as she passed by and she saw how its body was laden with yellow pollen as it weaved a drunken path back to the hive. She too felt intoxicated by the sweetness of the day. There was no doubt in her mind why she would always remember this moment. For the first time in her life, Maire knew what it was to be completely and utterly in love.

***

Iain Macdonald was just leaving the house as they arrived. He gave Alasdair a cool look which was almost hostile and then glanced at Maire with something approaching disapproval. She became aware of her dishevelled appearance and tried to tidy her hair quickly. What must Iain think? Then she thought with impatience that it did not matter. What was more to the point was that she had better present a more groomed appearance to her aunt and uncle. Still, it annoyed her to have Iain look at her like that as if – as if she were a kitchen maid caught in the bushes with her lover! She excused herself hastily and went to her room.

The rest of the day passed quietly for Maire. She kept her promise to Jamie and went fishing with him. They failed to catch anything but the activity soothed her. She felt calmer now and less as if she had been struck down by a fever. The sun was setting as they came home from the shore of the loch. Maire had never seen sunsets like the ones in the Highlands. The whole western sky was aflame with gold, blending to orange and pink at the verges of the horizon. For some reason, the incredible beauty brought tears to her eyes tonight, as if she would never see it quite like this again.

Maire sensed that something was wrong as soon as she arrived home. There was a heavy silence and the murmur of voices from beyond the door of her uncle's library. The words could not be heard but she was sure one of the voices belonged to Alasdair. How different it sounded now from the one that had whispered words of love to her that very day on the hill. It was hard, serious and, yes – worried.

She learned what the trouble was later that evening. Davie, whom she now realised she had not seen all day, had left early to fetch home something of great importance. Maire could guess what, remembering the conversation at the ceilidh. It could only be part of the buried treasure. She could also guess for what purpose it was to be used – the coming rebellion, no doubt. It was with dismay that she learned the cause of the worry that gnawed at Alasdair and Uncle Ewan.

Davie had not returned. He had completely disappeared.

Chapter Seven

The next two days passed drearily, with no-one able to take an interest in anything very much while this problem remained unsolved. It hung over the entire household, like an invisible cloud.

The Laird mounted a search and his hunting dogs were also pressed into service to see if their quivering, sensitive noses could pick up Davie's scent. The dogs started off eagerly enough, but at some point along the loch, they always came to a halt, sniffing the air in a puzzled way. Maire realised Uncle Ewan's dilemma: he could not disclose exactly where the French gold was hidden, and yet he had to search as close to the spot as he dared. She wondered briefly why Davie Hamilton had been sent alone on his quest. Then the answer came to her; one man would not arouse attention. The location of the treasure must obviously be a well-guarded secret. It had lain in the earth, Maire learned, since the last days of the '15 Rebellion when it came too late to be of use. Loyal Jacobite that he was, the Laird had buried it at a secret spot until it could be used once more to help the Stuart cause. Maire wrinkled her brow in deep thought as she stabbed viciously at her embroidery. *Someone* had known, however. If not the exact place, certainly that Davie was carrying gold.

Unable to concentrate on any activity for long, Maire decided to go to the kitchen to see if she could help Janet or the others with any tasks that needed doing. Alasdair and the others were out searching, as usual. She had glimpsed him early that morning. He was increasingly grey-faced with anxiety. The two men had been very close. Maire knew that the longer it took to find Davie, the less hope there was that he was alive. She was deeply sorry, for the quiet, modest man had made quite an impression on her.

The kitchen only contained two occupants, one of whom, she was sorry to see, was Fiona. The girl was preparing bannocks for the iron griddle, dipping each in oatmeal before cooking them. She worked quickly and deftly. The cook, an older, slow-witted but well-meaning woman, was gutting a salmon on the table and grumbling to herself.

"Salmon again. That's the fifth time this week. I dinna ken what the others will say, at all, at all! The master disna' notice what he eats but he should think o' other folk."

Maire was both amused and exasperated by this. It was true that salmon was one of their staple diets at the moment. It was cheap and plentiful. The Laird's rivers were teeming with it, and the beef and pork had to be salted and laid away against the lean days of winter. She pointed this out to the cook and also added with a touch of asperity that if the servants turned up their noses at salmon, they ought to try the diet of a poor cotter who was lucky to have a bowl of oats and whey to keep him alive. The cook sniffed but said no more. During this exchange, Fiona said nothing but prepared and chopped herbs while the bannocks were cooking on the iron griddle. She was smiling to herself as she worked, as if she was in a world of her own, a secret place where no-one could follow her. It struck Maire that there was something "fey" about the girl. She had a quality that was unearthly, eerie almost.

Fiona looked up suddenly and met Maire's eyes. Maire received a cold shock; it was like looking into the eyes of a snake, green, shiny and pitiless. The moment passed and Maire scolded herself inwardly. Now Fiona was smiling at her – a rare occurrence; she ought to put away her prejudices about the girl and try to be friendly. Maire tried to think of something agreeable to say.

"That's a pretty necklace, Fiona. What is the stone? It looks most unusual."

She had said the wrong thing after all. The delicate chain which gleamed round Fiona's white neck was quickly twitched so the lustrous, many-faceted stone was hidden in her dress. It was a green stone that matched the girl's eyes. Maire was no expert on jewels but, had she not known it was impossible, she'd have taken it for an emerald. That could not be, of course. It must be made of paste, a clever replica. She wondered idly where Fiona had obtained it but thought it better not to probe further. The girl was so touchy. Anyway, thought Maire, I'm not really interested. I only wanted to be kind.

They did not find Davie Hamilton until the third day after his disappearance. His body lay behind a dry stone wall, buried in a thorny tangle of undergrowth and bushes. A stone lay nearby with blood on it - clearly the weapon used to smash his skull. There was nothing in his pockets, no sign of any gold.

Alasdair was beside himself with grief, but typically, kept it to himself and went about dry-eyed and grim. The Laird was angrier than Maire had ever seen or dreamt of. This was a different Uncle Ewan - the chief of his Clan. It was a terrible disgrace to him that a visitor whom he had welcomed to his home should meet such a fate. Murdered on Macdonald land! There was a lot of talking behind closed doors, a lot of comings and goings and questioning of various servants and tenants. It was, Maire thought, like a secret court in session – or certainly, if not a court, an investigation. The chief of the Clan, she knew, had judiciary status; he had the power of life and death over his clansmen. This was, she realised, a long way from Edinburgh. She was glad to be kept out of it.

It made her sick at heart to think of how poor Davie had lain there, dead and alone. There was something gruesome about such a fate; it reminded her of the macabre ballad of the "Twa' Corbies" where the two ravens gloat over their coming feast on a dead man's body:

> Many a one for him maks mane,
> But none shall ken where he is gane;
> O'er his white banes, when they are bare,
> The wind shall blaw for evermair.

Maire shivered involuntarily. She'd been so happy a few days ago. Now it was as if a dark shadow had come to them all. She only hoped it was not a precursor of what was to come. She forced her thoughts away from this line of thinking. She was in danger of becoming morbid!

The trouble was that another worry niggled at her also – one she did not want to think through. That necklace Fiona was wearing. It looked too valuable for a kitchen maid to afford.

Who had given it to her? Who had the money to buy a jewel like that? Maire felt uncomfortably that she could guess the answer to that question. The murderer. Was Gavin the killer who struck down Davie?

She wondered if she ought to go to her uncle and report the business of the necklace. After all, if it was only paste and worthless, Fiona – and her lover – had nothing to fear. And yet, Maire hesitated. She hated the thought of getting the girl into trouble unnecessarily. The fact that she found it hard to like or trust her was not relevant. Maire was very fair-minded in matters such as this. The result was that she took no action at all.

It turned out that she didn't have to. Someone from the Laird's household brought back an interesting report from a nearby village. A young man, clearly of the servant class, had been observed with more money than he should have and, which was more damning, trying to change French *louis d'ors* into local money. The description fitted Gavin perfectly and he was at once sent for. There was no difficulty in proving his guilt for he still had some of the money hidden in the straw of his stable. At least, the Laird was thankful for one thing. When he learned details of the murder, it transpired that Gavin had no idea where the main treasure was buried. He had simply taken the opportunity of waylaying Davie on his way back home. The Laird received a shock about the eavesdropping at the ceilidh; he had better be more circumspect in future.

Maire wondered what would happen now. She tried to ask her uncle and aunt but was brushed off; it was as if she had once more become a Lowland outsider. The Clan kept its business to itself.

All the servants avoided speaking to Fiona more than was necessary. The girl was not openly blamed for collusion but nevertheless, she had become a social leper. Maire wondered from the looks the girl gave her, whether Fiona suspected her of telling about the necklace. In fact, Maire had told nobody.

The next night, there was a strange brooding silence about the house. It made Maire uneasy, as if they were all waiting for a thunderstorm. And yet, the sky outside was clear and bright with a moon rising over the silver loch. No-one had spoken much at dinner; her uncle was preoccupied and Alasdair, too, seemed to have something on his mind. Maire was disappointed. She'd thought she meant more to him than this. She was beginning to realise that for a Jacobite, politics came first and love second.

Maire was glad to retire to bed. Everyone was out of sorts tonight. Of course, they had not yet had time to recover from the shock of Davie's death. She tossed and turned for a while, finally falling asleep as the moon rose high over the corrugated mirror that gleamed below.

Several hours later, in the early hours of the morning when everyone in the house was in their deepest slumber, a rowing boat put out across the widest part of the loch. Within half an hour it returned, its blades entering the water so softly that they made barely a splash and the squeak of the oars on the gunwale muffled into silence. The boat went out with four men in it; it returned with only three.

There was no sign of life in the sleeping house; no candle guttering at a window to betray the presence of a watcher. One person was awake, however, and saw the boat come back. Her green eyes glittered in the moonlight, not with tears but with an icy, terrible fury.

She swore to have her revenge on this family for what it had done to Gavin – and to her. She didn't care how long it took. Time was immaterial since life now stretched empty before her like a long corridor that had no end.

One day, Fiona promised herself. One day!

Chapter Eight

The young man from France had a cold, windy welcome as his ship landed at Arisaig. The *Doutelle* had not had an easy passage from Brittany; buffeted by gale force winds at intervals, the passages of calm brought other dangers. Pursued by a British warship, which engaged its escort in combat, Charles's frigate had to finish the journey alone. It was lucky to make it to Scotland. On 25th July 1745, the Stuart Prince landed with a small number of friends, for ever after known as "the Seven Men of Moidart".

The news of his landing was not greeted immediately with overwhelming enthusiasm. His first visitor was Macdonald of Boisdale. He looked with dismay at this young man of twenty-four who seemed to think that he could perform miracles. Did he really think that he could conquer a kingdom for his father with a handful of followers? Surely, Charles could not be serious about this foolhardy venture!

Firmly, Macdonald advised the Prince that the best thing he could do was to turn and go back home.

"Sir," said Charles Edward with simple dignity, "I *have* come home."

It was Macdonald's first experience of that devastating mixture of charismatic charm and wilfulness that the Stuarts were famous for. He gulped and could not think of an answer.

One by one, the Macdonald chiefs came, partly out of curiosity, partly to pay homage, but always to talk Charles out of his folly. There was no braver fighter in the world than a Highlander, but the chiefs were not fools. The memory of the defeat of the '15 still rankled and though many had hidden their weapons after the Disarming Act of 1725, they were not bent altogether on suicide. A Stuart rising with French help was one thing; a rash foray into the jaws of disaster was quite another.

The tall young man listened, his handsome features set in

obstinate lines, his dark, liquid eyes already full of a vision no-one else could see. One day, he swore to himself, and that not too far off, he would sit in Holyrood, the palace of his ancestors. All he needed, he told the cautious chiefs, was a small body of loyal men to follow him and the whole of Scotland would rise. Then the French, seeing a Jacobite army in the field, would keep their long delayed promise and send help. This could all be achieved, argued Charles, if only they would trust him.

"Will you not help me?" cried the young prince, who had a fine sense of drama. The older men found this appeal hard enough to resist, but it went straight to the heart of young Ranald Macdonald.

"Yes, I will follow you," he exclaimed, "though no other man in the Highlands will draw his sword!" This emotional declaration from a youthful kinsman won over the doubting chiefs. One by one, the great Macdonald clans were pledged to fight for him – Clanranald first, then Keppoch and Glencoe. From his arrival with seven men, Charles was making progress.

He had a bitter disappointment when he heard that "the men from Skye are not coming". He had counted on the support of the Lord of the Isles and also the McLeod chief. That, he had to admit, was a severe blow to his hopes.

Still, Charles was of a sanguine temperament and was never down for long. He had still to see Lochiel. The Camerons were sure to support him and they were one of the most powerful clans in the Highlands. He brightened up when he thought of them. If Lochiel threw in his lot with him, others would follow. He was downcast when he received a letter from the Cameron chief, telling him that he could not commit his clan to such a venture. Charles's answer was direct and typical. If Lochiel thought that, he should tell it to his face!

Donald Cameron, known as "The Gentle Lochiel", was nothing if not a man of honour. He accepted the invitation. On the way, he met his brother who had already spoken with Charles to no avail and had some experience of the spellbinding charm the young Prince could exercise when he chose. He warned Lochiel not to meet Charles.

"Brother," he said gloomily, "I know you better than you know yourself. If this Prince once sets his eyes upon you he will make you do whatever he pleases." Lochiel, understandably, refused to listen. He thought that forewarned was forearmed and he had all his arguments ready.

So did Charles Edward, and he put his with a passionate intensity that bowled Lochiel off his feet. The Prince was set on raising the standard within days, with or without the Camerons. He was going to win or perish in the attempt. His final sarcastic remark caught Lochiel on the raw. He could, Charles said hotly, stay at home if he liked and learn from the newspapers the fate of his Prince.

That did it! Lochiel capitulated like the others. "No," he found himself saying. "I'll share the fate of my Prince, and so shall every man over whom nature or fortune has given me any power." A Cameron was known never to break his word, and Charles rejoiced to have Lochiel on his side. He knew that this was a turning point. Others would come in now when they heard he was raising a Jacobite army.

The clan chiefs departed to raise their clans for the rendezvous at Glenfinnan fixed for Monday the 19th of August. The Prince would raise the standard on that day to mark the official beginning of the Rising. It was time to send the Fiery Cross once more round the glens.

Chapter Nine

The news reached Loch Mhor a week before this date. The custom of carrying the "*Croshtarie*" – two burning sticks in the shape of a cross tied with a strip of bloodstained linen – was an ancient way of raising the clans in warfare. Like all primitive rituals, it struck a deep chord. Maire felt her own Highland blood stirred when she saw it.

The excitement was infectious. There was a great flurry of activity in the normally sleepy glen. Claymores and dirks, broadswords and rusty muskets were brought out from various hiding places. The Laird and Alasdair were very busy, out rallying the clan and taking an inventory of arms which had long lain deep in Uncle Ewan's wine cellar and were now brought up for inspection and sharpening. It was all very brisk and businesslike. Maire was impressed by it, though she could not quite share completely in the jubilation she saw around her. She was haunted sometimes by a feeling of foreboding. Also, she knew that soon she would have to say goodbye – or at least, *au revoir* – to Alasdair. Having found the man she loved, she was soon to lose him.

She became aware too of a jarring note in all these hectic preparations for war. The Laird called out his small Clan but not everyone, Maire found, was eager to flock to the Prince's side. She saw Sandy Macdonald in his element as he bullied and chivied some of the tenants who were loath to exchange their farming implements for weapons. There was ugly talk of burning the roofs over their heads should any tenant fail in his duty to his chief.

She witnessed another confrontation between Morag-of-the-hill and the tacksman. Allan, Morag's son, was called out and his mother refused to let him go. She faced up to the Laird himself with equal maternal ferocity.

"Ye took my man in the '15," she said accusingly. "And

now it seems ye want my son as well."

The Laird did not seem to have an answer to this, by which Maire guessed that it was true. She'd known that Morag was a widow – no wonder she had no love for the Stuarts.

The situation was saved by Allan, a gentle-eyed giant of a man.

"I want to go, mother," he said calmly. "Not because of threats but because my father would have wished it." Morag, for once, was speechless. There was nothing more she could do. She knew that, like many quiet men, once Allan made up his mind, it was useless to argue.

There was a worse scene in the case of Iain Macdonald, however. His farm lay on Macdonald land and he was of fighting age. He came himself to the house and gave his reasons for refusing. He was dedicated, he said, to the preservation of life, not to the taking of it. Besides, he added with a curl of the lip, he did not support the Stuart cause which had only led to bloodshed in the past.

Alasdair was furious and accused Iain of being afraid to go. The young medical student blanched at this. Maire knew that if there was one thing Iain was not, it was a coward. She felt very bad on his behalf and knew it was anger that took the colour from his cheeks. She was about to speak up for him when the harsh tones of the tacksman cut her short.

"We'll see what ye have to say, laddie," he jeered, "when there's reek rising from your mother's farm. There'll no' be a stone left by the time I've finished wi' you."

Maire caught her breath in alarm. Iain's eyes had become grey steel. She had seen that look before at the Grassmarket. Any moment, this could turn into a violent brawl. She was glad to see her uncle arrive and ask what was going on. He listened impassively to Sandy's biased account of the row. To the tacksman's great annoyance and Maire's tremendous relief, he refused to take any action against Iain's family.

"His father was one of my friends," he said curtly. "He saved my life during the '15 and I will never harm a hair of his widow's head. As for his son, he must make up his own mind. Perhaps," added the Laird, "we cannot all be soldiers. Now there's an end of the matter!"

Iain turned on his heel and left, still taut and pale with anger. He might have thanked my uncle, thought Maire. She regretted very much being part of this scene; it seemed to make her and Iain enemies.

The last days went very quickly. It was strange how time seemed to gallop when you did not want it to. Alasdair also seemed aware of their imminent parting and in spite of his duties, spent many bittersweet hours with her. His eyes shone warm and golden with love and any doubts Maire had felt were quickly dispelled. His seeming neglect of her before was simply due to his total involvement with the coming rebellion. He knew Prince Charles well and never tired of telling Maire of his fine qualities.

"He could charm the bird from the tree," said Alasdair. "Never was there a Prince more suited to lead us to victory."

Maire wondered what charm had to do with military skill but she did not say so. She hoped with all her heart that the Rising *would* succeed because then she would have Alasdair back again.

He became increasingly passionate as the time to leave drew closer. There was a desperate quality now in their snatched meetings, each knowing that their time together was limited. And yet they had to be careful not to attract attention. Maire was under the care of her aunt and uncle and they would not approve of anything which could damage their niece's reputation. So the pair lived from one day to the next, coming together for stolen kisses in a fever of unfulfilled longing.

Maire found it unbearable and came to the biggest decision of her life so far. Alasdair had made no secret of his desire to love her completely. She felt the same. Why then should she hesitate? There were dangers in such a course of action but Maire was in no mood to care. She wanted to grasp hold of this precious time and live it to the full. She agreed to spend the last night with the man she loved. After all, thought Maire, God knows when we will see each other again.

They arranged discreetly for Alasdair to come to her room that night. He was to lead the men of the Clan tomorrow. It was an honour for him and a tribute to his dead father. Maire was happy for him and also glad that it put Sandy's nose out of joint.

He had assumed he would replace the Laird, whose bad leg prevented him from going.

That last day flew and dragged at the same time. In some ways, Maire counted the hours and grudged their going. Yet the minutes also tortured her with their secret promise of the night to come. At dinner, her heart fluttered and beat so fast that she feared her face might betray her.

Luckily, the Laird and Alasdair had plenty to occupy them with talk of the coming campaign. Somehow, Maire got through the meal and retired early to her room. She undressed and put on her night-clothes, shivering in the evening air. She made sure the log fire was built up for it was a chilly August evening. As the house gradually settled down for the night, Maire sat by the fire and gazed into its flames. The only sounds were the occasional spitting of the logs and the loud beating of her own heart.

At last, he came. She heard his light step and the tap, barely perceptible, on her door. She flew to open it and he entered, closing the door softly. In a moment, she was in his arms. For once, there was no subterfuge, no fear of hidden watchers.

Maire had been a little worried about knowing what to do, that she would perhaps be awkward or clumsy. She marvelled now at how easy, how natural, it was to love Alasdair. It was as if all her life had been waiting for this moment.

He held her close to him, kissing her eyes, her lips, her throat; Maire felt her body respond as if it had a life of its own. Her flesh tingled at his touch. Instinctively, she arched her back and her copper hair fell in a shining cascade over her shoulders.

His questing lips moved downwards and she felt impatient fingers fumble with the strings which tied her nightgown. At last, they gave way and the flimsy garment slipped to her feet. Suddenly, he was kissing her breasts, fondling them so that the rosy nipples stood erect and proud, an invitation to his hungry mouth.

Maire had never known such passion, such extreme physical sensations. Her whole being ached for him and it felt as if her insides had turned to water. Nothing in the world mattered except this new world of love and there was no question of holding back or any thought of tomorrow. Now, was all that existed.

Just as Maire felt her legs would no longer hold her, she felt herself lifted and carried over to the hearth. Her eyes were closed but she felt the soft warmth of the goatskin rug beneath her. Alasdair knelt beside her, kissing her, crooning words of love in the language which came naturally to him.

Maire opened her eyes and saw her lover's face outlined in a halo of golden firelight. She reached out her hand and traced the lines of his features as if she could somehow hold this memory for ever.

"Alasdair," she whispered again and again. The word sounded like a prayer.

His hands stroked her skin, soothing and arousing her alternately, prolonging the pleasure and delaying the moment of complete surrender. Gradually, his caresses became more demanding. With tender proficiency he aroused her to a pitch of wanting which made her body cry out for his. Finally, when she thought she could bear it no longer, they came together with a fierce sweetness that she had not known existed. There was one moment of sharpness when he entered her, but it was swept away in the ecstatic union that followed. Alasdair knew very well how to pleasure a woman; he had had plenty of practice. This time, however, was different, and he knew it. Here was one girl he would not be able to love and forget.

"*Ma belle*," he murmured, burying his head in her hair, glinting russet in the soft light. "*Ma petite rose blanche.*"

***

His little white rose stood forlornly the next morning outside the house in the misty dawn. The hills around Loch Mhor were hazy silhouettes in the gradually lightening sky. Aunt Isobel joined her, and Jamie who, one could tell, longed to be going too. Uncle Ewan was a few yards away, in deep discussion with the man he had chosen as leader. Maire noticed the surly face of the tacksman, sitting on his horse just behind. If she had not felt so sad, she would have smiled to see Sandy taken down a peg or two.

It wasn't a big sept of the Macdonalds. The Loch Mhor contingent consisted of about thirty-eight men, but they were

66

armed better than some that would march that day to Glenfinnan. The Laird and Alasdair had seen to that. It was strange to see men she knew and normally saw working at their crofts standing to attention with swords and muskets. Each man had a claymore, the basket-hilted broadsword, at his belt. In his left hand, he carried a targe, the leather shield used by Highlanders. Many also had muskets or pistols and Alasdair had a silver dirk, which befitted the leader of the clan. As the day grew lighter, the many varied colours of the tartans worn by the clansmen made the occasion almost gay. No clan wore a special tartan in those days and a man could wear several at one time, according to his choice – and means.

The clan was now assembled, all the names had been checked off and Maire knew that the moment for departure had arrived. In a way, it was a relief. She could not guarantee to remain dry-eyed for ever. Better to get it over.

Her eyes were fixed on her lover, wheeling his horse around, drawing his sword and calling on the men to fall in behind him. She could see now why Uncle Ewan was wise to choose Alasdair as leader. A professional officer, he was clearly in his element; the men would follow him with confidence.

Maire's hand went involuntarily to her mouth as they rode away. Her lips were still tender, bruised from his kisses. They gave her back the memory of last night's loving, a comforting confirmation which she felt she needed. The truth was that as she looked at Alasdair, resplendent in Highland dress and every inch the Jacobite leader, she had the oddest feeling that already she was looking at a stranger.

Chapter Ten

August dragged on to its close and signs of autumn began to appear in the landscape round Loch Mhor. Green leaves crackled to yellow and crimson and swirled round in the gusts of wind that were a foretaste of winter. The hills round the loch began to change colour, imperceptibly at first, until one day purple heather coated them completely with a vibrant hue which dazzled the eye. Maire was captivated by the sight; she had never seen such a dramatic change take place before her eyes and the sheer beauty of it made her heart ache.

It ached for other reasons too. She missed Alasdair terribly. Fate seemed to be very cruel, offering her a taste of love's sweetness one day and snatching it away the next. Luckily, she had plenty to occupy her waking moments. Since the clansmen marched away, the house and estate were short-staffed and there was much to see to. Both Maire and Janet were very practical and made themselves useful in all kinds of ways. Jamie was not neglected though; he now had lessons with Maire who began to teach him French and the rudiments of dancing. Her Gaelic now was much more fluent. The household settled down to an ordered if rather quiet existence.

This peace was rudely shattered one day and completely without warning. It was about the middle of the afternoon and Maire had just finished a lesson with her cousin. The scream that came from her aunt's apartment made her heart stand still. Dropping her book, Maire rushed to see what had happened.

It was Uncle Ewan. He had been taken ill suddenly and was doubled up in obvious agony, his face contorted in a grimace and his breathing hard and rasping. The violence of the attack frightened Maire. There was clearly something terribly wrong. She flew for Janet who came at once, wiping her hands on her apron.

The Laird was writhing on the floor by now, rolling from

side to side as if in an effort to find relief from the pain which seared him internally. Aunt Isobel was weeping and wringing her hands, powerless to help him.

"What ails you, laddie? Tell me, Ewan, what is hurting you so? In God's name, what are we going to do?"

Janet bit her lip. This was very serious; she knew that at a glance. Something was torturing the Laird but until she knew what it was, she was afraid to act. However, she went quickly and fetched her medical supplies. Then she bent down and felt the Laird's stomach; it seemed to be distended and tender to the touch. Unfortunately, that could have several causes. If she guessed the wrong one, she might do more harm than good. Thinking desperately, Janet bathed the patient's forehead and face with a damp cloth. He was soaked in perspiration; there seemed to be some kind of fever. She had a feeling that time was limited. He was growing weaker, and at times the thrashing movements seemed to turn into convulsions. The man could be dying before her eyes. Yet still she hesitated, afraid to administer the wrong remedy.

Her worried eyes met Maire's. "Can't you help him?" The girl spoke in a whisper, her eyes large with distress.

"Aye, maybe I could, lassie, if I could only ken what was wrong with him. The attack has come on so suddenly. He's had nothing like it before. I've an idea it might be best to purge him and get rid of what he has on his stomach. But if I am wrong, there is a risk of bursting something internally by forcing him to vomit. If only I knew what had caused it."

On her way to the kitchen to fetch more cold water to bathe the Laird, Maire struggled to think rationally in spite of her terror. What had Uncle Ewan eaten that day? Perhaps there was a clue there. She met the cook outside the kitchen door. The woman was weeping into her apron and moaning to herself. News of her master's illness had flashed round the house like lightning. When the chief was ill, it was a disaster for the whole Clan. Maire spoke to the woman gently.

"I want you to think. What did the Laird have to eat today? Did he have anything unusual that could have made him sick? You must remember!"

The cook raised a tear-stained face and puckered her brow

in thought. "No. He had his favourite breakfast – a slice of cold beef and fried mushrooms. He often has it. There's no-one can blame me for anything!" She dissolved in another wail under the apron.

Helplessly, Maire left her and pushed open the door of the kitchen. She heard the soft singing before she saw Fiona over in the corner, sitting at a table and crooning to herself at some task or other. The girl as usual was in a dream world of her own. She looked happier than Maire had seen her for some time. A little smile curved her lips; obviously this was one person who was not affected by the tragedy unfolding upstairs. Perhaps Fiona had not heard yet.

Maire, tight-lipped, went to fetch a bowl of water to take back. She could not bring herself to speak to Fiona at that moment. Besides, there was no time for long involved explanations. The others might need her. She was almost afraid to go back upstairs because of what she might find.

Carrying the bowl carefully, Maire left the kitchen and walked along the passage. With a spurt of annoyance, she heard the singing start up once more behind her. Fiona had at least fallen silent when she was there. Tactful of her! thought Maire bitterly. Not that the girl would care what happened to Uncle Ewan; she probably hated him.

Maire froze suddenly, immobile, with the bowl of water still clenched carefully in her hands. That song Fiona was singing – the tune was vaguely familiar, though the words were slightly different in Gaelic. Something told Maire that the song was sending her some kind of message – a disturbing message. She forced herself to remember some of the words she used to know. She mouthed them silently to herself:

Oh, what is it ails you, Lord Randal, my son?
Oh what is it ails you, my bonny young man?

It was a mother speaking to her son. The song suddenly spilled into Maire's mind with a rush, bringing with it the dread realisation of why it had struck her with such a ghastly echo. It was a tale of murder. The son's answer rang clearly in her mind with all its stark and terrible simplicity:

I fear I am poisoned, mother; mak' my bed soon,
For I'm sick at the heart and I fain would lie doon.

It took Maire just four seconds to burst into the kitchen. The bowl of water was dropped and lay unheeded, spilling over the passage. She confronted Fiona, her eyes blazing.

"It was you, wasn't it? You poisoned my Uncle Ewan! What was it you put in his food? Tell me at once or I'll shake it out of you!"

Maire was beside herself. She hauled the girl out of her chair and slammed her against the wall. She never doubted for a moment that she was right. And if she *had* known any doubt, Fiona's reaction would have convinced her. The girl, startled and a little frightened at first, soon recovered. Her eyes gleamed green with a venomous spite which took even Maire by surprise. She realised with a shock that she was looking at pure, undiluted hatred.

Fiona recovered her balance with catlike speed. She pushed Maire aside and darted over to the door. Desperately, Maire threw herself after her, terrified to lose the one source of knowledge that could save Uncle Ewan. She managed to catch the girl at the door and the two girls struggled for a moment, Fiona scratching and tearing at Maire's clothes and hair but being gradually forced down to the floor. Sitting on her enemy, Maire put her hands round the girl's slim throat.

"Now!" she gasped, hardly recognising herself. "You will tell me what you used to poison my uncle or I will kill you!" She fervently hoped that her bluff would not be called. Fiona narrowed her eyes and with all the strength she could muster, spat viciously at Maire's face. However, she realised she was beaten and finally broke down and confessed.

She'd been sent to pick the mushrooms that morning, a task she had often performed. Only that day, she took the opportunity to slip a few toadstools in with them and the cook, being short-sighted, did not notice. Maire drew in her breath with horror and misgiving. She knew that her uncle might be doomed. Toadstools were a very virulent poison. Janet must be told at once so she could try an antidote.

The cook returned and Maire left Fiona in her keeping,

emphasising that on no account should the girl be allowed to leave. Taking the stairs two at a time, Maire rushed back to Uncle Ewan, fearing the worst. When she arrived, she was completely out of breath, her clothes torn and her hair dishevelled. The scene was much as before. Uncle Ewan, thank God, was still breathing but Janet was reaching out for a bottle of medicine. She could wait no longer, though her heart was in her mouth because of the risk.

"Toadstools!"

This one word was all Maire could manage as she stood there, her chest heaving. It was enough for Janet, however. She wasted no time in asking questions. Within minutes, she had dosed the Laird with one of her herbal medicines and waited calmly until the expected result. Painful vomiting and terrible stomach cramps followed but Janet proceeded to give yet another dose of the elixir. At last, the Laird fell weakly on to his bed. It seemed the sickness was over. It remained to be seen whether he would recover. His stomach was now empty but Janet could not be sure that it had not been damaged irreparably.

"Now all we can do," she told the Laird's wife, "is pray."

Aunt Isobel went away to find and comfort Jamie who had been excluded from these harrowing events. The two of them sat by the Laird's bed, watching over him while he fell into an exhausted slumber. Janet thought this a good sign.

Suddenly, Maire remembered about Fiona. Something had to be done about her. Aunt Isobel was much too occupied and upset to bear any more strain just now. Maire decided she must deal with the girl herself.

Fiona was sitting at the table in sulky silence with the cook mounting guard as if she enjoyed it. The girl's acid green stare was like a blast of ice. Maire took a deep breath.

"Why did you do it, Fiona? Was it because my uncle sent Gavin away? Was that the reason?"

The girl's mirthless laugh chilled the others to the marrow. There was something inhuman in the sound. It occurred to Maire that perhaps Fiona wasn't altogether sane.

"Sent him away? Oh, he sent him away all right – to the bottom of the loch! And don't pretend you knew nothing about it, Miss Innocent. You are all to blame – all of you! You took away the one thing I loved in all the world and now it is a cold and dark place without him."

Maire could not believe this of her uncle. Surely it could not be true! And yet, she knew such things happened. A little voice inside her whispered that it could be the truth Fiona spoke. If so, her action was, if not excusable, at least understandable. Maire was uncertain now how to proceed. She had fully intended to hand Fiona over to Aunt Isobel and, if he recovered, her uncle, for punishment. Now she hesitated. If such summary justice was the norm here, Maire wanted no part of it. Besides, when it became common knowledge what crime Fiona had tried to commit – the murder of her Chief by poison – the vengeance of the Clan would be swift and terrible.

She decided to give Fiona a chance. "Let her go!" she ordered, paying no attention to the cook's gasp of disapproval. "You will leave this house at once and never return to it. Do you understand?" Maire fixed her eyes sternly on the girl's pale tense face.

Fiona ran across to the door with her usual feline grace and speed. She turned for a moment to face the girl who had dismissed her, hate welling up in her like a sickness.

"God damn this whole cursed family!" It was said with all the passionate fervour of a prayer and that made it dreadful to hear. Then she was gone.

Maire stood for a moment, feeling shaken by the vehemence of the ill will which had been unleashed on them all. Then she shrugged; she had hardly expected Fiona to thank her for being sent away. It would have been worse for you if you had stayed, my girl, thought Maire grimly.

Iain Macdonald arrived suddenly, having received a message to come quickly. He looked curiously at Maire and asked about the girl who nearly knocked him down in her hurry to leave. Maire found herself telling him briefly what had happened. He was remarkably easy to talk to, listening gravely until she had finished and then congratulating her on her detection of the crime.

"That was clever of you," he said admiringly, "to realise that what was in her mind was betrayed unwittingly by the song she was singing." She knew he meant what he said; Iain was not given to flattery. Far from it. Maire felt ridiculously pleased by his praise because she knew it was hard to win.

They went up together to see the Laird and were pleased to see him now awake and looking a little better. There was even some colour in his cheeks though he was still as weak as a kitten. Aunt Isobel sat by him, holding his hand and tenderly soothing his brow from time to time. She knew she'd never come nearer to losing him. Not since the '15 Rebellion thirty years ago.

The Laird stirred and his dry lips opened to speak. His wife leant forward, anxious to catch every word.

"I would like to live," whispered Ewan, "long enough to set eyes on my rightful Prince. If only I could live to see that day, I would die a happy man."

Isobel swallowed hard. "Och, man, away with you!" She smiled to hold back the tears pricking her eyelids. "You've never died a winter yet, nor are you going to. You'll be here to plague us yet awhile. But I'll tell you this, laddie! When Prince Charles holds court in Edinburgh, we will be among the first to pay our respects to him. I promise you that!"

Isobel's eyes were shining as if she could see the glittering throng already at Holyrood. Watching her, Maire felt her own spirits rise. So far, they had received little or no news of how the Jacobite army was faring. She hoped that no news was good news. She hoped it with all her heart.

PART II

AUTUMN – 1745

Chapter Eleven

The Jacobite army was, in fact, doing well so far. Fortune seemed to smile on the young Prince who had dared to arrive with hardly any supporters to claim the throne of his grandfather.

The Raising of the Standard at Glenfinnan was a day no-one who was present could ever forget. The blue water of Loch Shiel sparkled and the towering mountains, their tops wreathed in mist, were majestic witnesses to the simple ceremony as the Duke of Atholl unfurled the flag to mark the official start of the Rebellion. Up to then, the only sound was the mewing cry of seagulls wheeling high above, but the moment the red, white and blue standard fluttered in the breeze, the hills resounded to the echo of a thousand voices. Blue bonnets were thrown up in the air and the clash of steel disturbed the peaceful day as swords left their scabbards to be brandished in the air. Lochiel and the Macdonald chiefs had kept faith; Prince Charles now marched at the head of a small army. It was a good beginning.

He heard with mischievous delight that he was now considered enough of a threat to the Government in London to have a price on his head of thirty thousand pounds. Charles responded by issuing a cheeky proclamation of his own. He would himself offer a reward of thirty pounds to the man who arrested the Elector, George II! It satisfied his impudent and irreverent wit to read this out with mock solemnity to the assembled clans.

Moreover, Charles Edward had more idea of military tactics than anyone had so far given him credit for. He had taken part personally in the siege of the Italian city of Gaeta when he was only thirteen years old – much to his father's dismay. He was not afraid of making quick decisions, either. They accorded well with his impulsive nature. When General Sir John Cope, in charge of 3,000 soldiers at Stirling, committed the incredible blunder of taking his troops north to Inverness, Charles could not believe his luck. The way to the south now lay open! Such ineptitude on the part of the English must be seized upon at once, Charles reasoned. He promptly marched straight to Stirling and occupied it.

Cope was furious. He had been outmanœuvred by a callow young man with little or no military experience. It made him look a fool, and he could not wait to teach Charles a lesson on the field of battle. He hurried south as fast as he could, knowing that Edinburgh was the next prize that could fall to the Highland army. That would be a terrible blow to morale, if the Scottish capital was taken by the Jacobites. It must not be allowed to happen. For speed, Cope embarked his troops on ships and sailed to the Firth of Forth, hoping to prevent Charles from taking Edinburgh.

Meanwhile, the Town Council of "Auld Reekie" was playing for time. The City Fathers did not fancy fighting in the streets of Edinburgh so they tried to parley with Charles Edward in the hope that General Cope would arrive and settle matters with his regular troops. A wild bunch of tattered Highlanders would hardly stand against a trained, disciplined army. So the Town Council reasoned, as it sent deputation after deputation to sweet-talk Charles without actually handing over the city to him. The gates were still firmly closed on all sides.

Finally, the Prince lost patience with all this delay. He ordered Lochiel and his Camerons to try to take the city by peaceful means, if at all possible. Charles did not want unnecessary bloodshed; he never forgot that these were his father's subjects.

The Camerons took up their position outside one of the city gates, the Nether Bow Port at the Canongate. They watched and waited their chance. Once more, Fate played into their hands. The coach carrying back the latest deputation of time-wasting councillors came rumbling up to the gate to enter the town. The Nether Bow Port swung open to admit them and Lochiel and the Camerons rushed in as well. The guard on the gate fled and the town of Edinburgh was in Jacobite hands without the sleeping townspeople knowing anything about it until the next day. One Edinburgh citizen, seeing a guard in Highland garb on duty at the gate, asked curiously what he was doing there. He was courteously informed that the guard "had been relieved".

Huge crowds gathered to see the Prince enter at the head of his army. Word had gone round the streets like wildfire that he was coming and no-one wanted to miss the spectacle of a Stuart Prince entering the home of his ancestors.

Charles knew the people wanted a show so he gave them one. He always had a fine sense of theatre and his triumphant entry into Edinburgh was beautifully stage-managed. Everyone who saw it knew they were taking part in a historical event they would one day describe to their grandchildren. Charles did not disappoint them.

He was on horseback, which always suited him as he rode extremely well. Tall and handsome, his face sunburnt from his days of marching; he wore Highland dress with a short tartan coat and a blue bonnet. On his breast was a ribbon with the star of St Andrew. His hair under a wig was reddish gold, which earned him the sobriquet of "the Flaxen-haired Laddie" and provided an unusual contrast with his fine dark eyes. He was everyone's idea of a prince and the ladies of the town fell instantly in love with him. He was now "Bonnie Prince Charlie" and the city was at his feet.

After he had shown himself sufficiently to the people, he proceeded to Holyrood and took up court there in the palace. The dream he had arrived with and which seemed so unlikely on the cold, wind-swept coast at Moidart, had come to pass after all. The Highlanders were jubilant. Everything was going their way. King James was proclaimed at the Mercat Cross amid enthusiastic crowds waving white handkerchiefs, though it could have been observed that they were mostly women. Few men were there to cheer.

The Castle, too, still held out for the Government under a doughty octogenarian, General Guest, who from time to time let loose a defiant burst of cannon. And there was still the threat of General Cope hurrying south to engage the Jacobites in battle. It was one thing to capture Edinburgh by a clever trick; it might be another to keep it.

At last, Cope arrived and drew up his army to the east of the city. He chose his ground carefully. This time, there must be no mistake. Prestonpans was an ideal spot to defend because the marshy ground in front rendered his army safe from direct attack. No-one could approach him from that direction. The English army settled down to sleep on 20th September with every reason to feel secure.

The early hours of 21st September were dark and misty. A man could hardly see his hand in front of him. The Highlanders were used to these conditions; they were also adept at moving silently and by stealth. Guided by a local laird of Jacobite sympathies, Robert Anderson, they crept through the marsh in single file on a little known path until they reached within a few feet of the enemy.

The English woke to find themselves face to face with the clansmen in their midst. Their sentries had no chance to give warning. A swift rush led by the Camerons caused panic among the English. The mounted dragoons galloped away leaving the infantry to face the savage-looking Highlanders. Bayonets were no use at close quarters. The claymore was an old-fashioned weapon but when used with ferocious stabbing efficiency, it proved to be deadly. The infantry fell over themselves in their attempt to get away, even trampling their own officers in the confusion. The battle was over in just seven minutes, almost before it had begun.

A dreadful scene of carnage was revealed as the morning gradually lightened. The clansmen had sustained few losses but Cope's army was completely routed and the wounded and dead lay all around.

The Prince, who had last night slept on a straw pillow under his plaid in the open air so he could be with his men at the attack, was overcome by pity for the groans he heard. He sent for extra surgeons from Edinburgh so they could attend the wounded of the enemy as well as his own. This kind of humanity to the foe was unheard of, but no-one argued; his wishes were obeyed.

For the second time, Prince Charles entered Edinburgh in triumph. The town went wild. All the way up the High Street, windows were thrown open and caps and hats were waved to greet him. Cheers resounded through the narrow streets. It became fashionable now to be Jacobite and the town was gay with white cockades and tartan sashes. Once more, the Prince set up court at Holyrood.

That autumn, a jaunty new air was whistled around the streets of Edinburgh:

> *Hey Johnnie Cope, are ye waukin' [awake] yet?*
> *Or are your drums a-beatin' yet?*

You could hear the catchy tune and taunting words at every street corner; it was a sign of the times.

Chapter Twelve

Maire could sense the excitement in the air as soon as she arrived in Edinburgh. There was a festive atmosphere in the normally staid capital whose citizens usually had their minds firmly on business. Now it seemed as if someone had declared a public holiday; there were smiles on all sides. Even the prim landlady who greeted them at her premises in the Lawnmarket sported a white cockade in her grey curls.

She made a fuss of Uncle Ewan and his wife, having seen them before on their previous visits. It felt strange to Maire coming to her own city like an outsider. She was part of the family now and assumed to be a Highlander. In a way, she found it an interesting experience; she saw Edinburgh with fresh eyes as a stranger would have done. She certainly was in no hurry to visit Cramond, but went happily with Aunt Isobel to visit the shops near the Luckenbooths. Uncle Ewan was only too glad to rest after the journey. Though he had made a good recovery from his illness, he became quickly tired. Besides, nothing would stop him from going out that evening to achieve his lifetime's ambition. They were to attend a ball at Holyrood Palace and set eyes for the first time on the Prince everyone was talking about. The thought of that moment had spurred him on to regain his health as quickly as possible.

Maire herself was keen to see Prince Charles but that was not why her heart was skipping with a mad rhythm that made her want to dance in the street. Soon, she would see Alasdair again, for it was certain he would attend the ball. The Laird had already sent word of their arrival to the army encamped near Edinburgh. He would be bound to receive the message, wherever his duties took him around the city.

"Look, Maire! I'm told these are all the rage in Edinburgh just now. Shall we buy them for this evening?" Aunt Isobel held out two tartan sashes, one red, one green, and two silken white cockades. Her niece nodded approval and the purchase was made. The canny shopkeeper stowed the money away with a satisfied smirk. He had no feelings about the Jacobites one way or the other but white cockades were selling like hot cakes just now. The seamstresses could hardly make enough of them. For his own part, he'd have sold purple cockades if there'd been a demand for them.

As they approached the Mercat Cross, the women saw a bunch of raw-looking recruits being issued with white rosettes of their own to stick on their bonnets. These were volunteers for the newly formed Edinburgh Regiment under John Roy Stewart. They seemed to consist mainly of apprentices, their young faces bright with idealism as if war was a great adventure.

"Down wi' the wee German Lairdie! We'll mak' him run!" someone shouted to cheers, as they passed by. Prince Charles's success had encouraged more clans to join the Jacobites and he now had an army of six thousand men. No wonder his hopes were riding high.

Maire accompanied her aunt to the lodging house and then excused herself for a while. She wanted very much to visit her old friend, Sheena Ferguson, whom she knew would be thrilled to see her.

Rasping the iron tirling-pin up and down, Maire smiled to herself as she waited for someone to answer the door in the High Street. It seemed as if years had passed since she was here last, yet it was only months. So much had happened since she went to Loch Mhor.

The welcome was as ecstatic as she could have hoped, reminding her for a wry moment of that other day when she had not been expected. No such shadow of fear pursued the Ferguson family now. Like all the other closet Jacobites, they were now in the full sunlight, exultant at Prince Charlie's success and sure of his ultimate victory. Maire did not ask after Neil though she would like to have known what became of him. She was afraid of wounding the family at their moment of joy.

Sheena's happiness was complete when she found that Maire was to attend the ball given by the Prince that evening.

"Then I shall look for you!" she cried. "We shall be there also."

Maire wondered what her friend would say if she knew how completely her outlook had altered since she had fallen in love. That was a secret she hugged to herself, not willing yet to share it with anyone. Those hours of stolen sweetness she had spent with Alasdair seemed now to have the unreality of a dream – a wonderful dream – but she had a superstitious fear that to speak of her love would in some way detract from it.

She spent the rest of the day recovering from the last lap of their journey and preparing for the ball. Her white silk gown seemed to have travelled best and would look good with the red tartan sash slung over her shoulder. She missed Janet to help with her hair but Aunt Isobel proved quite skilful at taming the copper mane into some kind of order.

"It's a simple style but it becomes you," said her aunt, combing Maire's curls so they fell on to her shoulders. She herself wore maroon silk and the green tartan sash over it. Both ladies fixed the seemingly obligatory white cockade, Maire in her hair, Aunt Isobel at her breast.

Uncle Ewan had the foresight to order sedan chairs for them in plenty of time. He had foreseen the crush there would be down the High Street and spilling into the Canongate. Carriages would be next to impossible. Even chairs were at a premium because of the ball; some people simply arrived on foot. As they alighted outside Holyrood, Maire caught her breath at the magnificence of it all. Linkmen were everywhere, carrying torches which lit up the courtyard as if it were day. Chattering, laughing crowds, dressed in velvets, silks and satins, wearing jewels which had probably been dug out of bank vaults for the occasion, made their way slowly into the palace in a kind of queue. Everyone wanted to meet the Prince; people had come from miles around to do so. She saw the Ferguson family a long way in front. It was as if, thought Maire, the campaign was over and the Stuarts were already restored.

At last, their turn came and they were admitted to the ballroom. More dazzling sights met their eyes. Blazing candelabras shone down on what must have been one of the most colourful scenes this sombre palace had ever known. The sheer variety of tartans, added to the rainbow shimmering silks and satins made Maire blink as she entered the room.

In a moment, a hand touched her arm and she whirled round, hoping to see Alasdair. To her surprise, it was Mr. Ramsay, her old lawyer friend from Cramond. He was happier than she had ever seen him and there was a new determination to the set of his chin that she had not seen before. Politely he asked her uncle if he could have a few private words with Maire and, curiosity mounting, she followed him to a small side-table.

"First of all, lassie, I am glad to see you in such good care," he began. "It is obvious that you are happy with the Macdonalds. And why not, when they were your mother's folk? It is of your mother that I wish to speak for there is something I have to tell you."

Maire was astonished to learn that her mother before she died had left a will. This left the house and money to her daughter when she was twenty-one and gave Hector Grant the right to live in the house till that time, provided he cared for Maire. The will had been suppressed by Hector Grant for obvious reasons.

"And I'm ashamed to say," said Mr. Ramsay, "that I took part in that lie for he has had a hold over me these thirty years, the blackguard!"

Maire's eyes opened even wider; it seemed this evening was full of revelations about her past. It transpired that Grant had in his possession a letter of Mr. Ramsay's written to the court of "King James" and clearly damning him as a Jacobite spy. Such secret correspondence with the Pretender's Court was treasonable; a man could hang for a lot less.

"He has bought my silence with my fear since the '15 Rebellion," said the lawyer bitterly. "And the more shame to me. But not any longer! Now the boot is on the other foot and it is Whigs like Grant who will have to look to themselves. Most of them have fled the city." Ramsay's good-natured face darkened. "But I hear that Hector is still here although I have already served legal notice on him to quit the premises. I intend to visit Cramond tomorrow to make sure he does so as soon as possible and takes that trollop, Burt, with him. This is one task I'd like to perform personally. Would you care to accompany me, my dear?"

At first, Maire was taken aback. Then a vivid memory

washed over her as she recalled her miserable days in that man's house. Her house now! Exultation filled her and with it, an understandable desire to confront her old enemies under these new circumstances.

"Yes," she said. "I'll come with you, Mr. Ramsay. I wouldn't miss it for the world."

This dream-like evening was becoming more unreal by the minute. Maire looked around the glittering ballroom and had the strange feeling of being an actor in a stage play. If so, it was a drama in which she was happy to play a part.

The lawyer's tone changed as he asked happily, "Tell me, Maire, what do you think of our Prince?"

A murmur of excited voices alerted them to the fact that Prince Charles had entered and was graciously greeting all the people who were being presented to him. Many of them had contributed generously to his Cause and he thanked them personally with that Stuart charm, which he had in abundance. His magnetism could be felt even from a distance, Maire thought, looking with fascination at this young man who was determined to change history.

"Oh, I would willingly die for him!" sighed a young lady behind Maire, ready to swoon with hero-worship.

"Luckily, my dear, you will not be required to do so," was the somewhat dry, cynical reply from her swain. "That privilege will belong to others, no doubt."

This last remark struck a cold note of realism in the warm room. Maire was reminded unwillingly that this gay, scented crowd was only so much pomp and circumstance, an impressive panoply which was only a front. The Stuarts had as yet no real power. Prince Charles still had to win the throne of England and war was not a game.

These dark thoughts were swept away when she met Alasdair. Suddenly, he was there before her, his hazel eyes kindling golden as soon as he saw her. He looked very handsome in Highland dress, the proud and triumphant soldier. He told them all about Prestonpans and how the English had run like hares before the furious Highland charge. Listening to him, Maire wondered how she could ever have doubted. It was not worthy of her. Of course the Prince would win! He already said that one Highlander was worth ten other men and considered his clans to be invincible. Looking at Alasdair's confident and happy face, she was glad to share his optimism.

The time passed swiftly; hours seemed to become moments. Maire danced mostly with Alasdair and could not spend enough time with him. She longed for them to be together as before and wondered secretly how it could be managed. She noticed to her surprise that the Prince never danced, but Alasdair explained it.

"He says he has quite another tune to dance to and until he performs it, he will dance no other." Maire saw the wisdom in not selecting one lady above another; since so many were in love with him, the Prince avoided giving offence by not choosing a partner.

As all dreams must, the wonderful evening came to an end. Maire followed her aunt and uncle out of the brightly-lit palace into the darkness of the Edinburgh night. There was a hint of autumn chill in the air and she shivered, pulling her velvet cloak tightly round her shoulders.

"Are you cold, Maire?" Isobel was concerned. "You Lowlanders seem to feel the cold more than we do."

Maire reassured her with a smile. "Not at all, Aunt. I only felt the air cold after the heat inside."

It was true. And yet it was not the whole truth. As Maire looked up at the brooding mass of Arthur's Seat which towered above Holyrood, she could not rid herself of the feeling that all this brittle happiness would have to be paid for.

Chapter Thirteen

Next morning, Maire woke up feeling much more hopeful about the future. Last night had been a historic occasion and she had been privileged to be part of it. She had a memory to treasure for the rest of her life, like everybody else who had witnessed the Stuart prince back in the home of his ancestors.

It seemed the weather smiled on them too; the sun was shining on an Edinburgh which for once had lost its dour grey image. The castle on its rock resembled an oil painting as it stood out in theatrical splendour against the skyline. Maire admired the view as the carriage she shared with Mr. Ramsay swayed and jolted its way to Cramond. This was the historic city she had grown up in and it would always be a part of her.

Her feelings were mixed however as they approached the house she remembered so well. It was associated with many youthful experiences, most of them bad. The familiar stomach lurch came unbidden but Maire reminded herself firmly that this time there was no need for it.

The carriage halted outside the elegant house and Ramsay descended and helped Maire out. She was dressed very differently from the previous night's finery. A sober, grey and lavender outfit conveyed the right business-like impression. At least, Maire hoped so. They walked up the path and Ramsay jangled the bell. Maire was again struck by the change in her old friend. He was clearly enjoying the situation and she couldn't blame him. He'd lived with fear for so long because of Hector Grant.

To her surprise, it was her uncle who opened the door. The servants had obviously departed already or he would never have performed such a menial task. His florid face was paler than usual and his eyes were bloodshot. It was still morning but he had the look of a man who had already been at the brandy. His slightly dishevelled appearance lent him an air of hectic desperation. Maire almost felt it in her heart to feel sorry for him. Almost but not quite.

She was rather relieved when Grant began to bluster with some semblance of his old bullying self. He raked Ramsay with a glance of contemptuous loathing.

"So it's you," he growled. "You meddling scoundrel! After all the dinners you've had under my roof. Plotting and planning like the vermin you are. And turning my own niece against me with your black-hearted lies." His scowl faded as he turned a pleading gaze on Maire. "You'll not believe a word of it, my dear? He's a lying toad! Lawyers were aye thieves. You know how fond I always was of you. I promised your dear mother I'd look after you and so I have."

This was a tactical mistake on Grant's part. The mention of her dead mother was all Maire needed to harden her resolve. Like all children orphaned early in life, she kept a private and sacred place in her heart for the dead mother she had never known. Grant flinched from the icy blue eyes she turned on him.

"Looked after me? Oh yes, you did that all right, uncle. By trying to marry me off to that drunken reprobate of a son of yours. All to get your greedy hands on the property you had stolen and wanted to acquire legally."

Maire paused for breath, amazed at her own passion. She realised that her anger was like a dam bursting after being pent up for so long. Hector Grant took a step backwards. Clearly, he was dealing with a different proposition from the young girl he had controlled for years. He stumbled and nearly fell over an obstacle; it was then that Maire saw the boxes which filled the hall. It was obvious that Grant knew the game was up and was preparing for a hurried departure. This was just a last attempt to reverse the situation.

Muttering sulkily about "ingratitude" and "legal sharks", he withdrew and his place was taken by Wilhelmina Burt who had heard the commotion. Maire looked steadily at this woman who had darkened her childhood. The housekeeper seemed smaller, somehow. Her hair wasn't as tidy as usual and her hands, Maire noticed with a certain satisfaction, were grubby as if she'd been doing unaccustomed work. Another indication that the servants had left. The woman's eyes were the same though – still pebble hard.

"Come to gloat, have ye?" was Wilhelmina's opening greeting. "Lady High-and-Mighty now, I suppose, and no thought of thanks for those who looked after ye all those years!"

This was too much. The woman's brazen hypocrisy was staggering. Maire opened her mouth to reply but Ramsay, who had been quietly enjoying the scene, interposed by shoving a legal document under the housekeeper's nose. "This is your final notice to quit the premises by the end of the month. The rightful owner will expect full vacant possession by that time. Any failure to comply with this order will result in legal action being taken against you. And you may think yourselves lucky," Ramsay added warmly, "that Miss Drummond is not filing a suit against you for illegal occupation, let alone suppression of a will."

Maire could tell how much he was relishing this moment. He seemed quite different from the kindly old man who had once been her only friend in that house. This was the lawyer in action. She wondered how Wilhelmina would react. Explosively, no doubt, but even Maire was surprised by the venom with which the housekeeper suddenly spat at them.

"You pair of vultures," she hissed. "Plotting to turn us out on to the street. A filthy rat of a Jacobite lawyer and a lassie I treated like my own flesh and blood. You little turncoat!"

This last piece of invective was hurled at Maire who was beginning to tire of the doorstep confrontation. "That's enough!" she said with curt authority. "You know the situation; insults will only make matters worse. Quit this house by the required date or face legal action. I'm sure," Maire added, "that my uncle would not welcome the authorities looking into his business affairs."

This struck home. Wilhelmina gulped and stepped back without another word. The door was unceremoniously slammed in their faces. Ramsay grimaced, shrugged and fastidiously wiped the spittle off his jacket with a lawn handkerchief. "That woman is straight out of the gutter to which, I have no doubt, she will return. Well done, lassie! I'll see to all the legal formalities and write to you at Loch Mhor when they are complete."

Maire assured him that she was in no hurry to return to Edinburgh in the near future and was happy to leave everything in his capable hands. Of course, she was delighted about her unexpected inheritance but at the moment, it did not seem greatly to matter. That was for the future. It was the present which concerned her now: the dangerous present where the only certainty on the horizon was her love for Alasdair.

Chapter Fourteen

The two lovers did manage to be together for several occasions during the next two weeks. Alasdair arranged for them to visit a lodging-house where he was known and where he could count on the landlord's discretion.

Maire felt strange the first time she met Alasdair there. It seemed furtive and underhand – not worthy of their love. Yet she knew it was necessary. For the moment, their relationship had to be kept secret. The time would come, she promised herself, when they could declare their attachment and walk in the full sunlight. For now, she would settle for what she could have. Being in love with a soldier, she thought ruefully, had its drawbacks. But to be with her lover at last after all the long weeks without him – Maire would have paid any price for that.

She had tried to recall their one night of love so many times. Her hands remembered the shape and feel of his face as she had traced it that night as they lay together on the goatskin rug. The touch of his body on hers and his passion, arousing her own hunger, was a constant memory, which she carried in secret during those lonely days at Loch Mhor. It had kept her going.

But now, the joy of being with him again and reliving that physical ecstasy was almost too bittersweet to be borne. She dared not ask herself how long it would last this time before the future pain of inevitable separation, but gave herself up willingly to the happiness of the present.

Maire had a nasty, sickening moment of doubt when they were about to enter the house for the second time and by chance, a group of fellow officers passed by. They recognised Alasdair and called out bantering remarks accompanied by lewd whistles, asking whose reputation was he ruining this time? Maire shrank back against the wall, suddenly conscious of her position, and angry to find herself in it. What kind of madness was she indulging in? She was well aware of the risks she ran, not only of loss of reputation, which was serious, but also of unwanted pregnancy, which would mean ruin. She was thankful Janet was still in charge of the household at Loch Mhor; she could guess with uncomfortable accuracy what Janet would think of her behaviour.

And yet, strangely, when she was in his arms at last, Maire ceased to care about any of these things. She felt like a person with no past and no future; only the present existed. Her body hungered to be touched by him, and when it was, it seemed to leap to flame as if only then was she truly alive. Other activities became dull and repetitive, simply times of waiting till the next session of lovemaking. It was Maire's first experience of the enslavement of passion. She had not known till now that love could be such a tyrant.

She was taken aback one day to see in the mirror how her face had subtly changed. Her eyes had a large, dazed look like someone who had taken too much laudanum. Perhaps love was a drug, and more powerfully habit-forming than any other. Her lips were fuller than she remembered and there were light violet shadows under her eyes. To run a secret love life, she was discovering, involved a certain amount of strain. Maire had a suspicion that Aunt Isobel knew something of her clandestine meetings with Alasdair. If so, like a true romantic, she was turning a blind eye. Uncle Ewan would be a different matter.

The situation could not continue and it came to an end when the Macdonald family decided to return home after a fortnight. It was then October and the journey had to be completed before the Highland winter set in and made the roads impassable. Maire accepted the fact of leaving, almost with a feeling of relief. To live life at this feverish level of ecstasy was almost painful and certainly exhausting. She began to pack with Aunt Isobel in quiet resignation.

In any case, Alasdair would soon be leaving. Everyone knew about the imminent departure of the Jacobite army. There was talk of invading England in early November. The Prince had been set on it for some time and persuaded the clansmen that this was a necessary step in claiming the crown for his father.

A Scottish crown was not enough – it was the triple crown of Scotland, England and Ireland that was the Stuart birthright.

The Highlanders were reluctant. They wanted to stay and consolidate their success in their own country. Charles however was adamant. He would cross the Border and the sooner the better. It was already late in the year, he urged.

It was indeed. These valuable weeks spent in Edinburgh were a godsend for the Government in London. After an initial panic after Prestonpans, when the south reeled with the news that a crowd of undisciplined clansmen had cut through both dragoons and infantry, sending them scattering like toy soldiers in seven minutes, the Prime Minister, Pelham, rallied his craven Cabinet. The respite granted to them enabled troops to be recalled from the Continent, including George II's favourite son, the Duke of Cumberland. Marshal Wade, who had built the famous roads through the Highlands, took charge of an army. The rumbling of the English war machine became louder and more menacing though it could not be heard by the Jacobites far away in Edinburgh.

Nevertheless, it was clear to everyone that the time for dancing was over. As Maire and her aunt mounted the coach bound for Stirling on the first part of their journey home, the girl noticed a worried frown on Isobel's face.

"What is it, Aunt?" she asked anxiously. The older woman's face cleared for a moment but Maire could still see the lines of tension round her eyes.

"Och, it's nothing, child. I was just thinking of our brave men who will be marching south any day now. May God be with them!"

Amen to that, thought Maire. "But Aunt Isobel," she said reassuringly with more confidence than she felt, "the Prince has been victorious so far. He has defeated all who have come against him."

Her aunt smiled sadly. "Aye, you are right, my dear. So he has. But England is a big country and a powerful one, and once our clansmen have crossed the Border, I am thinking they will be a long way from Scotland and home."

Chapter Fifteen

Winter came early to the Highlands that year of 1745. The end of October brought with it gusts of hail and strong wind to accompany the celebrations of:

Hallowe'en, Hallowe'en,
When all the witches are to be seen.

Children from the crofts and farms around visited the house in disguise, their faces blackened with soot. They said rhymes or sang songs and received a coin for their efforts. The "guisers" were an annual tradition. Dolina, the new kitchen maid who had replaced Fiona, made special bannocks which, she claimed, had the property of informing the woman who ate one, the name of her future husband. Her eyes sparkling with fun, she offered one to Maire who took one to please her. She had no interest any longer in these girlish games. Maire knew perfectly well whom she was going to marry.

November saw the first flurries of snow and by December it lay thick on the ground. Streams were frozen and even part of Loch Mhor looked sluggish with ice. Cattle were penned up and given such fodder as could be found for them until the spring.

Maire wondered how the poorer crofters were faring at this lean time; they could barely scratch a living the rest of the year. She discovered to her pity and horror that some of them were reduced to bleeding their poor beasts and mixing the blood with oatmeal in a sort of cake, in order to exist. She went to her aunt and uncle with this information and found them sympathetic though by no means surprised. Hardship was nothing new in the Highlands.

"Aye, it is a severe winter right enough," agreed Uncle Ewan. "We have some extra meal laid by for an emergency such as this though we do not usually need it until the month of

January. You can help us to distribute it, Maire, if it pleases you."

She was delighted to do so. The needy recipients who came to collect the extra meal consisted mainly of old men, women and children, bringing home to her once more how depleted the clan was since the men had gone. They accepted their portion with a dignity which impressed her, as if it was their right. Of course, she realised, in a way it *was,* since it was produced largely by their labours.

Seeing such want and suffering, in a way brought Maire to her senses and restored her sense of proportion. The Edinburgh visit became a distant memory, like something that had happened to another person. The details were no longer so vivid in her mind but blurred at the edges. The sharpness of her need for Alasdair, which on her return tormented her with its physical ache of longing, became bearable. The horizons of her life moved back to show her what in fact she had always known – that love was only a part of living, though of course by far the most important. She was her own person once more and, though she only partly realised it, she was growing up.

Christmas came and went with an attempt at festivity to welcome the New Year, which everyone hoped would bring longed for success to the Jacobites. This no longer seemed so certain. News was sketchy but what facts were gleaned from the odd clansman returning to his glen were not promising. There was no mention of a defeat but the Jacobite army had turned back and was marching northwards once more. Apparently, desertions were rife and it was considered inadvisable for them to invite a major confrontation in enemy territory. England had not been conquered; that much was certain. Maire felt uneasy about the future but rejoiced at the thought that at least the men were on their way back home.

She saw Iain Macdonald from time to time. He passed through on his way to see crofters who had fallen ill through the severe winter. It was comforting to see him and Maire began to look forward to his visits. He was always gravely polite when they met and sometimes she fancied she saw a warmth and softness in his grey eyes which was not there for anyone else. However, she could have imagined it.

One day, there was a great commotion. One of Morag's cows had broken out of its byre and fallen into a drift. The unfortunate animal could not move. The more it struggled in the snow, the deeper it was wedged in. Morag had a halter round its neck and by means of tugging and shouting encouragement, was desperately trying to rescue the beast. It constituted half her herd.

"Ach," she growled to Maire, "if only Allan was here, he would have it out in a moment." She was red-faced with effort. Maire offered to help and the two women attempted to free the cow, Morag pulling at the front and Maire pushing from behind. All to no avail. They kept slithering into the snowdrift themselves. They were about to admit defeat when Iain chanced to pass by. Maire was never so glad to see anyone and flashed him a smile of such warm invitation that he felt his heart lurch. He frowned to hide this moment of weakness. He could not help the feelings this girl aroused in him but there was no reason, he thought savagely, why she should know of them.

Clambering down to help them, Iain issued curt orders to the women about the best way to extricate the cow.

"You are in danger of strangling the poor beast," he scolded Morag who for once did not answer back. Then he fixed a dour gaze on Maire.

"And as for you pushing it forward, can you not see that it has a broken leg?" Maire was mortified. She was sorry she had caused pain to the cow but after all, she had simply been doing her best. There was no need for Iain Macdonald to speak to her like that in front of Morag! After all, she thought in a rare moment of pique, she was the Laird's niece. But of course, she already knew that Iain Macdonald was no respecter of persons. Social position meant little to him. It was – it *had* been, she corrected herself sternly – one of the things she most admired in him. There were limits however, and Maire detested rudeness.

The cow however under his efficient directions and greater strength was at last freed. It clambered on to the solid crust of snow and lowed in gratitude. Now that it was at liberty, it looked distinctly sorry for itself and Maire saw with dismay that its back leg did indeed jut out at an odd angle. There was nothing for it but to half carry the beast back to shelter. This was managed and

Iain became engrossed in the task of setting its leg in a makeshift splint. Maire watched his deft, sure movements with reluctant respect. There was no doubt that he would make a fine doctor.

He accompanied her back to the house in spite of her protests. "What if *you* fell into a drift?" he said with mock seriousness. "One rescue is enough in a day!" It was hard not to like him when his eyes twinkled like that. He offended her one moment and was kind to her the next. Maire decided that she would never understand him.

Their progress was slow, impeded by a fresh snowfall. As they made their way up a hillock which hid the house from their view, Iain stole a glance at this girl he couldn't get out of his mind, in spite of his efforts. He saw a change in her which intrigued him. She was no longer the young woman he had met at the Grassmarket that day, nor even the one who had charmed him utterly the night she sang at the ceilidh. There was now a voluptuous curve to her lips and the line of her cheek. With a needle stab of jealousy, he wondered if Maire had a lover. If she had, he thought ferociously, he could guess who had won her heart. Alasdair Macdonald had all the requisites to win a woman.

The thought depressed him and made him angry, and not purely for selfish reasons either. He was concerned for Maire. If Alasdair loved her, it was his duty to protect her and that did not involve claiming her body as well as her heart. It exposed her to several kinds of risk. Also, what future would she have with him, if indeed there were any future at all for a Jacobite officer?

His mind was so far away that he did not notice Maire stumble over a hidden obstacle in the snow. She exclaimed and fell against him. In a moment, she was in his arms and without thinking or self-conscious awareness of his action, Iain bent and kissed her full on the lips.

It was clear to the startled Maire that this was no ordinary, teasing embrace. There was pent-up emotion behind it and a barely concealed passion, which for a moment called to something in her own blood. She felt herself begin to respond to his kiss, then pushed him away violently, angry with herself and unable to believe her own reaction. If there was one quality Maire rated above all others, it was loyalty. She hated herself for betraying Alasdair, even for a moment. Her self-disgust caused her to glare at Iain, who was already furious that he had exposed his emotions so openly. The two stared coldly at one another until Iain broke the silence.

"I am sorry I offended you, Miss Drummond. It will, I can assure you, never occur again."

He gave no further explanation; Maire was left to wonder what exactly he had meant by the kiss but there was no way her curiosity could be satisfied. This incident spoiled the easy relationship which had grown between them over the bleak winter months. Maire regretted it because she had few other people of her own age to talk to, and she had grown to rely on Iain's dependable and understanding presence from time to time. It was always the same with men, she thought crossly. Sooner or later they complicated things.

* * *

The winter seemed to tighten its grip even more firmly during the early months of 1746. Movement was restricted and there were few items of news from the outside world to disturb their calm existence.

The retreat – for that is what it was – continued and the Jacobite army was once more back in Scotland, pursued closely by the enemy. One piece of heartening news did reach them, however. The Prince's army had turned on General Hawley's troops at Falkirk and defeated a Government army which greatly outnumbered them. Once again, the furious Highland charge which the English dreaded, carried the day. If the Scots could have read the letter sent that night of 17th January from Hawley to the Duke of Cumberland, it would have given them something to smile about for never was a more pathetic letter of excuse received by a commander:

'My heart is broke. We had enough to beat them for we had 2,000 men more than they, but such scandalous cowardice I never saw before. The whole second line of Foot ran away without firing a shot!'

No more news of any battle was heard after this. It seemed

that the two armies had settled into their winter quarters until the spring enabled them to move again, Cumberland at Aberdeen and the Jacobites at Inverness.

Alasdair returned unexpectedly. She had hoped for his coming for it was entirely possible to make the journey now the thaw could not be far off. He looked pale and thin and, she thought, exhausted. There was a bitterness in his face she had not seen before. As luck would have it, she was with Iain Macdonald who had paid them a visit to see how they all were – a rare thing these days. Maire was just congratulating herself that they seemed to be regaining something of their old friendship when Alasdair came.

He stood at the door of the room, leaning against the wooden frame and raking Iain with a glance of utter contempt. Maire's heart raced suddenly. Mingled with her delight at seeing him again was a feeling of apprehension. The hostility in the room was palpable; you could almost hear the clash of steel.

"So," Alasdair said the word from between clenched teeth. "This is how you spend your leisure time, *Doctor* Macdonald." He emphasised the word "doctor" as if it were an insult. "You have the effrontery to sit here in comfort while finer men than you risk their lives in battle – aye, and give their lives, too. There are some Macdonalds who will not be returning when this is over, and there are others who could well do with your medical skills, such as they are. We have wounded men at Inverness but of course, that does not concern you. A man who does not have the stomach to fight will hardly find himself with an army!"

Maire heard a sharp intake of breath from Iain and waited for the inevitable outburst. To her surprise, it never came, though he was pale with anger. She had the feeling that some other emotion, however, was troubling him as well. In his grey eyes, she thought she saw signs of compassion as if Alasdair's words had stirred him in a way he did not expect.

Curtly and with few words, Iain took his leave. Maire was glad that at least the confrontation had been brief. She sent word to the rest of the family that Alasdair had come home. It turned out that he was only there for a brief visit, to obtain the last of the gold for the dwindling Jacobite coffers and, if possible, to drum up some more support. The army was smaller now than before, having suffered from desertions since its retreat back home.

Over dinner, Alasdair told them why the army had turned back. It was the main cause of his savage disappointment.

"We managed to reach Derby," he said. "Within striking distance of London! The Prince was all for making a surprise dash to take the city and I think he was right. We would have taken them unawares and the capital would have been ours. Why, a rumour reached our ears that King George was packing his trunks ready to scuttle to Hanover if we came any closer. And what happened?"

There was silence at the dinner table: they all knew the answer was coming.

"The Prince was advised by all his lieutenants that we should march north again, back to Scotland. We were too weak to engage with the enemy on his home ground. We had suffered too many desertions. Back home, we could wait the winter out and raise another army in the spring – all very convincing arguments, no doubt, but the counsels of old men! The Prince knew that it was a mistake to lose the chance of having London fall into his lap like a ripe plum. He pleaded with them with tears in his eyes. But what could Charles do? In the end, the Prince gave in and we began the retreat."

Alasdair bowed his head over his wine as if to hide his own tears. Maire and the others sat silent, appalled by the incipient tragedy that was unfolding before them. They have lost their best chance, thought Maire and as if in answer to her thoughts, Uncle Ewan quoted bookishly, which was something he was given to doing in moments of stress:

> There is a tide in the affairs of men
> Which taken at the flood, leads on to fortune.

He sighed and did not finish the quotation, nor did he want to.

The family retired soon after this. Alasdair and Maire met briefly for a few minutes and for the first time, she saw that terrible bitterness leave his face. He assured her of his continuing love for her but said that since he had to leave early next day and was much in need of rest, he would say "*au revoir*" now. Maire willingly agreed. It was an unexpected gift to have seen him at all. At least now she knew that he was still safe.

No-one noticed Jamie, who had sat quietly listening at dinner to all the troubles that beset the Jacobites and in particular the lack of resources and manpower. The Prince was his idol and Alasdair only marginally less so. As the house fell silent and asleep, the boy lay awake for a long time watching the moon rise over Loch Mhor.

Chapter Sixteen

Maire woke in the early hours with a vague feeling of loss. She started awake and sat up in bed wondering what was wrong. She must have been dreaming. Then she remembered that Alasdair was leaving today to return to the Prince's camp. That would explain her strange, indeterminate sensation that something precious was gone.

The morning began normally. They had a simple breakfast, early as usual. Jamie's place was empty and his mother went away smiling to get the sleepyhead out of bed. She was back within minutes. Maire took one look at her aunt's face and leapt up.

"What's wrong?"

Even as Aunt Isobel told her about the empty room and the few belongings taken, including a favourite penknife, Maire guessed what had happened. She blamed herself for not foreseeing that something like this was possible. Jamie's face last night came back to her – pale, set, determined, with that faraway look in the eyes his father had. The boy was an idealist and brought up in a Jacobite household. What was more natural than for a spirited lad like him to run away and join the army? The Prince needed men; Alasdair had said so.

Aunt Isobel was beginning to break down in hysterics. That, Maire decided, would do no good to anyone. Firmly, she took charge of the situation. Jamie could not have gone very far. He might even have lost his way. In any case, the sooner an attempt was made to find him the better. A search was mounted at once but to no avail. For two weeks the neighbouring countryside was scoured in ever-widening circles but in the end, they drew a blank. Isobel was beside herself with worry and Maire was increasingly convinced that eventually someone would have to set out towards the Prince's camp at Inverness. Jamie must be there, or on the road to it, and there was a chance that he had been seen by somebody. She felt she was the one to go. No-one else who could be spared was able to undertake the journey.

At first they would not hear of it. A girl – a Lowlander at that – alone on their hills! She would never manage. How would she even know the right direction to Inverness? Not that Jamie could be anywhere near there, of course. He was probably, said Isobel hopefully, on his way home right now. Perhaps it would be all right if Maire went just a little way to look for him? Uncle Ewan gave in. Cursing his bad leg and the fact that all the able-bodied men were at war, he could see no other solution.

Janet wasn't happy about it but did not try to stop Maire. Once the girl had made up her mind about something, there was not much point; Janet knew that. Besides, she was aware that in the last few months, Maire was maturing and making adult decisions of her own. Not always wise ones, thought Janet with a tightening of the lips. Nevertheless, she was glad to see the emergence of a strong, self-reliant young woman in the girl she was so fond of. If Maire had given her heart where Janet suspected, she would have need of all her strength before she was done.

Ewan and Isobel were reassured when they saw the businesslike preparations made by their niece before her departure. Maire dressed in very practical woollen clothes, a skirt and bodice and a pair of stout shoes fit for rough walking. Over her shoulders she threw a tartan shawl for warmth, for it was chilly in those early days of April. Spring still seemed a long way off.

What Maire did not show the others were a few other articles she carefully stowed away in case of need. Though she hoped to return shortly with her cousin, she had no intention of being caught unprepared on the hills. Something might delay her, or Jamie might be further away than they thought. Against this contingency, Maire took with her a sharp knife, a small cooking pot and a tinder box. At least she and Jamie would not starve if they had to spend a night or two in the open. Whether they died of exposure, she thought with a shiver, was another matter. In any case, the hidden articles were only in case of emergency; she hoped fervently that she would not be away long enough to need them.

The weather was kind to start with as she left Loch Mhor and struck out northwards in the direction of Inverness. There was a glint of sunlight on the surface of the water and a faint haze of green on the frozen hills. Maire's spirits lifted. Perhaps spring wasn't so far off, after all.

She made good progress and in a few hours began to keep a sharp lookout for Jamie. There was no sign of anyone except an old shepherd who looked at her curiously. It wasn't every day you saw a girl scrambling about on this rough territory. On an impulse, Maire asked him whether he had seen a young boy around, and described Jamie. To her delight, the wizened brown face nodded. Yes, he had seen a boy and that very day, too. He pointed in a direction which surprised her, to the north-east. Surely that was off course for Inverness? Still, it was in the right general direction. Perhaps Jamie had just strayed a little. It was natural, considering his youth. Forgetting that this was a boy who had been brought up in the country and whose sense of geographical direction from running wild in his native hills, was probably better than her own, Maire followed the shepherd's directions.

It was an hour before she began to notice that the weather had changed. It was a lot colder and, which was worse, a sudden mist was coming down like a blanket. Already the sound of her feet on the rocky stone was muffled and threw back a weird echo. It was as if there was another pair of footsteps following her. Maire began to feel uneasy and very alone.

Still, these hill mists could vanish as quickly as they came down. All she had to do was wait until she could see the way forward. It was dangerous to move around in these conditions. The path was clear one moment and swirling the next with white indecipherable shapes that resembled wraiths. It was a good thing; Maire told herself firmly, that she was not given to imaginative fancies. Nevertheless, there was the possibility of a crevasse opening under her feet in this visibility. She had better seek some kind of shelter.

An overhanging rock appeared which offered a fairly dry niche from the moist air. She scrambled under it, feeling her way rather than seeing it and glad to find the softness of springy heather underneath. Perhaps some animal had used it as a den.

She herself would not object to stretching out her weary limbs for a short time. Her hand went out to steady herself and then her heart seemed to jerk to a stop.

Another hand grasped hers in the semi-darkness! Maire had never known a moment of such utter terror. She was too frozen even to scream. Then she heard something. A low choking sound as if someone was crying and trying not to be heard. The fear left her. Whoever it was, was even more frightened than she was. She realised she was still clutching the hand and it dawned on her how small it was compared to her own. Surely this was the hand of a child!

She peered ahead with sudden courage and found herself looking at a young boy. Not Jamie. This lad was dressed in a somewhat tattered army uniform and Maire instinctively knew that it was an alien uniform. It did not take a military expert to recognise the famous colour of the English Redcoats and the braid and pewter buttons seemed to scream aloud that he belonged to the Government army. He was clutching some object that seemed to him to be very precious and which her wondering gaze revealed to be a drum.

Whoever he was, he certainly posed no threat. Maire noticed in the swiftly dispersing mist that the lad was pale and shivering – probably starving, too. He looked as if he had spent a few nights in the open. What on earth was he doing here? And – the thought struck her with trepidation – what was the English army doing near here? She had assumed it was far away at Aberdeen.

"Who are you?" It seemed a good way to begin; Maire could think of nothing else and this was no time for polite formalities. The boy's blue eyes blinked as if surprised, but pleased as well. A grin appeared on his face, reminding her of Jamie.

"You speak English!" He obviously hadn't expected it. Why should he when most other people around here spoke only Gaelic? She spoke slowly and carefully to him, allowing for the fact that each found the other's accent hard to interpret. Once started talking, he became quite garrulous.

His name was Tom. He came from a place in England called Kent. From what he said, it was apparently the nearest place to Paradise on earth. Apples and cherries grew there and the sun shone all summer long. Even in mid-winter, it was never as cold as this. He wished he had never joined the army. It was a big mistake and he ought to have listened to his mother. Instead, he had run away and enlisted as a drummer boy. This was his drum. He showed it to Maire proudly and she duly admired it. He had taken it with him when he decided to run away from a brutal sergeant who was always picking on him. Besides, the army was not as much fun as he'd thought. In fact, it wasn't fun at all. You didn't even get enough to eat and you were beaten for the least thing. The trouble was – Maire saw a tear start to glisten – now he was in even worse trouble. You could be hanged for desertion, or at the very least, flogged. He didn't know what he was going to do.

Maire felt a surge of protective tenderness. In spite of the fact that she had only just met him and he belonged to a different country, there was a frank honesty about the English boy which spoke directly to her heart. Also, he reminded her so much of Jamie in his youthful vulnerability. She wanted to help him.

"When did you last eat?" she asked with concern. He couldn't remember exactly. A long time ago. Maire suddenly became aware that she too hadn't eaten for some time. That settled the matter. The mist had cleared almost completely now and she could continue her journey northwards. Why could Tom not accompany her? He would be safer making for the Jacobites than returning to his own camp to be treated as a deserter.

Briefly, she told the drummer boy what brought her on this journey and about her hope of finding Jamie. She also showed him the accoutrements she had brought with her in case she had to find her own food. Given the chance of a travelling-companion and a hope of sustenance, Tom accepted with alacrity. Besides, this was the first kind voice he had heard since he left home.

The rest of that day, the two walked together over the hills. It was safer to keep away from the main road below, Maire decided. Both she and Tom had every reason to wish to avoid the Redcoats. She still felt the shock of discovering that they were so close. As they walked, they talked, and a warm friendship grew between them which had nothing to do with the time they had known one another and everything to do with circumstance.

They took shelter at night in an empty shepherd's bothy. It wasn't very clean but it was better than nothing. The weather had become sharply colder with that treacherous speed which could catch the unwary traveller in these hills. Maire was privately becoming more anxious than she showed her new friend. The culinary equipment she had brought had not done them much good so far. They had not managed to obtain any food to put in the pot. All they had eaten were the remnants of a couple of bannocks which, thank goodness, she had shoved in her pocket at the last moment. Also, she wasn't at all sure exactly – or even roughly – where they were any more. The mist had completely disorientated her. However, she kept these worries to herself.

The next day dawned so cold that their breath formed clouds of steam in the little hut. The only solution was to trudge on in a direction they hoped was north. To keep moving was their only chance of survival. Stomachs rumbling with emptiness, they tried to keep their spirits up by singing and telling stories. It was safe enough; there was no-one to hear them in that wilderness.

Then they had a stroke of good fortune. They were lucky enough to catch a rabbit emerging unwarily from its burrow. Tom pounced on it and wrung its neck quickly. There was a nearby stream which served to quench their thirst and also to fill the pot Maire had brought. She skinned and gutted the rabbit and put the pieces in the pot. The fire was lit easily by the tinder box and soon crackled merrily. A stew had never smelt or tasted so good and neither minded the absence of salt.

Maire felt they had walked enough for one day. She thought it wise to look for a suitable place for the night before darkness set in. It was obvious that they would have to sleep in the open. She was thankful she had brought the warm plaid with her. It would serve again as a blanket.

A whoop of triumph showed that Tom had found a cave, which would at least offer some degree of shelter. They dragged old bracken and heather in to cushion the floor as a rough mattress, and lay down exhausted but comforted by each other's presence. Each was grateful not to be spending the long night alone in that desolate place.

The only sounds in the Highland night were the odd cry of a curlew and the constant rushing water over the pebbles of the burn.

Chapter Seventeen

They slept better that night. The intense cold seemed to have
lessened and the food had been a great solace. On rising, they
prepared to continue their journey but a strange warning intuition
told Maire that it would be as well to spy out the land first. They
could not assume that they were the only ones on these hills.
Tom offered eagerly to climb to a high ridge and be the lookout.
He longed to be of use to this girl who had befriended him.
Willingly, Maire agreed and watched him disappear over the
rise.

There was silence on the hillside after Tom's footsteps
faded away, the undergrowth creaking and rustling under his
buckled army shoes. Maire looked down at the heather. Rusty
yellowed roots were giving way to fresh green shoots which
would mantle the September hills in a blaze of purple. Gorse
flamed with gold and the bracken unfurled delicate, serrated
leaves like miniature banners.

Maire suddenly felt a lightness of heart she had not known
since the start of her journey. A rare shaft of sunlight
transformed the grey landscape and the air she breathed seemed
balmy compared to yesterday's iron-gripping cold. It was an
unexpected touch of spring in that icy April. Above her, she
heard with delight, a lark spiralled and sang. It was difficult not
to feel hopeful on such a day.

While Tom reconnoitred the hills to see if it was safe to
move on, Maire remembered that she also had work to do. All
traces of their stay in the cave must be got rid of. The relics of
last night's meal, the crushed undergrowth where they had
rested, any sign which would betray their presence had to be
carefully hidden.

She scattered the ashes from the fire among the heather and
buried the rabbit bones and skin deep under a boulder. The taste
of the meat was still fresh on her tongue and made her mouth

water at the memory. It was the best meal they had enjoyed for days and Maire felt stronger because of it. "A full belly makes a brave man." She smiled as she remembered Janet's old saying.

Her cleaning-up operations completed, Maire decided to freshen up by washing her face and hands at the burn. Also, she was thirsty after her exertions. Slinging the tartan plaid loosely round her shoulders, she walked down through the fast-dissolving shreds of mist to the diamond-winking stream. She could just see its source in the mountain above, a white brushstroke of frozen water, but here it gushed and frothed over brown pebbles.

Maire slipped off her plaid and unbuttoned her bodice to wash. She felt the grime of days float away as she splashed water on her face and neck, cupping her hands again and again. It was icy, tingling cold, making her gasp, but it was invigorating.

The rock she leant on was over a part of the burn which resembled a pool, more still and deep than the chattering water below. It was so clear that Maire could see the silver dart of fish in its depths. Perhaps, she thought, we may catch a trout before we leave and then Tom and I will not starve tonight either.

The sun made the brown trout pool into a mirror and Maire caught sight of herself for the first time in days. She was appalled at her dishevelled appearance and tried to tidy her hair as best she could, without the benefit of a comb. She cursed her lack of foresight in not bringing one, but she had been intent on remembering to take essentials, such as the knife, the cooking pot and the tinder box. On reflection, she thought that she had done the right thing. After all, who was here on this desolate hillside to see her untidy state? And finding Jamie was the only thing that mattered.

The warm sun fell like a blessing on her neck and shoulders and Maire felt stiff, knotted muscles relax after her uncomfortable night on the cave floor. Last year's bracken had been too tinder dry to be much of a cushion. There was something soporific about the gushing song of the water and Maire began to feel sleepy.

Suddenly a movement close by caused her to start. A gleaming streak of brown flashed past her feet and dived gracefully into the pool. Maire saw the splash rather than heard it because of the rippling burn below.

Fascinated, she watched the otter swim downstream after a silvery trout. The ripples made by its entrance into the brown stillness gradually widened and Maire's face, momentarily fragmented, began to reappear as the water settled. It was like seeing a child's puzzle being reassembled by an unseen hand.

And then her heart jumped into her mouth. For hers was not the only face reflected in the shuddering mirror. A burly soldier stood behind her, his shape blotting out the sun. The day seemed suddenly to have gone very dark.

Maire could see the scarlet of his coat gashed by blue and yellow facings, with bright buttons and gold piping. He wore a black tricorne hat over pale blue, very hard eyes. The face was brutal and malicious. It was also smiling. Maire saw all these details in a flash with that astounding clarity which sometimes occurs in moments of sheer terror.

She tried to rise to her feet and flee but the Redcoat grabbed her shoulders and hauled her round to face him. Maire had a brief glimpse of white gaitered legs, buttoned up to the thigh and saw that hanging from the man's belt was a cartridge pouch, and on his left, a bayonet. She wondered for a fleeting desperate moment if she could perhaps manage to get hold of those sixteen inches of steel death.

As if he read her thoughts, the man barked a laugh and pulled her closer to him.

"Oh no, you don't, my pretty. I know what you'd like to do to the likes of me. Will Rogers wasn't born yesterday."

He stooped and picked up the plaid shawl from the rock. "A Rebel, if ever I saw one. And no-one cares what we do to Rebels. Vermin, that's what you are and the less of you we leave alive, the better. But not yet. I've got something in mind first, before I settle with you."

Maire opened her mouth to scream but the Redcoat hit her sharply across the mouth and she felt the salt taste of blood on her tongue.

"Shut your mouth! We don't want anyone to interrupt us, do we? Not yet awhile. Finders keepers, that's what I say."

The pockmarked face leered closer and the stench of his sour tobacco-laden breath made Maire want to gag. She felt faint with horror and disgust as she felt herself half dragged, half carried across the heather. Maire's hands scrabbled desperately at tufts of wiry undergrowth, seeking to find a hold to delay their progress to where? Where was he taking her? Her fingernails broke and bled as she was pulled inexorably towards the yawning black mouth in the hillside. It was the same cave she and Tom had used for refuge last night. But now that seemed like a thousand years ago and the welcoming cave had become dark and menacing, a gaping maw waiting to devour her.

The lark above was still singing, oblivious and uncaring about the scene below. Part of Maire's mind heard the sweet cascade of melody and she felt a bitter stab as she remembered how happy that song had made her only a few minutes ago. It wasn't the natural world that had changed; everything went on the same. Only *her* world had been shattered.

These thoughts took only a few moments to race through Maire's mind and suddenly, she found herself in the cave. With renewed energy, she fought and struggled, managing to scratch the Redcoat's cheek with two thin red lines. It only made him more brutal and since he was between her and the cave entrance, Maire could see no hope of escape.

Flung onto a pile of old and withered bracken, she rolled to one side and just evaded the outstretched calloused hands with their bitten nails. The soldier laughed and unbuckled his belt. He found this an amusing pastime. This wasn't the first Highland slut he had raped and by God, it wouldn't be the last. They fought like wild cats, these mountain women but then, he reasoned, that was only to be expected. They were half animals, these Highlanders, not really human. So it didn't matter what you did to them. And in fact, he chuckled to himself as he took off his jacket; it was much more fun this way. That little vixen had put up quite a fight but she was finished now. He looked at her coldly and totally without pity. The red gold curls were matted and torn, tears of fear and outrage still wet on her cheeks.

Maire knew in her heart that this was the end for her. She would never leave the cave alive but what she most dreaded was what would happen before she died. What was about to happen now?

She gave a despairing cry as the Redcoat leapt on her, but

she had no real hope. Who was there to hear her? Then her voice was cut off as one hand clamped over her mouth and the other clawed at her dress. She fought bravely against the crushing weight on top of her and the probing fingers that ripped and tore at her clothing. Her breasts were bruised with his rough handling and she wanted to cry out with pain. The rancid smell of stale sweat from his half-naked body made Maire retch. But the worst thing of all was that she could scarcely breathe and felt she was buried under a mountain of male flesh. She heard her dress being torn to shreds and felt her legs forced apart as the man dealt with her wild struggles with one heavy blow to her temple. Her head sang from the pain and she began to feel herself slipping towards a dark tunnel which would engulf her and from which she feared she would never emerge. Everything began to seem unreal as if it was all happening to someone else; she was simply observing it as a spectator.

As unconsciousness began to close in on her, Maire began to hope that she would indeed never wake up. It was easier that way. Pain shot through her loins and she was suddenly aware of the man forcing himself into her, grunting like an animal. All her strength had ebbed away and she closed her eyes against the nightmare and let herself drift towards the welcome blackness that awaited. Her bruised, beaten body could fight no longer.

Suddenly, there was a dull thud and the man slumped over her. She struggled to breathe, to push off the dead weight and hazily, as through a thick mist, she saw Tom.

He was standing rigid as if he were paralysed, looking down at the soldier he had hit, the stone still in his hand.

Neither of them spoke for a moment. Then Maire squeezed out from under the Redcoat and noticed as she did so, a trickle of blood running from the back of his head.

"Is he dead?" Tom's whisper sounded hoarse and unlike his usual voice. He seemed all at once to have become much older.

Maire sensed the fear in the boy, and tried to pull herself together. Painfully, she struggled to her knees and then her feet. Her head buzzed as if a swarm of bees had invaded it, but the darkness was receding from her eyes. She could see more clearly now, the dank interior of the cave with the sunlight beyond, and lying sprawled at her feet, the man who had raped her.

The half dressed Redcoat lay inert on the cave floor, but he was still alive. They could see the rise and fall of his chest, hear his stertorous, slow breathing. He was stunned, but for how long? And what would be their fate if they were found here with the soldier they had attacked? One of His Majesty's troops. They both knew they had to get away from that place, and as quickly as possible.

It was clear however that Maire was in no condition to move just yet. Tom looked with pity and horror at his friend's bruised, scratched body, the weals on her arms and legs turning an ugly purplish-red, even in the dim light of the cave.

"That brute nearly killed you!" He put his arms protectively round her and made a makeshift bracken couch for her to rest upon. His tenderness made Maire want to cry but she knew this was no time to break down.

"Rest here for a little, Maire. Get your strength back. I'll go out and see if it is safe for us to go on."

Tom knew that this time he must be extra cautious in spying out the land. Where one Redcoat was, there were likely to be others.

He picked up his drum and sticks which he had left in a corner of the cave, not really knowing what he was doing. The familiar touch of the instrument comforted him in some strange way. It reminded him of when things were normal.

Leaving Maire huddled in the cave beside the prone body of the Redcoat, Tom made his way down the hill and towards the valley. He jumped across a small stream and struck upwards again to see if the next hill was empty of danger. All seemed quiet. Reassured, he climbed further to obtain a clearer view of the surrounding countryside. The loch below was a silver slash in the morning sunlight and the snow-capped peaks in the distance reminded him with a pang of homesick longing of the sugar cakes his mother used to make. He stood for a moment, sniffing the wind and listening for any unusual noise.

It was as well he did so. He had some little warning of the party of Redcoats who were just below and from whom he was hidden by a rocky mound. The men's footsteps were muffled by a carpet of moss and it was a chance curse from one of the men ahead who stumbled over a boulder that alerted Tom.

Quick as the wild animal he was beginning to feel in his hunted state, Tom shrank back into the shadow of a cranny where two boulders met. It wasn't much cover but it would have to do. There was no time for anything else. He waited helplessly, his breath rasping in his chest. There seemed to be the steady beat of a drum near him and he realised with surprise that it was the pounding of his own heart.

The Redcoat, who had stumbled, puffed with exertion as he climbed the last steep slope to where Tom was hiding. Robert Wilkins, Sergeant in the Royal East Kents Regiment, was not happy on this fine April morning to be scrambling about on hillsides in this accursed country, looking for Rebel spies or deserters. In fact, truth to tell, he was not, at that moment, happy to be a soldier at all. A basically humane man, he did not feel at home in an army which treated its own men only a little less harshly than the enemy. Outspoken when he felt the occasion demanded it, he had been flogged more than once for daring to question his superiors. What rankled even more however, was the fact that his doxy, who accompanied him everywhere as a camp follower, had recently been put on the whirligig until she vomited her guts out, taking two days to recover. This cruel machine, a wooden cage set on a pivot, was used as a punishment for women who offended authority. In this case, the authority who demanded that Molly be disciplined was his commanding officer, who had taken a fancy to the girl – an advance which was, unfortunately for Molly, swiftly and ignominiously rejected.

Wilkins still broke out in a cold sweat when he remembered his choking helpless fury at seeing the girl he loved and who had given him such fidelity, tossed round in the air on the whirligig. She was strapped in and screaming until she could scream no more. It was much worse than being flogged himself. At least then, he could bite on a leather strap.

These bitter thoughts were in Wilkins' mind when he rounded the boulder. He saw Tom at once. The hiding place was totally inadequate and the boy stood out like a red beacon against the granite rocks.

The two looked at one another – the man and the boy, with instant recognition. The Redcoat opened his mouth to call to his comrades and Tom felt a wave of panic. His hand went out involuntarily in a gesture of pleading.

And then, unbelieving, he heard Wilkins call down to his soldiers, "Nothing up here, lads. We'd best try further on. Spread out and search the next hill."

Something flew through the air and fell at Tom's feet. He looked at it stupidly, not at first being able to recognise it for what it was. A piece of stale bread, still dusty from the soldier's pocket.

Wilkins had disappeared as quickly as he came and Tom bent down and picked up the hunk of bread. It was a gesture of friendship, of goodwill, and he felt tears start to his eyes. He had no right to expect friendship from such a quarter. He remembered Wilkins, though he couldn't remember his name. He'd been the kindest of the soldiers he had met in the army during those dreadful months.

Tom bit into the bread and chewed a piece off. It was leathery but still eatable. He masticated slowly, pondering on the strange event that he had just witnessed. It was beyond his comprehension why Wilkins had not betrayed him. But it was enough to be still alive, and he was thankful for it.

He heard the soldiers calling to one another as they moved to the next hill for their search. "Move up, there!" "Spread out!" "Flush the Rebels out, lads!"

The next hill! The hill where Maire was, hiding in a cave beside a Redcoat whom they had attacked. The thoughts collided in his brain in a fusion of sudden awareness and anguish. Maire would be captured and certainly killed if they found her. The circumstances were too desperate to allow of any reprieve. What could he do?

His hand reached down to the drum still slung around his neck. It was a ridiculous adjunct in his present plight. No use at all. Why did he hang onto it? Much better to ditch it and move more freely. Tom's hand automatically smoothed the skin of the drum and finding it loose, he tightened it as if he were going to play.

And then it came to him! He had no weapon but he did have the drum. Perhaps he could use it to draw off the soldiers from Maire's hiding place. Soldiers reacted instinctively to the drum signals they were taught to obey. He knew that. Many times he had seen men half asleep, tumble out of their tents, pulling on their uniforms to turn out for the Reveille.

His left heel went into the hollow of his right foot and he bent his left knee to balance the drum as he had done so often before. His elbows went up, poised to give out a military signal. Almost without thought, he went into the drag and paradiddle of the General Call to Arms. It was a strange relief to play once again and make the sound echo around the silent hills.

The result was immediate. The soldiers heard the familiar drum roll with its relentless left-hand beat and halted, confused. Curiosity led them to search for the sound. They left the hill and scrambled down towards the signal, which should not be happening, not here. It did not take them long to locate the drummer boy. He was not hiding now, but in the open, drumming proudly as if he was still part of the army.

Tom was arrested at once. It was quite clear that he was a deserter. His torn clothing and general appearance made it obvious. Also, a few of the soldiers recognised him as the drummer boy who had run away.

There were a few of the men who were keen to execute summary justice themselves on the lily-livered little coward. Dead or alive, what would it matter, as long as they took him back?

Wilkins stepped in and halted a punishment session where Tom was being slapped around the head and sent tottering round a circle of grinning faces. He knew only too well how one thing could lead to another, if the men got excited.

Quickly, he ordered the soldiers into an escort party surrounding the prisoner and himself struck up a verse of Lilliburlero as they marched down the hill. Savagely, he turned to Tom as the men took up the refrain from his lead. "Play, boy! It's all you're good for. So play while you still can!"

Tom obeyed and tapped out the martial rhythm as he was marched off in the midst of the soldiers. They felt happy now that they had at least found something.

Not much to show for a day on the hills but better than nothing. Their rations might be better tonight. Only the sergeant seemed strangely morose.

The drummer boy held his head high as he went. A strange calm had settled on him since he had used the drum again. He couldn't explain it. It wasn't that fear had left him. He knew what awaited him back at the army camp. At worst, death. At best, a flogging. But he couldn't regret what he had done.

He hoped Maire would understand why he'd had to leave her. She was the only person who had been kind to him since he last saw his mother. For a brief moment, Tom saw his home in Kent in all its greenness: the apple orchard in autumn, the cherry trees in spring. A terrible yearning filled him like an ache. He wondered bleakly as he marched through the valley among those foreign hills, whether he would ever see his home again.

Chapter Eighteen

High above on the hillside, Maire watched them go, their scarlet uniforms slicing through the valley like a streak of blood. She heard the singing: snatches of English words ringing a challenge to echo round the Scottish braes:

> *The Pope sends us over a bonny brisk lad,*
> *Twang 'em, we'll bang 'em and hang 'em up all.*
> *Who to court English favour, wears a Scotch plaid,*
> *Twang 'em, we'll bang 'em and hand 'em up all.*
> *To arms, to arms,*
> *Brave boys, to arms!*

She had not connected the singing with Tom, but some unformulated fear made Maire drag her bruised and aching body out of the cave and over to a vantage point where she could look down into the glen. Hidden behind a lichen covered rock, she saw her friend led away and hope withered in her heart. She doubted she would ever see Tom alive again. What had happened to lead to his capture, she could only guess. Instinct told her that it had something to do with the drumming she had heard earlier, but she could not think what strange suicidal impulse had led Tom to call attention to himself in that way. Unless – it was to draw the soldiers away from her! Suddenly, Maire knew with absolute certainty what Tom had done. And she would never be able to thank him! She swallowed hard to dispel the tight knot in her throat. A stiff gust of wind made her shiver and reminded her of her present predicament. The temporary spring-like lull in the weather had passed and the air once more seized her lungs with the grim reminder that it was still winter. It was like breathing ice; Maire saw hazy droplets of steam issue from her mouth with every harsh gasp she took. Even her feet felt frozen to the ground as she moved painfully away from the rock and pulled the woollen plaid round her body. There was snow in the wind, and the sky was grey and lowering.

She could not return to the cave. The Redcoat had shown signs of returning consciousness, emitting loud groans, which was one reason why she was glad to scramble here and find out what the noise of singing and drumming could signify. She'd known it was risky to be in the open but she *had* to know what had happened to Tom. Well, now she knew. She was alone once more.

Maire forced herself to try to think clearly. Her wits seemed to be leaden with cold and exhaustion. It seemed to her that there was only one course of action she could take. She had to get away from the vicinity of the cave and the brutal soldier who had attacked her. There was no longer any question however of continuing the journey in her present condition. She could easily die of exposure and then what use would she be to Jamie?

Refuge of some kind must be found, and the sooner the better. Warmth, food, drink and above all rest, was what her strained, exhausted body cried out for. There must be a dwelling somewhere down in the glen. She would walk till she found one and throw herself on the mercy of the inhabitants. If they turned her away to die like a dog in the mountains, or if they were Government supporters who gave her up to the authorities, what did it matter? At least it would be a solution to her present problems. Maire felt almost past caring. It was comforting in a way to reach a stage of such utter desperation. When you reached the end of your tether, there was nowhere else to go. One more short journey, she told herself; a few miles perhaps of clambering over razor-sharp rocks and slithering down slopes of heather, glassy with ice, and she might – *must* – find sanctuary.

She pulled her befuddled wits together and focused hard on the descent from the hill. She soon lost all sense of direction. All she concentrated on was going downwards, seeing a few feet in front of her, not looking ahead at all, lest she lose hope at the enormity of the task she had undertaken. The movement helped get her blood flowing again but the return of feeling to her frozen limbs brought pain with it, sharp and juddering; yet welcome, because now she felt she was at least on the move again and in control of her own destiny. Every step which took her further away from that dreadful cave, made her feel safer. Maire was not particularly religious but into her mind there filtered of its own accord, a half-forgotten childhood prayer and she chanted it to herself in time with her faltering steps. It was strangely comforting and made her feel less abandoned and alone. Also, the simple words reminded her of a time long ago when she was young and knew nothing of the nightmares which could overwhelm you in adult life.

Time seemed to stop as the past and the present became mingled in strange whirling confusion in Maire's head. She wasn't quite sure any longer where she was or what she was doing, slithering and stumbling down the brae with only one aim clear in her head, to find shelter. She felt light-headed and feverish, which was strange in that intense cold. Time was beginning to run out for her. She knew with terrifying clarity that if she fell down now, she would never rise again.

It dawned on her gradually that she was no longer slipping downwards. She had reached the bottom of the hill without knowing it and was in the comparative shelter of the glen. Her steps were now on the level and even the roughness of the ground seemed easy in comparison with the dangerous descent she had miraculously survived.

There was however a new hazard to contend with. Swirls of mist hung in patches over the path, making it difficult to be sure she was still on it. Grimly, Maire plodded on, afraid to stop in case she never started again.

Suddenly, an unearthly wail broke the silence and brought renewed terror to her heart. What creature was there waiting for her in the thick grey blanket ahead? Wild images churned through Maire's fevered imagination, born of old legends and folk tales told her by Janet when she was small. She had halted at the weird and dreadful noise, which surely could not be human! Then a figure gradually took shape through the mist and Maire laughed hysterically and weakly with relief. It was only a young heifer, tethered by a leather thong to a gate and lowing in protest.

She must be near a house or farm. Where there were animals, surely there were people? With a last burst of energy, Maire walked on, more firmly now and with a dawning hope.

The cottage appeared suddenly on a turn of the road. Dry stone built, it had a roof of tightly packed heather, lashed down against the winter gales. There was also a cattle byre and Maire could hear the clucking and scratching of hens in the kailyard behind the house.

She did not stop to think of her reception. The decision had been made on the hill. This was her only chance of survival. They must take her in!

It took Maire's last little remnant of strength to beat her knuckles on the wooden door. Weak as a child, she was appalled at the little noise she made. Perhaps no-one would hear her! She would die in the open after all and they would find her on the doorstep.

When the door did creak ajar, Maire fell forward almost into the arms of the woman who opened it. She managed to whisper the words, "Help me!" and then the darkness which had been threatening for so long to engulf her, finally swept her into oblivion.

She woke to unfamiliar noises and lay there for a few minutes, warm and content as a child, savouring the feeling of comfort and safety. She couldn't recall where she was for a moment but lay still with her eyes closed, trying to remember. The hiss of a peat fire and the sound of a spoon stirring an iron pot brought Maire back to full consciousness. She remembered now how she had come here. Her eyes opened to see a simply furnished room with a table in the centre and a big open hearth. She was lying on a straw pallet on the earth floor near the fire. Maire stirred and at once the woman turned from her work at the cooking pot and came over. Her face was thin and lined as if she had known much sorrow in her life. It would have been a hard face but for the eyes, which were a soft, velvet brown and filled with compassion as she looked down at the girl who was so obviously in trouble.

"Just like my Eppy would have been, had she lived." The thought struck the woman with the force of a blow because at that moment Maire's pale face and tousled copper hair did indeed resemble the daughter she had lost a year ago. There was something too in the girl's eyes – a wounded, hunted look – which went straight to her heart.

"How do you feel, lassie? Are you better? I thocht you were dead, when you fell down on our floor like a sack of oats. What ailed you?"

"It's a long story," Maire said wearily, wondering where to begin.

"Och, the story can wait! It's food you'll be wanting and Kirsty Fraser was never the woman to starve a visitor. But first you must take a hot drink. I've made some brose ready against your waking. There's nothing like it for putting strength into a body."

It tasted like nectar. As Maire sipped the steaming liquid, a blend of heather-honey, oatmeal, cream and whisky, it scorched down her throat and coursed through her body, filling it with a delicious and relaxing glow. Kirsty Fraser was right. It *did* make her feel stronger. She struggled to sit up and suddenly became aware of how filthy and unkempt she was.

"Perhaps," she said shyly, not wanting to give the woman any more trouble than she already had, "I could wash a little. If there is any water to spare –"

"Aye and plenty of it. I have a potful simmering on the fire. I thocht you would need it, for you look as if you had spent a night on the hills. How came a lassie like yourself to be in such a terrible state? Were you kidnapped by gipsies – or worse?"

And while Maire gladly stripped off her rags in front of the fire and washed her bruised body with Kirsty's help, she told her frankly and fully everything that had befallen her since she had left the Laird's house. The only part she kept back was about Tom, for she did not feel ready yet to talk about him. She still grieved for the little drummer-boy. Maire knew instinctively that this woman was to be trusted and it was a great solace to tell another woman of her terrible ordeal in the cave.

Kirsty Fraser listened carefully to Maire's story and when she heard of the encounter with the Redcoat, her face took on the hardness of granite.

"I thocht as much. It wasn't by chance that those marks came to be on your body. So it was one of those Redcoat swine who attacked you. Aye, and many another lass too, I'll warrant. But if you were searching for the Jacobite army, what were you doing so far to the east? Did ye not ken the Prince has been billeted at Inverness these two months past?"

Maire explained that she had been on her way there but had gone astray following a false trail after Jamie. She borrowed a comb from Kirsty and received a present of fresh clothes in place of the tattered rags she arrived in. There was a grey skirt of coarse homespun wool, a linen bodice, woollen stockings and a pair of good, stout shoes. Maire's tartan plaid was drying out in front of the fire.

The clothes fitted perfectly and Maire felt more human than she had for days.

"How can I ever thank you, Kirsty? They are the finest gift I have ever received. But are you sure you can spare them?"

She could tell by the simple furniture that this was a modest household, though by no means as desperately poor as many in the Highlands. There was a sack of oatmeal in the corner and also one of flour. A haunch of salt beef hung from the smoke-darkened beams, making Maire's mouth water and reminding her that she was ravenously hungry. However, she had a conscience about taking too much from a family that could ill afford it. If only she had money with her to pay for the clothes at least!

In a few moments, she was thankful that she had not raised the question of payment. It would have been hurtful to her hostess. Highland hospitality to strangers was a great point of honour. She must remember that, with her Lowland upbringing. Also, as Kirsty sat Maire down at the table and proceeded to feed her with a delicious beef stew and boiled kale, washed down with a home-brewed ale, she explained in calm, everyday tones that the clothes Maire wore, had belonged to her daughter Eppy, now dead.

"And glad I am to see you wear them, lassie. Better they keep you warm than they lie mouldering in a kist for the moths to eat." At that, Maire was even more grateful that she had accepted the clothes in the gracious spirit in which they were offered.

She began to wonder if Kirsty Fraser was a widow, and as if in answer to her thoughts, the older woman cleared the table and set out another platter.

"My man, Duncan, will be home soon from the hills," Kirsty said and Maire detected a nervous note in her voice that she had not heard before. "There is something you should know before he comes home," Kirsty went on, and Maire had an intuition that somehow the coming of Duncan Fraser spelt trouble for her.

While she stirred the pot of stew over the fire, Kirsty talked of the time when Duncan and herself were sweethearts over thirty years ago. The expression on her face altered as she spoke and a subtle transformation almost erased the lines of care and suffering. Maire could now see quite clearly the pretty young girl Kirsty had once been.

"He was a fine figure of a man, was Duncan, in those days. We always knew we were to wed. I had eyes for no other, nor did he, for that matter. We planned to marry when we were both eighteen. There seemed nothing to stop us."

Kirsty sighed and set the spoon down on the hearth. She sat down on the settle beside the glowing fire and continued.

"You told me you come from Edinburgh, lassie. I'll wager you will never think that mysel' or Duncan have ever set foot in the place! But you would be wrong, for we lived in the city for eight months, trying to gather enough money to buy a small piece of land and start a farm. Duncan built this house with his own hands, ye ken, and me and a few others helping him." Kirsty could not keep the pride out of her voice as she said this.

"What did you do in Edinburgh?" asked Maire, intrigued at the thought of the two Highlanders in the city she knew so well and wondering what they thought of it.

"I was a seamstress at the house of a rich advocate and his wife in the Lawnmarket. I've always been a fair hand with the needle. As for Duncan, he was a common chairman, like most of the Highlanders in the city of Edinburgh. They can't get any other work, speaking only the Gaelic, but to hump great fat merchants and gentlefolk round the city on their shoulders. Nobody cares what language a chairman speaks, for he is only a beast of burden, after all. I fared a little better in the great house because I had to learn a bit of your Lowland tongue to understand what the ladies wanted of me. I picked it up the more quickly when I discovered that I was treated a lot better when I could speak English. I was even given better food, whereas before I was fed with scraps like the cat and dog."

Maire felt uncomfortable at this, because she knew households where that sort of thing did happen. Her own, for example. She remembered the anger she used to feel at Hector Grant's attitude to someone like Janet: "Show me a Highlander and I will show you a thief." Yes, she knew that all Kirsty told her was true. Lalland prejudice was rife about anyone who came from beyond the Highland Line.

She saw Kirsty's face suddenly draw into the gaunt lines of grief and worry which it usually bore, and knew that she was about to tell of the tragedy which had blighted both her life and that of Duncan.

"Our happiness melted like snow off a dyke at the coming of spring. The Fiery Cross was sent round the glens, calling out the clansmen to fight for King James."

"The '15 Rebellion," murmured Maire, who knew about it from Janet. Tales of the '15 had filled her childhood, with stories of heroic exploits and deeds of daring. All to no avail of course, for the Scottish army and their supporters from the North of England had been thoroughly defeated and the Earl of Mar, who had raised the Standard, had fled to France.

"Aye, lass, that was the year," Kirsty's lilting voice was low and quiet. Maire felt it had the sad, musical quality of a lament. "1715. I'll not forget it, for it robbed Duncan of his only brother and turned him into the cripple he is today. It was at Sherriffmuir that his brother fell and Duncan himself was left for dead on the battlefield. A whole day he lay in the open with his leg shattered by cannon and no-one to tend him. He remembers looking up at the sky and seeing black wings circling over him. The hooded crows were waiting for him to die. By the grace of God, he managed to crawl to a bothy nearby and was found by a herdsman the next morning. The surgeons saved his life but he will never be the man he was. His right leg is useless and has to be dragged behind him like a lump of lead. He blames the Stuarts for his misfortunes and is bitter now against the Jacobites. It is best you know this, Maire, before he comes. I canna keep you here long, lassie, for I fear that Duncan will not stand for it. But this nicht I am determined you will stay, no matter what Duncan may say!"

As if on cue, the latch of the door was lifted and the man of the house appeared. He had a stick in his hand, which Maire took to be a shepherd's crook but would also serve as a support for his lameness. And lame he certainly was. She felt a pang of pity as she saw the gaunt, bearded figure shuffle over to the fire seeking warmth from the cold outside. A flurry of snow had entered with him and the little cottage which had been such a warm haven to Maire for the last few hours, suddenly seemed to have gone cold.

"What have we here?" His voice was querulous and menacing at the same time and Maire shivered as her eyes met his blue ones, which resembled chips of ice. Kirsty however started to bustle about serving his meal.

"Och, away with you, Duncan! You should think shame of yourself, to greet a visitor like that. She is but a lassie who came seeking help. Her name is Maire and she had an accident on the hills."

Duncan Fraser did not seem satisfied with this explanation but his attention was diverted from the stranger who had invaded his home by the smell of the hot food being set before him. He picked up a wooden spoon and set to with the kind of animal hunger of a man who had not eaten all day.

The meal improved his temper and it was with a more mollified expression that he asked for further details of Maire's arrival. On hearing that she was on her way to the Prince's army at Inverness, his lean face once more took on a hatchet look and he looked ready to throw her out of doors at any moment.

"So she is nothing but a camp follower! One of those loose women who go with the baggage train in the wake of that Young Pretender, as they call him. Another Stuart come to bring disaster to Scotland!" His face was suffused with an angry flush, which made his cheek-bones look more skeletal than ever. He broke into a fit of coughing and Kirsty hastily fetched him a jug of ale with the solicitude of someone tending a sick child. Suddenly, Maire saw the truth of their relationship. Kirsty loved Duncan for what he once had been, though he was now only a shadow of it. She was the strong one who made the decisions. Duncan, for all his bullying and bluster, leant on her absolutely.

Maire could not imagine herself ever being attached to a man like Duncan Fraser under any circumstances. Then she was struck by an uneasy thought. Perhaps Duncan in his youth had been rather like her own Alasdair. Young, strong, eager to fight, ardent for a cause – *the* Cause. But, Maire told herself, Duncan may have gone to fight under duress, answering the call of his chief. Yes, she decided, that would make a great difference between the two men. Alasdair would never be like Duncan, no matter what the future held. She held on to this comforting thought.

Chapter Nineteen

It was decided that Maire would stay the night and then move on if she was strong enough. Duncan grudgingly agreed to this and Kirsty made a night posset for them all. It was a hot oatmeal "Brochan" and Kirsty swore it was the best way to cure or keep away a cold or cough. There was a momentary feeling of truce as they all three sat together in the light from the dying peat fire, supping the gruel in almost companionable silence. It had been dark outside for some hours since and the little cottage seemed remote and cut off from any human contact.

There was no warning of the soldiers' arrival. Their footsteps must have been muffled by the light dusting of snow which coated the ground. The first intimation of their presence was a thunderous knocking on the door with what sounded like rifle butts. "Open up in the name of King George!"

"Heaven preserve us!" Kirsty exclaimed and jumped out of her seat as if she were stung. Duncan's jaw fell open with shock and a spoonful of gruel dribbled over his beard like grey thread. Maire watched it with fascination. She seemed unable to move or even to think. Her body felt paralysed, in spite of the way her heart was suddenly racing within her breast. They had come for her! She was sure of it. There was no longer anywhere left to run.

Her eyes met those of Kirsty, and she could tell by the expression in the dark brown ones that she had understood the situation as quickly as Maire herself. Kirsty knew the whole story about Maire's escape from the hill; Duncan had no reason to suspect that she was a fugitive.

Quick as thought, Kirsty strode across to a linen curtain hung up on the wall. She pulled it aside to reveal a box bed set into the wall with a narrow chaff-filled mattress on it. The space was small and uncomfortable but Maire did not hesitate. Obeying Kirsty's mimed instructions, she clambered into the bed and found herself in darkness as the musty curtain was pulled closed behind her. The dust and fragments of straw escaping from the mattress tickled Maire's nose and throat and she pressed her hands tightly over her face to prevent a fit of sneezing.

The door rasped open as Kirsty withdrew the bolt. Maire crouched against the dry stone wall, listening intently and trying to breathe in the dusty atmosphere. The linen curtain was impregnated with soot from past fires and this added to her discomfort. She prayed that her ordeal would not last long.

There were four Redcoats. The officer in charge was tall, thin and arrogant. He looked around the simple cottage and wrinkled his fastidious nose in distaste at the smoky atmosphere and spartan furnishings. How these Highland peasants lived! Even worse than the poorest farm workers on his own estate in the South of England. He only hoped he could communicate with these people. Apparently, many of them only spoke their barbaric Gaelic tongue.

"Woman!" he addressed Kirsty in a patronising tone. "Do you understand English?"

Her answer was disconcerting and not at all what he expected.

"Aye, sir. We speak two languages here. I believe in England, you have only the one?"

One of the soldiers, a Lowland Scot, sniggered behind his hand, but another tightened his grip on the pistol at his belt. He had a vague feeling that his captain had just been insulted. The officer shot a swift, suspicious glance at the woman who had spoken, but the expression on Kirsty's face betrayed no hint of veiled insolence; rather a blank innocence verging on imbecility.

This woman is clearly an idiot, the captain thought to himself, and the husband looks even worse. He noted with disgust, the smear of gruel on the man's beard. God! These people really were primitive. Disdainfully, he withdrew his gaze from that scarecrow of a man and decided to speak slowly and clearly, as to the deaf. After all, he had a job to do.

"We seek a woman of the tinker class, dressed in one of your outlandish plaids. She is wanted for attacking one of our troops and leaving him unconscious in a cave near here. She had accomplices, and we are also intent on arresting them. They will be made an example of, I assure you, because we intend to hang the lot of them from the nearest tree. Have you seen this woman? She would be likely to seek refuge somewhere as our wounded comrade says he fought bravely against the attack and gave her a few blows before he was struck down by the other assailants. This was a completely unprovoked attack against one of His Majesty's troops, and they will pay dear for it."

His eyes roved round the room as he spoke and landed on Maire's tartan plaid, lying in front of the peat fire. It had long since ceased to steam and was now quite dry. Kirsty followed his gaze.

"That is my shawl," she said. "And we have had no visitors here tonight."

Duncan opened his mouth, then shut it again, feeling it advisable to follow his wife's lead, though his eyes were full of horrified anger at the sudden discovery of the danger his unwanted guest had brought to his house. His blue eyes snapped an unmistakable message at Kirsty. He would have plenty to say when this was over.

The officer however was not so easily put off. He pointed to the three bowls which had contained the gruel. "Who was the third person?" he drawled with deceptive politeness. "I see only two in this room."

Kirsty heard herself answering without time to think.

"My daughter Eppy, of course. She returned unwell from the milking and has retired to her bed with a terrible fever. She is asleep in yon bed and I would ask you not to wake her if you please!"

But the Redcoat officer was already on his way over to the curtain. Maire could hear the dull thud of his boots on the earth floor. She braced herself for inevitable discovery and arrest. There was no chance that they would believe she was Eppy. She would easily be identified by the wounded Redcoat who had raped her, and who had made up this cowardly tale to cover his crime.

Then, unbelieving, she heard the footsteps halt, as Kirsty's words rang out in sinister warning.

"The doctor thinks it may be smallpox Eppy has, but I do not think so. Where would she contract a disease like that round here? As for the strange red marks all over her body, I have those mysel' – look! What do you think of this? And this? Perhaps an educated gentleman like yourself can tell me –?"

Wonderingly, Maire heard a splutter of rage and fear and the clatter of boots as the Redcoats hastily made for the door. The officer hurled imprecations as he withdrew, his former false politeness thrown to the winds.

"What do you mean by letting us enter your rat-infested hovel, you old hag? Keep your filthy skin disease to yourself, whatever it is, and think yourself lucky we do not burn the house down over your heads. Come, men! Leave these Highland pigs to fester in their own mire. We'll search no more this night."

They went as quickly as they had come and Maire was glad to crawl stiffly out of her hiding place.

"What frightened them so?" she asked Kirsty, whose face was bright with relief and suppressed laughter.

"Och, I don't know why they decided to go so quickly," said Kirsty with a mischievous glint dancing in her eyes. "They didna' seem to care for these marks on my arms. I canna think why, when they were only caused by the dyeing of my wool. Look!" Kirsty pulled her sleeves back and showed Maire her forearms. They were covered with lurid crimson and purple blotches which looked like weals and were made even more repellent by virulent yellow streaks here and there. In the dim light of the dying fire, the stains had a ghastly appearance, like some weird, suppurating skin malady, the yellow patches resembling septic wounds. Maire could well understand why the soldiers had baulked at the sight, especially after Kirsty had primed them with the mention of the dreaded smallpox. Association of ideas and fear had done the rest.

"My hands are clean with all the washing and cooking I have done, but it takes a while for the stains on my arms to fade," said Kirsty. "I make my own dyes from heather and lichen and the bark of trees. I am well known for it hereabouts but of course, the Redcoats were not to know that."

Maire looked at this remarkable woman who was calmly clearing away the bowls from the table and preparing a bed for her. This was the second time Kirsty Fraser had saved her life. Maire hoped that one day perhaps she would be able to repay her.

Chapter Twenty

That night, Maire slept as dreamlessly and soundly as a child. Emotionally sucked dry by the events of the longest day she had ever known, she slumbered as soon as her head touched the straw pillow.

It was just as well she did, because the next day was to see her on the move again. Miraculously refreshed, Maire woke feeling better than she had dared to believe possible. A little stiffness in her joints remained, but the heavy, feverish chill which had threatened to seize hold had been successfully thrown off. No doubt it was Kirsty's Brochan, Maire decided, and looked around for her saviour of the night before.

Kirsty was obviously up before her, and nowhere to be seen. The sound of a clanking bucket outside, drew Maire to the door. Her friend was walking back to the house, carrying a foaming pail of creamy milk, steaming warm from the cow, and leading a Highland garron with the other. It was a black, sturdy beast, with the sure-footed agility of all this Highland breed of horse. When Kirsty saw her guest awake, a smile broke through the concentrated expression which made her face severe. It was like the sun suddenly soaring out from behind a cloud; the full warmth of Kirsty's personality shone out of her eyes. Maire felt a rush of affection for her. Somehow, she knew that she and this Highland woman would always be friends.

"Good day to you!" Kirsty's musical voice rang out on the frosty air, as carefree and relaxed as if the previous evening had never happened. It seemed now like a bad dream, fled with the morning light.

Maire took the pail of milk while Kirsty tied the garron to a rusty ring embedded in the stone wall.

"He is for you," Kirsty said briefly. "To help you on your way to Inverness. It'll be too far for you to walk, just yet awhile. You need to get your strength back and you will not be doing that in one night. It's a pity you have to go at all as yet. But perhaps it is better so, for I think you will be safer away from here." She looked squarely at Maire. "By my reckoning, those Redcoats must be part of an advance guard. There will be an army behind them. Aye, it is better that you go, Maire, and put as many miles as you can between you and them."

"But Kirsty," Maire protested, "what about the horse? How can I return it to you?"

Her friend laughed, and once more, her face lit up the grey morning.

"Och, dinna fash yourself, lassie! Hamish has a mind of his own and he kens well the way back to his warm stable! Many's the time he's brocht Duncan back home, after he's ta'en too much whisky with his cronies over the hill. When you feel you are well enough on your road, just turn his head, slap his flank and order him home. I sometimes wish," Kirsty said with a smile, "that I could have the good fortune to meet a man with as much sense as a horse."

Maire laughed appreciatively. A horse-lover herself, she was delighted to have the loan of Hamish. But it suddenly occurred to her that Duncan might object. Where was he this morning? She had not seen him since she woke. She asked Kirsty who was airily evasive. "Och, he's away to his work. There is a wall to be mended, for the few sheep we have are beginning to stray through a hole in the dyke. He had to make an early start, so he will not be bothering us at all, at all."

Not a word, Maire noticed, about how angry Duncan had been about her presence, or the danger she had brought to them. What Kirsty and Duncan had said to one another last night, she could not tell, for sleep had claimed her so quickly. One thing was certain, however. As usual, Kirsty was having things her own way! She gave Maire some oatmeal bannocks for the journey, still warm from the iron griddle, and a slice of salt beef. Also, a flask of milk for when she got thirsty.

They breakfasted quickly on porridge and some bread and cheese, and then it was time to leave. Maire could not find words to express what she felt, but in fact, there was no need for words with Kirsty. She embraced the girl like a daughter, wrapped the tartan shawl warmly round her shoulders and bade her farewell in her soft Gaelic voice.

Maire took the little bundle of food wrapped in a square of linen and mounted the garron. She looked at Kirsty for a long moment. "Thank you," she said and knew it was all she needed to say. She dug in her heels and Hamish started forward, the sound of his hooves muffled by the snow which covered the path like thistledown.

After several miles, Maire decided that she had better dismount and send the horse home. She must be well on her way to Inverness, and she feared that Hamish, clever though he was, might lose his sense of direction in the white world, which changed contours and made everything look different. Strangely enough, since the snowfall, the cold had lessened its bitter grip and Maire did not shiver the way she had yesterday. She was aware of the almost uncanny beauty of the landscape which surrounded her with a magical, almost mystical, silence. It was as if time was suspended for this brief journey under a yellow, snow-filled sky; as if the whole world was waiting with bated breath. There was a total absence of sound.

Maire startled herself when she heard her voice echo on that quiet, bridle path. "Home, Hamish! Go home, now!" The horse obeyed at once, his intelligent eyes blinking in the dazzling white light. He set off at a trot as if he were perfectly sure where he was going. Maire hoped that he was. She wished she could say the same of herself!

It could not be very much further, though. She knew she was walking in the right direction. She was sure she had not strayed from the path, in spite of the misleading mantle which levelled everything in sight.

Maire walked on, hoping to see some sign of Inverness on the horizon. Then the road curved and she caught sight of a small band of men about half a mile away. That they were Highlanders was clear from their dress. One of them was on horseback with a bonnet on his head and something about the way he sat on the horse, even at that distance, made Maire's heart skip a beat. She could hardly catch her breath, but suddenly without thought, without conscious decision, she was hurrying on. Her feet in the deerskin shoes, began to slip and slither in the packed snow of the road. She left the path and continued on the soft snow beside it. Her feet squelched and sank into the squeaky softness, becoming soaked in no time, but Maire didn't care. She was afraid the man would ride off before she reached him.

At the top of a snowy hillock, she called and waved in the icy silence. Surely he would see her against the livid sky! And her call echoed strangely loud in the quiet air, unbroken even by birdsong. He should – he *must* – hear her!

With a lightening of the heart, Maire saw the mounted figure stiffen, stand erect in the saddle and gaze in her direction. There was a moment's pause, and then suddenly, he was trotting, cantering, galloping towards her. They met at the foot of the white mound. Maire half ran, half slithered down it, he leapt from his horse and met her with an embrace that swept her off her feet.

"Maire!" he kept saying. "Maire, my heart's darling! – *Eoghain – ma belle!*"

The endearments in three languages spilled out and fell around her like golden rain. Maire heard them with rapture and a singing heart. This was the moment she had dreamed of so often and feared would never come to pass; now that it was happening, the sweetness of it affected her with a kind of anguish. In the last few days, too much had happened to Maire too quickly. She could scarcely savour her new-found happiness because of the fear that it would swiftly be snatched away from her.

At last, they stood face to face, looking at one another with amazed delight. Maire noticed now with concern that Alasdair was thinner and there were lines of worry on his brow that had not been there before. She saw that the other Macdonald men had followed him and were standing in a sheepish group, uncertain what to do and afraid to interrupt this reunion. However, one of the Highlanders was smiling broadly in recognition and Maire realised with pleasure that it was Morag's son, Allan. She greeted him warmly and that broke the spell of embarrassed silence. The group came closer and surrounded her, full of curiosity about how she had got there and wanting news of home.

On the way back to camp, Maire rode Alasdair's horse, which he insisted on leading. She tried to answer all their questions as best she could. Their crofts had been safe when she last saw them and yes, Morag was well, and so was the Laird and his household.

Alasdair guessed that she had come for Jamie and was clearly relieved to have the boy return home. There were perils in war from which he might not be able to protect him.

"I have seen to the boy as well as I can," he said. "But I have many responsibilities here, many things to see to – " Alasdair's voice trailed off and Maire saw him cast an anxious look at the clansmen who loped alongside them with their running walk, which could cover miles, even in hard conditions such as these. She noticed now how gaunt and weary they looked, and that one of them carried a thong from which dangled a moorhen and a hare.

"You have been hunting?" Maire asked Alasdair and thought it strange that soldiers could have time for such a leisure pursuit. "Aye," said Alasdair in a sombre tone and she wondered at the grim way he said it. It was clear to her now that they were not hunting for fun.

"We have not been lucky today," he went on. "There are Macdonalds back at camp hoping we will return with more."

That was all he said and Maire did not like to press him. Whatever problems the army had, she would learn of them soon enough. As if he wanted to blot out his troubles, Alasdair changed the subject abruptly and talked animatedly of many happier topics as the horse jogged along with Maire swaying in the saddle. She enjoyed the experience of riding such a fine beast; it was quite a contrast to the sturdy little garron. They came near to Inverness and Maire saw a fine house on the outskirts of the town.

"That is Moy Hall," said Alasdair and she could tell by his voice that it must have a special significance to the Jacobites.

"Are they supporters of the Prince?" she asked and wondered at the laugh which rang from her lover. It was good to hear his laugh again, though. She had missed it, during all the lonely months without him.

"The answer to that is 'Aye' and 'No', Maire. Moy Hall is the seat of the Mackintosh chief, who prefers to serve the Elector of Hanover, because according to Aeneas Mackintosh, he can pay him 'half-a-guinea today and half-a-guinea tomorrow'."

Alasdair's voice continued scornfully, "In other words, the Laird of Mackintosh is a time-serving coward and a disgrace to the noble name he bears! The Mackintosh clan is part of Clan Chattan, which has always supported the Stuarts. Fortunately, the chief has a wife who does not share his views. Lady Anne is an ardent supporter of the Prince and when Aeneas was away on Government business, what did she do but raise the clan for Prince Charlie as soon as her husband's back was turned? She handed out white cockades with her own hands and led the men to join the Prince, with herself riding at the head of them. It earned her the title of 'Colonel Anne'. I wish you had seen it, Maire, for it was a grand sight!"

Maire wished indeed that she had. The story caught her imagination and she felt a great curiosity to meet this young woman – apparently she was barely older than herself – who was willing to risk everything for what she believed in.

She was to have her wish sooner than she expected. Alasdair sent the men on to the Macdonald tents, to deliver the meagre food they had caught, and with instructions to Allan to bring young Jamie back with him. Meanwhile, Alasdair decided that Maire needed rest and refreshments and so they repaired to a nearby inn.

She was glad of the opportunity to sit by a fire in the inn's parlour while Alasdair arranged to have a simple repast brought into them. She had become colder than she realised and stretched out numb fingers gratefully to the flames. She was hungry too and ate with relish the plain meal laid before them. It had been a long time since the milk and bannocks, eaten on the journey.

They talked while they ate and Alasdair told her many details about the successful battles they had fought so far, Prestonpans and Falkirk in particular. Maire had harboured some anxiety about relating her own story and the terror she had endured on the hillside at the hands of the English soldier. She knew she would find it difficult to speak calmly of the episode, but she had no doubt that talk of it she would, indeed must. It was too traumatic an event to be kept from this man who obviously loved her so deeply. No matter what pain it caused him, he must learn of it.

She felt a little puzzled and faintly disappointed that

Alasdair hardly asked her about her journey and any difficulties she might have experienced. After all, it had been quite a feat, for a girl not used to these Highland conditions, to succeed in such a hazardous undertaking, in order to find Jamie. She could not help feeling that her lover might have shown more interest, even concern. Maire stifled the criticism as soon as it was born. How selfish of her! Alasdair had so much on his mind just now, like all the Jacobite leaders. He had worries and responsibilities she could only guess at. With this loyal thought, she put all censure out of her mind.

Finally, Maire decided to broach the subject of her two encounters with the soldiers. It had to be done and since their meal was over and Jamie expected to arrive with Allan at any minute, it had better be done quickly. Quietly and with little drama, Maire began her tale but to her amazement, as soon as she mentioned the word "Redcoats", Alasdair reacted strongly and in a way she had not foreseen.

"Where? Not in this vicinity, surely? They cannot be so near. The last we heard was that Cumberland was on the other side of the Spey. Unless – he has sent troops in advance and that means that the river can now be forded. We thought the weather was still too bad to allow it. My God! If Cumberland is on the march from Aberdeen and on his way here to Inverness, then we must prepare for battle soon. Come Maire! We must go and tell the Prince immediately. There is not a moment to waste. Can you describe exactly where you saw these soldiers? How many? What kind of uniform?"

His questions came fast and hard as steel. This was the military leader she was seeing now – a side of Alasdair she knew existed but with which she was unfamiliar. It struck Maire as bitterly ironic that after the personal suffering she had undergone at the hands of these Redcoats, her most useful function at the moment was to report movements and numbers like an army scout. She did her best to be accurate in her memory of the enemy sightings and if her voice at times trembled a little, Alasdair did not appear to notice. He was in a state of fierce excitement, and all for going in search of the Prince at once. Maire however was firm in her resolve that she would not stir one step without Jamie. She had come long and far to find her young cousin and until she had him safe by her side, her quest would not be fulfilled. Besides, she longed to see the boy again.

Alasdair, though in a ferment of impatience, contained himself as well as he could and luckily, before long, they heard a boyish voice outside the inn.

"Maire! Where are you? Where is she, Allan? You said she would be here!"

Suddenly, he burst upon them, with eyes shining and his whole face lit up with joy at seeing her once more. It was with mutual delight that the two embraced, Maire holding Jamie close as if she never wanted to let him out of her sight again. Allan stood in the background, his gentle smile showing his delight at this new reunion. Secretly, he was glad that the boy was to be returned to his own folk, back home. An army waiting for engagement by the enemy was no place for a young lad, in his opinion.

Allan was able to give them news of the Prince's whereabouts. They learned that he was not far off but after a morning's hunting, had retired to Moy Hall to partake of some refreshment. The four of them decided to go there at once, and inform the Prince of the nearness of the enemy, and that with the coming of spring, his cousin Cumberland, was on the move.

Chapter Twenty One

Lady Anne Mackintosh herself greeted them warmly when she heard they had brought news for Prince Charlie. She led them into the drawing-room of Moy Hall. Maire was startled by the delicate loveliness of this young woman who had led her clan (or rather her husband's!) to join the Stuart cause. She was about twenty-three, Maire guessed, and not at all the Amazonian figure she had pictured in her mind. Far from it. Slender and dark, with clear eyes that shone with the light of idealism, Lady Anne was instantly likeable.

Prince Charles greeted them graciously and Maire was once more reminded of the charm she had felt all those months ago at Holyrood. His dark eyes were warm and welcoming, but Maire could see on his face, as on Alasdair's, the lines of worry. Also, he seemed to have a troublesome cough, as if he had been recently suffering from a chill.

His face tense, Alasdair at once gave the news of the near approach of the Redcoat army and both the Prince and Lady Anne listened carefully, aware of the seriousness of the situation. Maire was praised for her part in bringing the facts to their attention. Lady Anne was particularly impressed by what she insisted on regarding as heroism.

"You're a brave lass," she said. "To make that journey on your own and not knowing what you would meet. Just think! You could have been captured before you reached here." Maire said nothing about just how near to capture she *had* been, but she glowed in the praise bestowed on her by a woman whom already she admired greatly. Praise from "Colonel Anne" was praise indeed.

Flushed with excitement, Prince Charles decided to ride back at once to Inverness and inform his officers and chiefs. "We must make ready now," he said. "It cannot be long before there is a battle. We have to choose our ground and tactics. I have no doubt of the outcome but we must not be caught unawares. My brave Highlanders have routed them every time and God willing, they will do it again. Come gentlemen, to horse!"

Alasdair bade a hasty *au revoir* to Maire and left in company with Allan. Fresh horses were borrowed from the stables at Moy to enable them to carry back the news to the Jacobite camp as quickly as possible. Lady Anne insisted on lending the horses; it was clear that she would give her right arm, let alone her possessions, if it would help the Prince.

Maire was left with Jamie, clinging on to her hand, in that imposing room, with trophies of arms on the walls, mementoes of past victories and Stuart monarchs. She looked around; the house was steeped in history. Lady Anne saw her gaze and smiled proudly.

"Aye, you may well look, lassie. You'll not see arms such as these again." She pointed to the wall. "This sword belonged to King Charles I of blessed memory – he whom those traitors executed at the time of Cromwell. And that one belonged to the great Dundee who fought and died for the Stuart cause. You'll have heard of 'Bonnie Dundee', surely? Oh, if only we had him back again to fight with Prince Charlie! Still, it doesn't matter. We have heroes enough in our own army and I have small doubt that our Alexander MacGillivray will be one of them. It is he who will lead our Clan Chattan into battle for the Prince. If I were a man, I'd be glad to do it myself!"

Maire did not see any reason to disbelieve her, but she marvelled at the contrast between the loveliness of this young woman and her warlike words. Lady Anne suddenly recalled herself to the present.

"But this will not do!" she exclaimed. "What am I thinking of, to be prattling on about the past when I have guests to think of? You must both stay here for a day or so, until you are rested enough to start on your journey home." She brushed aside Maire's protests lightly. "No, no, it is all settled. It's the least I can do for a gallant lass who has dared everything to bring such important tidings to our beloved Prince. Come with me, and I will show you to your quarters."

Maire was led to a fine bedchamber, which provided a startling contrast to her refuge in the simple cottage the previous

143

night. She hoped sincerely that this time, her stay would not be so rudely and frighteningly, interrupted. Since Jamie showed no inclination to be parted from his beloved Maire now that he had found her again, it was arranged that he should sleep on a small mattress in the same room.

Maire learned that it had already been decided that the Prince and his main officers would dine at Moy Hall that night and that there was to be a ball as part of the evening's entertainment. Her heart leapt at the thought of meeting Alasdair again, but she looked ruefully at her mud-spattered and simple apparel, with the realisation that since she had no other clothes with her, it was not possible for her to attend the ball. She had better dine alone in her room.

Without a word on the subject being voiced, it seemed that Lady Anne had already thought of that problem. Sensitive to Maire's feelings and anxious not to cause offence, Lady Anne invited her guest to come to her room and asked Maire if she would be kind enough to do her the honour of selecting a gown from her own wardrobe. It was so charmingly put that no-one, including Maire, could be embarrassed by it. There was no question of being made to feel like a poor relation.

"This will perhaps suit you best, Maire," said Lady Anne, pulling out a beautiful gown of sapphire blue satin with tiny white cockades sewn to the lace around the low neckline.

"It will contrast well with your hair and is nearly the same colour as your eyes. I will send my girl, Alison, to help you with your hair this evening, after she has seen to me. She is a marvel and can do any style you wish."

It all seemed to Maire too good to be true. The rest of the day fled away and it was time to prepare for the evening before she could believe it possible. Jamie had made a friend down in the kitchen quarters where preparations were going on apace for the coming dinner, and had not been seen for over an hour. Knowing he was safe and happy, Maire did not worry.

With a lighter heart than she had known for some time, she began to dress for Lady Anne's ball. She undressed and laid the clothes given her by Kirsty carefully on a chair; she would need them tomorrow. It was only when Maire began to splash her face and neck with the warm scented water sent to her room, that her heart suddenly sank within her. Hitherto hidden by the warm clothes, the bruises from her attack showed clearly on her shoulders, red, purple and ugly. She tried to tell herself that they would be hidden by the dress but on putting it on, the bruises showed up, if anything, more clearly. There was no way of hiding them; she simply could not appear in public. It would arouse too much comment.

With tears of vexation in her eyes, Maire was studying her reflection dolefully and did not hear the soft tap at her door. Too late, she turned to see Lady Anne Mackintosh herself, slipping into her room, smiling and holding out a lovely pearl necklace and earrings in a velvet box.

"I thought these would match the gown," she started and then fell silent, as Maire's bruised and scratched shoulders met her appalled gaze.

"What in the name of God –" Lady Anne stopped, realising that the girl before her was overcome with embarrassment and chagrin.

"I'll not ask where you got those marks, Maire," she said softly. "Because I do not have to ask. It is quite clear that you were attacked, and I can guess by whom. It was a Redcoat soldier, was it not? One of those you told us you saw on the way here?"

Speechlessly, Maire nodded. She had not meant to keep the awful thing secret – it was just that there had been no opportunity, no time to tell of it. And it was not the kind of experience she could blurt out to anyone. Lady Anne, however, was someone she *could* tell and Maire did so with a feeling of relief. At least, she would not now have to make up some lame excuse for not appearing tonight.

However, she had not reckoned on Lady Anne's initiative. In very little time, she had looked out some Mechlin lace, as fine as gossamer, tucked it round the neckline to cover the worst of the angry marks, and powdered the rest with white powder.

"There!" she said approvingly. "I challenge anyone to see anything amiss now. You'll be the belle of the ball, my dear, as you deserve to be, and I am proud to have you here as my guest And I dare say," said Lady Anne with a teasing twinkle in her eyes, "that I'll not be the only one to be glad to see you here tonight. Anyone can see that Captain Alasdair Macdonald is head-over-heels in love with you."

Maire flushed with pleasure and surprise. She had not known that Alasdair's feelings were so easily spotted, especially when today she seemed to have been the last thing on his mind. Maire felt suddenly full of confidence and hope. This would be a marvellous evening and she intended to savour every moment of it.

She was pleased when Lady Anne invited her to greet the guests with her as they arrived. Dressed in a shimmering gown of crimson tartan silk, with a white cockade set on her dark hair, Lady Mackintosh looked every inch the Jacobite she was. Maire, in a way, envied the other woman her total conviction in the rightness of the Stuart cause. No shadow of doubt had ever seemed to cross her mind.

The Prince was in festive mood when he arrived with his principal officers. The news of Cumberland's approach seemed to have affected everyone with a new edge of excitement, of eagerness even. It had been a long enforced wait during those winter months when the Highlands were too snowed up to allow of easy movement. Now nerves were once more strung up and ready for the inevitable confrontation. All the more reason to enjoy an evening in the company of good friends, with music, laughter and dancing.

Maire looked out expectantly for the arrival of Alasdair and her pulses quickened as she saw him enter in his Highland dress. His face lit up with admiration as he saw her; Maire knew she had never looked better than she did tonight. The dress suited her to perfection and excitement lent a glow to her cheeks and a sparkle to her eyes. Other officers too gave her interested glances, but Alasdair quickly made it clear to the assembled company that he looked on Maire as his own. He placed a proprietorial hand under her elbow and led her out to dance again and again. Reels and Strathspeys followed one another in breathless succession and Maire danced them all with one partner. She desired no other and felt that her cup of happiness was full.

It was when she was dancing an eightsome reel and turned in the figure of eight to face a new partner, that she almost cried out in surprise. Facing her in the dance was the last person Maire expected to see here, at this Jacobite gathering.

Iain smiled at her gravely and held out his hand to steady her as Maire almost missed her footing. They passed one another in the intricate figure of eight, Maire recovering her composure and annoyed with herself for being so easily caught unawares. Why should Iain's presence disturb her in the least? It was certainly surprising to see him here, but no doubt there was a good explanation. In fact, Maire admitted to herself, it was good to see him again. There was something secure and steadfast about Iain. She wondered however what on earth he could be doing with the Prince's army.

Her curiosity was satisfied as soon as the dance ended. Iain joined Alasdair and herself and Maire gathered from the conversation between the two men that Iain had offered his services as a surgeon, when he heard how hard-pressed the Jacobite army was, on its return to Scotland. Maire pondered on this strange twist of events. She was willing to hazard a guess that Iain had not changed his mind about the Cause. It was simply for humane reasons that he had joined his fellow Highlanders, to minimise their suffering. He had been with the army now for a few weeks. Maire observed the two men with interest as they spoke of army matters. There was still a tension between them; she could feel it, even though they were now on the same side. She began to listen.

"I will be leaving in the morning, just after dawn. The men cannot stay here or they will die. There is hardly enough food for the able-bodied men, let alone those who are wounded. I intend to take them back to their glens before it is too late." It was Iain who spoke and his grey eyes had an angry light in them.

Alasdair shrugged elegantly. "That is up to you, Iain Macdonald. If you have no stomach to stay when we are preparing for battle –"

"It is not a question of my having no stomach!" Iain rapped out the words. "It is a question of having no food to put in the *men's* stomachs. And when they are ill or wounded, they will not survive. It is my duty to look after their welfare and I cannot do it when the daily supply of meal is here today and not tomorrow. So I will be gone at first light and I will return when I have delivered them safely. I have the approval of the chief surgeon in this, and as far as I am concerned that is all the permission I need."

"Very well," Alasdair agreed, tight-lipped. "You may take the wounded men home, but return as soon as you can, for you may be needed before a week has passed. At least, there is one advantage to your plan. The fewer sick men we have, the more food will be left for the rest who can fight."

"Aye, that is true," said Iain dryly and Maire caught a glint of sarcastic fury in his eye as he said it. He turned to her before leaving and said abruptly, almost roughly, "I hope you will not be staying long here, Maire. It is no place for you! There will be a different kind of dancing before long."

"Miss Drummond," said Alasdair stiffly, "is returning home in a day or so with Jamie. She only came to fetch him. Not that it is any of your business. And now, if you will excuse us, we wish to dance again."

Alasdair swept her away into the dance before she could say a word. Not that Maire was sure what she could have said after this bitter exchange. Still, as she entered into the graceful Strathspey, it was not with quite her former light-hearted enjoyment. A shadow had entered that gay, brightly-lit room with Iain; a shadow from the outside world, of cold, hunger and pain, of wounded and sick men, longing for home and safety. She had a swift vision of that world which Iain worked in, and felt herself wishing with all her heart that his mission would succeed.

Chapter Twenty Two

It was to be an eventful evening for Maire. An incident occurred during dinner that she could have done without. She was sitting at a table beside Alasdair and had almost recovered her previous gaiety, helped by the wine and good food, plentifully supplied by Lady Anne Mackintosh. Some guests had arrived late and Maire paid little attention as they took their seats at another table from her own. One of the men was capering round, arousing laughter from the guests and Maire turned to see what was the cause of all the mirth.

Her heart seemed to stop for a second; her breathing became rapid, her breast heaving painfully with the effort not to scream aloud. For there, close to her, leering in what seemed a comic way to others but grotesque to Maire, was a Redcoat. The uniform in all its details swam hideously before her eyes, the braid, the shining pewter buttons, the colour of the coat so reminiscent of blood – the evidence was before her eyes though her mind told her this could not be true. She turned instinctively to Alasdair, laying her hand on his arm in a mute desire for protection, for reassurance. But Alasdair was laughing as heartily as the rest, and did not realise her distress. Of course, he could not know how it would affect her. It dawned on her seconds later that this was one of the Macdonald men who had donned a uniform, taken from a captured Redcoat in the past, simply to amuse the company. It seemed to do so hugely. The Prince was showing his approval as much as anyone. The entire incident only lasted for a minute but as Maire recovered her self-assurance, her eyes met those of Iain Macdonald, further down the table. His grey eyes looked at her steadily and she felt uncomfortably that he had seen right into her heart with that piercing gaze. He had seen her discomfiture, her fear, and perhaps he guessed why. Unreasonably, Maire felt cross with Iain. How dare he read her like a book! She felt annoyed also

149

with herself for losing her composure, even for so short a time.

She threw herself into the party with even more abandon after that. She flirted and laughed, danced and chattered with almost feverish gaiety. Alasdair was entranced and she received many admiring looks from other officers and also gentlemen from Inverness, though less approving glances from their wives. She was treated as a heroine for having brought the news of enemy movements so swiftly, as if indeed that had been her sole reason for being here. Though she could see the irony in this, Maire was not averse to a little adulation. She enjoyed it. After the fear and privation of the last few days, she luxuriated in the joy of feeling totally alive again. And, she had to admit, it was good to be desired as she was, by a man like Alasdair. The message in his eyes, in the touch of his hands round her waist, during the dance, was unmistakable She was proud to be loved by him.

Flushed and hot from a particularly hectic Highland reel, the two lovers left the dance floor and retired to the quietness of the cool hall. There was a little room off it, into which Alasdair pulled Maire, and having closed a curtain behind them, started to kiss her passionately. Maire was at first startled, then feeling her own yearning for him rise fiercely within her, returned his kisses as ardently as they were given. It was when she felt herself lifted unexpectedly by strong arms and placed on a couch in the darkened alcove, that Maire felt her heartbeat alter its rhythm from the quick thud of passionate desire to the racing, fluttering throb of panic. The male figure bending over her, gripping her so tightly that she could hardly breathe, ceased to be Alasdair, whom she had longed to hold, for so many months. Once more, Maire felt herself back in the cave, helpless, degraded and threatened. She began to resist the kisses raining down on her shoulders, to push away the questing, eager hands that were already plucking delicately but with determined assurance at the creamy Mechlin lace round her neck. Desire had completely left her, and she felt cold, trembling, sick.

At last, Alasdair realised reluctantly that his attentions were no longer being received gladly and drew back, offended and puzzled at his love's change of attitude. His breathing, which had been hard and fast in his hunger for her, gradually slowed down and a cold, disappointed look replaced the golden warmth in his hazel eyes. As Maire saw this, she wept inside. But she could not help herself. It was too soon after – that thing which had happened to her. She just wasn't ready yet to accept a man, even the man she loved. She tried to explain, she wanted him to know that the blinding panic which had swept over her, had nothing to do with him or her feelings for him, but already, the moment had passed. He made a stiff bow in apology as if he had become a stranger, and held out his arm for her to be escorted back to the ballroom. Feeling broken, Maire set her lips in a determined smile; no-one should know how she felt, not even Alasdair. Or perhaps, she thought with a spark of anger, *especially*, Alasdair! It was all very well being wanted, she reflected sadly, but she longed to be understood as well.

Soon after, the company sat down to talk, and Maire found herself at His Highness' table. Once again she saw the famous Stuart charm for herself.

The Prince was in very good spirits and told a story which, though known well to most of the company, was new to her.

"Mistress Drummond," he called down the table. "Have you heard about the famous Rout of Moy?"

Maire had not, but she saw Lady Anne Mackintosh smile with pleasure at the mention of it. Maire guessed that it concerned her hostess in some way and listened with interest as Prince Charles continued.

"It happened about two months ago when I was staying here at Moy Hall. Lord Loudon learned of my whereabouts and decided to capture me and earn for himself the thirty thousand pound reward which has been put on my unworthy head. I did not know I was worth so much!" Everyone laughed with him and he went on. "His lordship took a grand force with him from Inverness – about fifteen hundred men, I believe – and marched in secret and in the dark towards Moy Hall to take me by surprise. And he might well have succeeded, had not word reached us that he was on his way – a young lad from Inverness dodged the cordon of troops he had placed round the city and ran hell for leather across the moor to reach Moy Hall before Loudon. Tell the rest of the story, Lady Anne, for it was your men who carried the day."

Lady Anne coloured but took up the story gladly, her eyes

shining at remembrance of it.

"We had few men here to defend His Highness but I sent Donald Fraser, our blacksmith, and four others to try to hold them off. They put up such a noise in the dark, letting off pistols and calling up imaginary regiments of Camerons and Macdonalds and I don't know who else, that the Redcoats were utterly terrified and ran away like hares, trampling their own officers as they went. Lord Loudon did not get his thirty thousand pounds that night!"

Everyone laughed and Maire laughed with them. It was a wonderful story! She could just imagine it happening, and was very glad that Lady Anne had such a memory to keep with her for always.

The evening finally ended and the guests prepared to leave for Inverness. Just before the last of them left, Maire overheard raised voices near her and wondered what the altercation was about. It had been such a merry evening. She saw two men, one of whom she knew was Lord George Murray, the Commander-in-Chief of the Jacobite army. He was a dark man of about forty-five and he was glaring with undisguised contempt at the other man, whom Maire did not recognise.

Lord George seemed angry about something. Maire wondered what it could be. Then she heard the high-pitched quavering tones of the other, "Come now, Lord George, there is no need for all this constant carping. I have told you before, that I have it all in hand. Everything will be got!"

The only answer Maire heard from Lord George was a loud snort of derision before he swept out of the room, without even taking leave of his Prince or his hostess. It was an abrupt and rude departure. Disapproving glances followed him and Maire asked Alasdair what it was about.

"Who is that man," she said, "who so annoyed Lord George Murray?"

Alasdair frowned as if the subject was unwelcome to him, and there was a hint of impatience in his reply. "That is Mr. Hay of Restalrig," he said. "He is the Prince's Secretary but since he has only recently taken over the post, he has much to learn about running the Commissariat. Lord George was no doubt complaining about the irregular supplies of food. The men are being paid in meal now, since money has run out. However, all this is no concern of yours, Maire." His voice took on a harsher, more vindictive note. "And it would become people like Iain Macdonald more, if he would cease to criticise the way the army is run, and attend to his own business! We all know we need surgeons, but they are hardly the men to win His Highness' father his throne again. That will only be accomplished by fighting men!"

Alasdair did not add the words "like myself" but Maire felt he did not need to. The implication was quite clear. His face had hardened as he thought of army matters again, and his chin rose in a slightly arrogant tilt, as if he were facing an adversary. He suddenly changed from the charming companion she had danced with, to the soldier he was. He looked, if anything, more handsome than ever, in this mood. It was evident to Maire that Alasdair despised Iain for what he was, and for what he did. There was certainly no love lost between the two men, she reflected, and wondered for a fleeting moment, whether this could have anything to do with herself. She found her feelings aroused slightly on behalf of Iain; she respected his dedication and his determination to relieve suffering. However, Maire decided that it would be wiser to say nothing at this juncture to Alasdair. She understood perfectly why he would have no sympathy with her attitude.

And facing the imminent prospect of battle, as Alasdair did, he had enough on his mind, like all the Jacobite leaders.

They parted on the steps of Moy Hall, planning to meet the next day when Alasdair's duties would permit him to call again. They both knew that the next meeting would be their last for some time as it was planned that Maire should leave with Jamie, the day after. Knowing that she would see him tomorrow, Maire wondered at the strangely empty feeling in her heart as she watched him ride away to Inverness. It was as though she had lost him already.

The next day was happily and peacefully spent with Lady Anne Mackintosh, sewing white cockades for the army. Anne had recently bought a plentiful supply of white ribbon at Inverness and was glad to share the task with Maire. The two chatted as they sewed and the cold April day sped as quickly as the passing grey snow clouds in the sky outside.

In the late afternoon, Alasdair came. Maire heard the sound of horse's hooves outside the window and went quickly to peep behind the velvet curtain at the dark courtyard. He had kept his word, as she knew he would. There had been the odd anxious moment when Maire doubted whether some military crisis would perhaps prevent their meeting. Now that anxiety was gone.

The two spent their last half-hour in the warm drawing room at Moy Hall, alone except for the two hunting dogs, Dougal and Fergus, who sprawled their long length before the spitting log fire. Lady Anne had tactfully left them alone, being fully aware of the romantic attachment between them. Afterwards, Maire could recall little of what was said.

Her only clear memory was of the glowing warmth and comfort of this little island of safety in the cold and hostile world which waited outside. That feeling of temporary refuge, of snatched happiness, made the time all the more precious. There was no awkwardness between them now. Last night's misunderstanding was as if it had never happened. They held each other close, not talking much. Alasdair's face relaxed and lost some of the tense lines that had been etched there. Maire was glad to see it; for a short time, he belonged to her, and not the army.

All too soon, it was time for Alasdair to go. Maire and Anne retired shortly afterwards, having ensured that all necessary preparations were made for Maire and Jamie to depart early the next morning.

Lady Anne insisted on sending a guide with them to escort them for the first leg of their journey. "This is Clan Chattan territory," she said, "and I will not risk you losing your way for lack of a Mackintosh to help you." The chosen guide was a freckle-faced lad called Douglas who was not much older than Jamie and engaged in animated conversation with the boy as they set off on horses borrowed from the Moy stable.

"They say there is to be the biggest battle ever seen in these parts," said Douglas excitedly to Jamie. "What a pity you're going to miss it. Can you not stay just a wee while longer?"

Jamie turned a pleading glance to Maire. He had been

thrilled at the thought of going home and seeing his mother and father again. He had been terribly homesick before Maire arrived though he'd have died before admitting it to Allan and the others. But now, it seemed as if they were leaving just when things were about to happen. It was a shame! "Couldn't we –" he began, but did not continue. Maire fixed him with a sterner glance than he had ever seen from her before.

"I have not come over the hills in this weather to fetch you back, laddie, only to change my mind at the last minute. What would I tell your mother? I'll thank you to stop making stupid suggestions and keep your eyes on the road ahead. We have much need to keep a lookout for there is no telling what we may meet on the way." Or who, she added silently to herself. Cumberland was thought to be on the road to Nairn but it was always possible that some of his army scouts were scouring the roads around Inverness. The quicker we move south towards home, the better, thought Maire.

They reached a bend in the road and she turned round for a last brief look at the Jacobite army. Its tents and makeshift shelters, scattered around Culloden House, looked pathetic at that distance, resembling fragile toys liable to be blown away to destruction by a winter gale. Maire feared for the men she had left behind and wondered with a dull ache in her heart what their fate would be. That it would be decided in the next few days, she had little doubt. Everyone was unanimous that engagement with the enemy could not be long off, and it was likely to be final, one way or the other.

She remembered Prince Charlie's happy, confident face during the dinner at Moy Hall: his total certainty of victory and the rightness of his Cause. Some of Lady Anne's words also resounded in her mind.

"Mark my words, Maire, next time we dance with his Highness, it will be at Holyrood!" Maire hoped with all her heart that this would be true.

The wind was rising now, whipping her face with colour and stabbing her eyes with cold, icy rain. Maire looked her last and turned her horse's head south towards the Great Glen. She felt tears on her cheeks but could not, for the life of her, tell whether they were caused solely by the biting wind.

Chapter Twenty Three

It was three days later. Cold grey light furtively fingered its way from the east across a sullen sky. Clouds, full of snow, hung dark and menacing as a steady sleet drove remorselessly into the faces of the clansmen lined up for battle on Drummossie Moor.

They stood huddled in their plaids, blue bonnets with white cockades pulled down low to protect their eyes from the frozen rain. Many, dazed with fatigue and dizzy with hunger, slept on their feet, leaning on their broadswords. Others still lay on the heather, wrapped in tartan, oblivious to the fact that the call to arms was taking place around them.

It was a sadly depleted Highland army that gathered together on that Wednesday 16th April 1746. About 2,000 loyal clansmen were missing, just when they were most needed. The confrontation which loomed had come sooner than expected and several regiments, away on other business, though now hurrying desperately to answer the Prince's call, seemed unlikely to arrive in time. Apart from that, there had been a certain amount of desertions from the Rebel army and these had increased of late. It was not to be wondered at, since the men were starving. Some were, at that very moment, out in the countryside or at Inverness, foraging for food. For three days, the men had been miserably fed. The Prince's Secretary, John Hay (he who had answered Lord George Murray's criticisms with the petulant, "Everything will be got!") had signally failed to get *anything* in the way of sustenance for the men, whatever else he managed to get. Apparently, organising carts to carry supplies of meal six miles from Inverness to Culloden was a task which seemed beyond him. At any rate, it hadn't been done.

The men standing on the icy moor had eaten one biscuit each for the whole day. There had not even been enough of those to go round. That was the ration on which they were to face one of the best-fed, best-disciplined armies in Europe.

The clans' extreme weariness and unreadiness for battle was easily explained. A plan the night before to make a surprise attack on Cumberland's camp at Nairn, had badly misfired. Having tramped for hours in dreadful weather conditions in the teeth of a biting wind, slowed down by the muddy moor-road on one of the darkest nights of the year, the Highlanders arrived too late. It had been hoped by the Prince and his advisers that the Government troops would be enjoying a deeper than usual slumber after carousing with brandy the night before in celebration of Duke William's birthday. Memories of the spectacularly successful surprise attack at Prestonpans buoyed up the Highlanders' hopes as they stumbled and squelched through bog and quagmire on that nightmarish forced march.

All to no avail. Cumberland's white tents were being drummed awake before they had a chance to catch them off guard. An attack now was out of the question. There was nothing for it but to return to Culloden. The entire fruitless episode took twelve hours and the men had no chance to shut their eyes. Back at camp, they slept where they fell.

It was with disbelief that, an hour or so later, they heard their own drums and trumpets call them to boot and saddle, though in fact, few had had time or energy to take their boots off in any case. Word had arrived that Cumberland was on the march and that Redcoats were approaching steadily. The Rebel army was frantically and hurriedly drawn up on Drummossie Moor in the thin lines with which the Prince hoped to stop the inexorable advance of his Royal cousin and enemy.

Prince Charles himself was haggard from want of rest since returning from the night march. He had not slept at all but spent the last couple of hours trying vainly to arrange the transport of food for his men. He had refused to eat a meal of roast lamb his cook had prepared for him. "How can I eat," he said, "while my men starve?"

Now he was riding among them on his grey gelding, cheering them on by reminding them of past victories and trying to instil a confidence which, perhaps, in his innermost heart, he no longer felt. If he did have doubts, no-one could tell, for he was a gallant sight in his tartan coat, blue bonnet on his red hair and a light broadsword in his hand. Always seen to advantage on horseback, he looked at that moment, more of a prince than ever.

The battleground could not have been worse chosen. In Lord George Murray's words, there "never was more improper ground for Highlanders", and the day before, he tried to persuade the Prince to place his Jacobite army on the boggy, uneven ground across the River Nairn. There, the enemy cavalry would have difficulty in moving with any speed and the Highland Clans would have a chance to do what they were best at, what they had become famous for. That wild, headlong charge downhill with claymores aloft and the shriek of Gaelic war cries had struck terror more than once into the Redcoat army and brought victory every time up till now.

But the Prince had not as yet known defeat in battle and was full of optimism that this time, as in the past, his "brave Highlanders" would carry the day. In vain had Lord George Murray argued and pleaded for a change of battlefield. Drummossie Moor had been selected by the Quartermaster, General O'Sullivan, who had not even examined the ground personally, but who had the ear of the Prince. Charles Edward had the Stuart obstinacy as well as the Stuart charm. In the past, he had been forced to agree to decisions that were abhorrent to him, such as the much argued retreat from Derby. He was determined this time to have his way. Besides, he now listened more to his Irish friends like O'Sullivan than to the Scottish ones who had sacrificed everything to follow him. On the question of Drummossie Moor, he was obdurate. Here was where they would fight. Aye, and win too! And in this battle Charles decided, he would for the first time in the campaign, take command himself.

There was no more to be said. The experienced commander-in-chief swallowed his chagrin and carried out the battle-plan of his Prince, though it must have been with a heart heavy with foreboding. The ground might have been chosen for Cumberland's cavalry and infantry: flat and offering no cover, it stretched out bleak and desolate under the leaden sky. Even the elements that day seemed to favour the Government army. The harsh hissing hail in the faces of the clansmen, borne on the north-east wind, all but blinded them.

Alasdair stood with Allan in the ranks of the Macdonalds

on the left wing of the front line. They had taken part in the night march to Nairn and had only just drifted into an exhausted slumber when they were jerked into bleary-eyed action in the midst of these hectic preparations for battle. Their hearts were heavy for another reason also, as were all the Macdonalds that day. For some reason they did not understand and which was never satisfactorily explained, their usual place in the lines had been taken away from them. Everyone knew that the Macdonalds had a hereditary right to fight in the place of honour on the right wing. It had been granted to them in the days of Robert the Bruce. And yet, here they were, on the left, their fighting ardour dampened by more than the constant sleet soaking into their clothes and chilling their bones.

Above gusts of hail, pipers played the gathering rants of each clan, drones tugged by the wind into a distorted version of the pibrochs which have always stirred the heart of every Highlander. The skirl of the pipes was punctuated by regular cries of "Close up! Close up!" as the lines were made ready by officers and clan chiefs anxious not to be taken unawares by a sudden enemy attack.

The men were as ready now as they would ever be. As was their custom, they had tied their kilts high between their thighs so they could move freely and some had thrown away their plaids the better to wield their swords. They waited from dawn on the cold, wet moor for Cumberland to come, but it was 11 o'clock before the Redcoats arrived and stretched out in solid, menacing, well-disciplined lines. The only sound from those orderly ranks was the steady, blood-chilling beat of battalion drums. One of those drums was being tapped by Tom, who had survived a flogging less merciless than usual, thanks to Sergeant Wilkins who had undertaken the duty of administering the punishment.

When the battle began, it was like a thunderclap. Cannon pounded great iron waves in rhythmical succession at the Jacobite army, scattering men like rag dolls and covering their lines in smoke and confusion. Cumberland's gunners knew what they were about; they had a well-drilled routine and the enemy, five hundred yards away, were easy targets. For the Highland army, it seemed like death falling from the sky. They had little artillery with which to reply but fired their few guns with more desperation than skill. This was not the kind of fighting the clans were used to and they were helpless against an enemy too far away to attack. They stood their ground bravely enough but seeing men fall all around them, cut down by the pitiless cannonade, some eventually threw themselves flat on the heather.

When would they be given the order to charge? Why did no-one tell them to advance? For what seemed an age, they stood in the wind and sleet, longing to fight in the only way they knew: the swift charge and then face-to-face combat. They longed to hear the shout, "Claymore!", the signal to move forward, but still it failed to come. What the Highlanders did not know was that the order was finally, if belatedly, sent out but the young lad carrying the message was killed by a cannonball before he reached the clans.

At last, the Rebel army could take no more of this punishment. They had closed up the gaps left by their dead as often as they were asked, but enough was enough. Colonel Anne's regiment of Mackintoshes and McGillivrays broke away first and charged forward, swiftly joined by Lord George Murray's Athollmen, the Camerons and Stewarts of Appin. Other clans followed as the order to advance came through at last, somewhat after the event.

The yells of "Claymore!" and other Gaelic war cries were accompanied now by a new sound – the murderous whistle of grapeshot. This took a terrible toll. The cannonballs were replaced by old iron nails and leaden balls, which savagely tore into the Highland charge. The clansmen stumbled, many fell, but the remainder continued their rush towards the red lines. Those that did reach the enemy fared little better, for a new hazard was waiting.

Cumberland had not wasted his time during his enforced winter stay at Aberdeen. He had taught his men a new bayonet routine. As a Highlander rushed on a soldier with his claymore brandished high, he held his targe, if he was lucky enough to have one, on his left arm, thus leaving the right side of his body vulnerable. Each Redcoat now stabbed, not at the clansman who faced him, but at the man on his right, under his sword-arm. Those hours of bayonet practice paid dividends and many

160

Highlanders who had survived the cannon and grapeshot, fell now, impaled on that bristling steel wall.

The grey sky now wept with a fine drizzle and the ground wept too, not only with rain. The air choked with acrid yellow gun smoke blown about in eddies by the constant, biting east wind. At last, the rain and sleet stopped and revealed a scene of utter confusion and carnage. The Highland army was routed. Many had already taken to the heather and the hills. Those left on the field were dead, dying or unable to move.

The Prince was led away from the moor, tears of grief and disappointment streaming down his face, having been told by his Irish friends that the day was irrevocably lost. O'Sullivan was heard to shriek in graphic terms, "All is gone to pot." At least, this time, he showed a true grasp of the situation.

The battle, destined to be the last ever to be fought on British soil, was over in less than an hour. The formerly unbeaten Jacobite army received its first and final defeat.

Yet even now, the slaughter continued. While Government surgeons moved over the field, seeing to their wounded, other Redcoats were at a different task. They systematically killed, with rifle-butts and bayonets, every wounded Rebel they could find, both on the battlefield and on the road to Inverness, now crammed with fleeing Highlanders. Even innocent bystanders, women and children among them, who had come to see the battle, were cut down by the swords of the Redcoat dragoons if they were unlucky enough to be wearing tartan.

The vision Janet had seen so reluctantly all those months ago, had come to pass, and the flowers of the forest were once more all weeded away. As for that other flower, the white rose, symbol of hope to the Stuarts for so many years, its petals were scattered for ever on the bloodstained earth later known as Culloden Moor.

Chapter Twenty Four

Maire mercifully knew nothing of this yet, as she approached the end of her journey. She and Jamie had parted with young Douglas Mackintosh and the horses on the first day, and then continued on their own. They made slow progress after that since Maire made sure that they kept well away from General Wade's road and used paths which were not nearly so direct, but a lot safer. Steadily, they came closer and closer to home and at last they reached the familiar shores of Loch Mhor. In a few minutes, they would round the final ridge and see the Laird's house in full view, reflected on the shining water.

Jamie's pace quickened in spite of his tiredness, for he had tramped many a mile in the last four days. His brief stay with the army had toughened him up, Maire decided. She looked fondly at her cousin. He had become taller, and certainly thinner, but the eager face still had a child's roundness and his eyes were clear and bright with thoughts of home. He obviously couldn't wait to see his parents again. He had forgotten all about his regret at leaving the Jacobite army. Maire smiled to herself and envied the swift resilience of youth. Then in a moment of self-realisation, it struck her that she too had come through some horrific experiences better than she could have hoped. Not unscathed, of course. There would never be a time when she would not be haunted by the memory of the cave. It was a scene which she stifled whenever it took shape in her imagination. But here she was, alive, in good health, and with much to be thankful for. She hurried forward to catch up with Jamie as he broke into a sprint at the last bend.

Maire saw him stop and stand, staring ahead, and something about his very stillness set off a trigger of alarm somewhere within her. Jamie made no sound; it was as if he had suddenly been turned to stone. She caught up with the boy and looked across the narrow stretch of loch to his home. The house was still there, its old grey walls warmed to a rosy glow by the flaming gold of the setting sun. In fact, now Maire looked closer, even the wooden barn looked red in the evening twilight. Too red. A plume of smoke snaked like a thick rope above the barn and in a moment Maire saw the shape of the building stand out against the darkening sky like the ribcage of a skeleton. Crimson flames licked their yellow tongues around the remaining planks. As the two of them watched in silent horror, the last supporting logs gave way and were consumed in a mass of fire, which lit up the sky for miles around. The whole scene was mirrored in the still waters of the loch, which threw back to the sky the image of a second fire like some eerie echo.

Jamie sprang into action at last. Running down to the shore, he sought for and found a disused boat with fishing-nets inside and these he threw out in an anguish of impatience. "Come, Maire!" His voice was urgent, compelling. "We may yet be in time –" In time for what? Maire dared not pursue this thought but, trembling, ran down to join him. Together they pushed the boat, squeaking and scraping over the pebbles, down the shore to the water. They waded out in the shallows and scrambled aboard. It occurred to Maire that they had not stopped to check if the boat was seaworthy. It might well have leaks. There was, she decided grimly, one sure way to find out.

To her relief, the little boat glided out with no sign of water seeping in and Jamie pulled strongly on the oars towards the opposite shore. It was the swiftest way of reaching home; to walk round the strait would have taken much longer. The twenty minutes it took for the crossing was long enough to see the total destruction of the barn. By the time they waded their way through the mud on the other side, it was clear to Maire and Jamie that nothing could be done to save the building. She hoped that there had been no animals inside. But how had the fire started? And why was no-one to be seen fighting the blaze? There was something uncannily quiet about the house. They both had a sense of foreboding that something was very wrong.

Skirting the burning barn, which was now a smouldering ruin, emitting flying sparks and flaming remnants into the night air, Maire led her cousin by the hand towards his home. And hers, for most of the last year. Jamie hung back at the last moment, as if afraid of what he might find, and Maire went alone into the empty house. She knew at once that it *was* empty. It wasn't just the lack of everyday sounds coming from the kitchen or the drawing-room; there was a brooding quality about the stillness which wasn't natural. Always intuitive, Maire guessed that something bad had happened here. Something which had caused Jamie's family to flee – and quickly, too. Her sharp eyes picked out small but unmistakable signs of hurried departure.

The kitchen door was ajar and Maire walked in quietly, the soft pad of her footsteps now being joined by those of her cousin on the flagged floor. Together, they looked round at the chaos in the once-neat centre of culinary activity. Pots and pans lay where they'd fallen, as if someone had hastily grabbed a few of them, scattering the rest The big iron cooking-pot above the grate contained remnants of an unfinished meal, congealed now and unappetising. And yet – Maire sniffed cautiously. There was still a smell of food lingering in the air and when her fingers touched the stone slab below the pot, she felt a distinct warmth. The fire had not been out for longer than a few hours.

"Where are they?" Jamie's voice was only a whisper but it sounded loud in the quiet kitchen.

"I don't know," Maire answered him. "Wait here!"

In the courtyard outside, she saw a sight which saddened her. It was old Murdo, the hunting dog which had never been far from the Laird's side. He was lying on the cobblestones, his head half in a puddle, sightless eyes looking up in puzzled agony at whoever had struck him down. His side was gashed open by what looked like a sword wound. Who carried swords and who would have done this? Maire asked and answered her own question with miserable certainty. Dragoons! Mounted Redcoats, who specialised in the military technique of riding down the enemy and cutting them to pieces with one sword-slash. Murdo had been one victim; how many others would she find?

Her strained nerves leapt at the abrupt snap of a twig in the dusk. Someone was there; someone whose approach she had not heard. Maire clenched her hands into fists to summon up all her courage and before she could think better of it, she deliberately walked over to the source of the tiny sound she had heard. She forced herself to concentrate on one feeling – anger. It would combat her fear and, after seeing Murdo, it was not a difficult emotion to summon up or sustain.

It turned out that the figure in the gloaming, waiting with bated breath for discovery, was more frightened than she was.

"Dolina! I can't believe it – what are you doing here, hiding like a thief in the night and nearly scaring me to death? I thought you were a bogle at least!" Maire's relief was so great at finding the servant-girl that she hugged her tightly. Here was a member of the Laird's household, alive and well, if scared out of her wits. If she was safe, there was a chance the others were also.

Maire led Dolina into the house though it took some persuading to get the girl to enter it. They found Jamie, and Maire set out some overturned stools for them to sit on. She searched and to her delight, found a jug of fresh milk which had miraculously escaped destruction. Encouraged by this discovery, she looked further and in the recesses of the larder, found some bread and cheese, a little stale but still edible. It wasn't a banquet but it was, Maire reasoned, better than nothing. She set out the repast before her two companions and ordered them to eat. She had discovered recently that in times of crisis, it was practical measures which helped most in the matter of survival. Dolina's story could as well be told over a few bites of food and if she stopped shivering, as Maire noticed she was doing uncontrollably, it would improve her coherence.

The two of them obeyed Maire implicitly and began to eat and drink. They seemed glad to have someone take charge. I know how they feel, thought Maire with a sudden rush of sympathetic insight: I felt the same with Kirsty Fraser. It struck her with surprise that she was no longer the same person who had set out to find Jamie. In age, not much older; but she could barely recognise the light-hearted girl she had been such a short time ago. Now she found it quite natural to lead the others. A new responsibility had entered her character.

"Drink up, Dolly," she said kindly but firmly to the girl, "and tell us what has happened. Where is the family? What happened to make you all run away?"

Dolina told them of the coming of the Redcoats without warning. She had been about to serve supper when the soldiers rode up and accused the Laird of being a Jacobite sympathiser. All the men of fighting age had gone and the family were unprotected. The soldiers killed the dog who sprang growling to his master's defence and then they turned their attention to the livestock which they drove off. They set the barn on fire and meant to do the same to the house but the brands had been set carelessly with green wood and a lucky shower of rain had extinguished them after the soldiers' departure. The Laird, his family and a few servants had escaped out of a side entrance, unnoticed by the soldiers, while the latter were busy looting the house and rounding up the animals.

"We ran as fast as we could," recalled Dolina, trembling again at the memory of it, "and took shelter in a bothy about a mile away. We saw the barn go up in flames and it was by the mercy of God that this house did not share a like fate. They were fully intent on murdering the Laird and his family and on burning the house over all our heads. 'So perish all traitors!' one of them kept shouting."

"But why?" wondered Maire aloud. "What brought the Redcoats to this house and with such a ferocious desire for vengeance? We're quite a long way from the Prince's army."

Dolina looked at her, her eyes dark with a ghastly message. "It was the battle," she said in a voice scarcely above a whisper. "The battle near a place called Culloden. Our Highland army suffered a terrible defeat and many clansmen have fled to the hills. Thousands lie slain on the field and Cumberland has sent his soldiers out to search the countryside, hunting down Rebels. Did ye not know of it, Mistress Maire? Ours is not the only house to be thus attacked and set on fire. God only knows whether any of our men will return, for news has reached us that the clans were cut to pieces and even those that were lying wounded were put to the sword."

Dolina's words, softly spoken though they were, seemed to fall on Maire with the savage force of hammer-blows. This was the news she'd been dreading, but worse, far worse, than she had ever expected. The two armies had been engaged in bloody conflict while she and Jamie were on the last lap of their journey home. She looked at the boy; he was as stunned by the news as she was. Maire pulled herself together. There was nothing to be done but go and find the Laird and his family. News would follow soon enough, she had no doubt, of the fate of the Macdonald men. She dare not think of it now.

"Come!" she said to her companions. "We will go to the bothy. It is time Jamie was reunited with his parents. That at least, will bring them solace, and we can decide what to do next. What did you come back for, Dolly? You haven't told us yet." It turned out that Dolina had returned to see how much damage had been done to the house and also to pick up some firewood from the yard outside. She had been engaged in the latter task when Maire disturbed her.

It was a sad trio who made their way, guided by Dolly, to the little bothy a mile away. It was a good hiding-place because it lay on low ground and was hidden by a coppice of trees. The joy felt by the Laird and his wife at finding their son returned to them, brought stinging tears to Maire's eyes, the more easily because she was already weeping inside for the men who had marched off so bravely the previous autumn. How many of them would return to tend their crofts and plant their crops in that dark and bitter spring?

No-one spoke much as they huddled round the small fire they had made with the firewood Dolina had salvaged. It did not give out great heat but the flickering, golden centre of warmth represented a comforting reminder of home, a bulwark against the darkness yawning outside. Maire looked round at the people she'd grown to know so well during her stay here. The Laird's face was mostly in shadow but Maire detected the unmistakable gleam of tears running down his cheeks. It shocked her, because he'd always been so controlled, so in charge of his own destiny and that of others. And why shouldn't the Laird weep, she asked herself. He had plenty to weep for. This was the end of all his hopes for a Jacobite victory, the end of the dream of having a Stuart king, perhaps even the end of his clansmen. As Maire watched the grief-stricken chieftain, a hand reached out and clasped his tightly. It was Maire's aunt who had always seemed the weaker of the two, the one who was delicate and had to be cosseted. Strangely, now that they were facing disaster she seemed to have found a strength no-one knew she possessed. She had Jamie back again, and now it seemed as if she could face anything.

Dolina was the only servant who had stayed with the family. The bothy was too small to accommodate the others and so they had scattered in different directions, making for kinsmen who would give them shelter. Dolina whispered in Maire's ear, asking her to come outside for a moment. She was glad to do so, because the smoke-filled air was beginning to make her cough. Maire longed for the comfort of the big house but it was not yet safe to return. Perhaps in a day or so, when they were sure the Redcoats had left the district.

The two girls scrambled outside and Maire stretched her cramped limbs gratefully. She'd never before had to live in such a small room and wondered how on earth they would all manage to sleep there tonight.

"What is it, Dolly? Don't cry – please don't! You've been such a brave lass up till now, and the others rely on us. It will all come right – I promise," said Maire rashly, uncomfortably aware that it hardly lay in her power to change the course of fate. She put her arm round the young girl's shoulders. At last the shuddering sobs stopped and she was able to speak. "It – it's Allan," she gasped. "Allan Macdonald, son of Morag-of-the-hill. We are betrothed and were about to ask the Laird for permission to wed when – when –"

"When Prince Charlie landed at Moidart," said Maire dully, as if she were reciting a lesson already learnt. It almost seemed as if she were, because there was a sharply poignant familiarity about the situation she was witnessing. She had seen this grief and heard these lost dreams before. Of course! It was the story of Kirsty Fraser and her Duncan that reverberated in her memory with uneasy echoes. Maire sighed. How many times would history repeat itself in this heartbreaking way? A wave of sympathetic understanding of the girl's plight nudged Maire into an awareness that they were both in the same boat, as it were. She looked at Dolina in the fitful moonlight and saw a reflection of her own private anguish on the girl's pale, drawn face. Fellow-feeling enabled her to speak directly and without holding back.

"I know how you feel, Dolly. I too am waiting for news of the man I love. If it is any comfort to you, the last time I saw Allan at the Jacobite camp, he was well and full of thoughts of home. As for my Alasdair, God knows where he is now, where they both are –"

The two young women clung together for comfort in the despairing night, and as an owl hooted softly and was answered by the barking cough of a fox, it seemed to Maire that the two of them were adrift, shrouded in a darkness to which morning would never come.

Chapter Twenty Five

The next two days were endured rather than lived. Maire sorely missed the company of Janet, who had always shared her troubles, and whose down-to-earth philosophy of life seemed to lessen any burden. Janet had gone to relatives in the Black Isle after receiving a message that one of them was seriously ill. That had happened just after Maire had left in search of Jamie and so Janet had escaped the attack on the house. Maire was at least glad of that. It was enough that the five of them were in this miserable situation, marooned from friend and foe alike, in what seemed a desert island which no boat would ever find.

The third day saw a lightening of the gloom with the arrival of two visitors. Morag-of-the-hill and Iain's mother came bearing gifts of food, fuel and blankets to comfort the refugees. Word had gone round the glen that the Laird's house had been attacked by Redcoat soldiers and that all inside had fled.

"It's taken us a wee while to find you," said Morag in her gruff, kindly way, "but I can see that you would hardly light a beacon to let us know where you were. Not with those Redcoat murderers in the vicinity."

"At least they have moved up the loch again towards the Great Glen." It was Iain's mother who spoke as she delved into her basket for eggs, cheese, milk and butter. She had raided her farm and her own meagre larder for these provisions and well the recipients knew it, as they received them with gratitude and not a little surprise. Iain's mother, Moira Macdonald, had no reason to love the Laird and certainly did not share his adherence to the Jacobite cause. Maire knew this from Iain. Besides, it was the wounds his father had received during the '15 Rebellion which had led to his premature death. No, Maire thought to herself as she looked at the small woman giving out her gifts with such quiet dignity and grace, Moira Macdonald had no cause to help them in their plight. She looked into the steady grey eyes and at once realised she was in the presence of someone very special. Now she knew where Iain had got his humanity from, his integrity, his sense of values, which sometimes made him seem an oddity and even got him into trouble. It was strange. Maire felt that she knew Moira Macdonald already, and yet they had hardly met. The eyes of the older woman fell again on Maire and crinkled into a smile. Maire smiled in return, and once more she was struck by that odd feeling of familiarity. It was almost as if the other woman knew all about her.

Since the two visitors were sure that the Redcoats had moved on, Maire and the others decided that they would risk returning to the house. Another day of such privation could hardly be borne. It was very cold at night and there was barely enough room to turn round when they were all stretched out on the floor in an attempt to rest.

Moira and Morag accompanied them for the mile walk home and told them of the latest news which had filtered through after Culloden.

It was almost universally bad. Men who had escaped told of atrocities which could hardly be credited, on the part of the Government soldiers. Wounded clansmen left on the battlefield, bayoneted or clubbed to death on the orders of Cumberland. A hut near the battlefield, full of Highlanders who had just managed to crawl there for shelter, set on fire deliberately and burnt down amid the screams of the unfortunate men inside.

"They are burning and looting their way through the Highlands," said Morag in a voice harsh with anger, "and killing everyone they suspect of any connection with Jacobites. They murder first and ask questions afterwards. Anyone wearing the tartan is seen as an enemy. It will soon be against the law to wear it. Do ye ken what they are calling the Duke now? 'Butcher Cumberland' they are calling him and it's a name he richly deserves."

Maire listened to these details with a gradually increasing revulsion. It was far worse than she had ever dreamed. Defeat, she had known, would be a disaster for the Jacobites, but she had never foreseen a campaign of vengeance carried through the entire Highlands.

"I believe the Redcoats call it 'scouring the Highlands' as if they were bent on ridding them of dirt and vermin," came Moira Macdonald's quiet tones, which Maire instinctively knew concealed as great an anger and disgust as Morag's.

No-one spoke after that. They were all busy with their private thoughts, tormented by anguished uncertainty about their own loved ones. It was a relief to arrive at the house and have definite tasks to do. There was much to see to. A certain amount of valuables had disappeared during the looting, but the heavy furniture still remained intact. There was a scorched patch on the roof and side of the house, but no serious damage had been done by the fire.

They all busied themselves in various parts of the house, Jamie and his mother inspecting and clearing the bedrooms, Maire seeing to the main rooms and the Laird rushing to his beloved library to see if his books were still there. As for Dolina, she found her steps drawn naturally to the kitchen, which was where most of her work took place.

Maire was busy brushing down and shaking dust out of a tapestry hanging which had been pulled down during the soldiers' brief rampage in the drawing room, when she became aware of Dolina's presence. The girl had been running, and her eyes were wide and glistening with excitement. Maire asked her why she had left the kitchen and in such a hurry. If she didn't know it was impossible in these circumstances, she'd almost have thought it was joy that sparkled in Dolina's blue eyes. The girl held out her hand for Maire to see. In her palm there lay a small metal object. It was difficult to tell what it was at first, and Maire was puzzled. What had got into the girl?

"It was on the kitchen table," said Dolina breathlessly. "It is a sign, sent by Allan. He must be hiding nearby; waiting till it is safe to show himself."

Maire was nonplussed at this, wondering if Dolina, through wishful thinking, was willing Allan to return. And yet, it wasn't like Dolly to make up tales. She was usually very level-headed. It was only when Maire examined the piece of metal more closely that she realised what she was holding. It was a broken half of a coin, known as a "bawbee". She had heard of lovers dividing such a token between them as a symbol of their fidelity. Until the two halves were put together again, each swore never

172

to marry. She looked at Dolina with a question to which she already knew the answer.

"You have the other half?"

Wordlessly, the girl smiled and nodded, her lashes wet with the happy tears brimming from her eyes. She reached into her clothing and produced a similar object. The two fitted together perfectly as Maire knew they would. They lay nestling on her hand, the metal cold on her skin, and she felt almost giddy with sudden hope. For days she had been merely existing, surviving automatically but with a heart numb with despair. Now, if Allan had escaped and was nearby, there was surely a chance that Alasdair could also be alive.

"Oh God," she prayed inwardly, "please let him not be dead. Let me see him once more, and I'll never ask for anything else."

Dolina was sure she knew where Allan would be hiding. She did not mention the exact whereabouts but Maire gathered that it was a place the lovers had kept as a secret rendezvous. All Maire knew was that it was near a waterfall. Dolina let that slip. Maire gladly gave Dolly permission to go in search of Allan and bring him back if possible. Meanwhile she herself went and told the news to her aunt, uncle and Jamie whose faces reflected the same dawning hope which was now raging in her own breast.

It was too soon however to rejoice. Until they actually saw Allan, they had no way of knowing how many of the Macdonald men had succeeded in taking to the heather. They did not even know if Allan was wounded.

That thought reminded Maire that she must go and inform Morag that her son was skulking nearby and had sent a sign. It was news Morag would be praying for daily and Maire was glad she would be the one to bring it. There was little enough good news these days in the Highlands.

She covered the distance to Morag's house as if her feet were airborne. It was amazing how all the leaden, weary lethargy of the last few days had dropped away since hearing of Allan's return. She felt revitalised and hardly able to contain her impatience for news of Alasdair.

Morag turned white and then red by turns when Maire told her that her only son was in the neighbourhood. She was puzzled and a little hurt when she learned that it was not her that he had first contacted. But Maire, sensitive to her feelings, pointed out that since Allan had no way of knowing if the coast was clear of Redcoats, he had done a very sensible thing in sending the token to the Laird's house. It meant nothing to anyone but Dolina and if it had been seen by the wrong eyes, it would have no significance. At this explanation Morag's brow cleared; she could see the sense in what Maire said. She snatched a shawl from her chair and was keen to accompany Maire at once back to the house.

They all waited together in the kitchen. It was the nearest room to the path which Dolina had used on her way to the hills. Any arrival would first be heard here. Morag could not sit still but walked back and forth, her shawl pulled round her, anxious fingers plucking at the fringe.

Maire helped her aunt tidy the kitchen – a task which Dolina had left unfinished on her discovery of the broken "bawbee". She was glad to keep her hands busy; it somewhat stilled the fluttering sensation in her stomach. That there was news of some kind on its way here, she had no doubt. She forced herself to cease speculation on what it would be and scrubbed the wooden table till her fingers were raw. Then she began to scour the pots.

It was Morag who heard it first – a soft footstep at the door. She leapt across the room to open it and in a moment Allan was enfolded in her arms, she cradling him against her, rocking back and forth and murmuring Gaelic endearments as if he were a child again. The six-foot Highlander submitted willingly to this embrace, bending his head down awkwardly so it could rest on his mother's shoulder. Dolina stood beside them, proud at having brought about this reunion and glad for Morag to have this moment alone with her son. Maire noticed that the girl's face had a new serenity which spoke of her inner joy. She could hardly recognise her as the same grief-stricken girl she had comforted a few days ago.

"She has her heart's desire now," thought Maire, and stifled an unworthy pang of envy. "Would that I could have mine!"

Allan was starving after living out in the hills like an animal. He ate the food put in front of him with more relish than manners and there was none to reproach him. Morag leant against the doorpost as if she was on guard, her dark, brooding face peaceful and happy as no-one had ever seen it. Her eyes seldom left her son.

At last, his ravenous hunger was satisfied and Allan was ready to talk. There was an awkward silence for a moment as if no-one wanted to be the first to ask for details. They might be too dreadful. But they had to know the truth of the men's fate, Maire decided. And how else could they find out?

"Allan," she said in a low voice, trying not to sound as if she was pleading for reassurance. "How many men escaped with you after Culloden? What happened to Alasdair Macdonald?"

He looked at her and her heart sank, for she was sure she saw pity in those kind eyes. Pity and anxiety – and also some other emotion which she could not quite place.

"The left wing was cut to pieces," Allan said with bitter brevity. "How many of our men managed to get away, I cannot say. Many fell, that I know. One of them was Alexander Macdonald, the tacksman. He was killed by the cannon in the first onslaught."

His eyes went automatically to the Laird as he told him of the loss of his right-hand man. The Laird sighed and shook his head.

"So Sandy will not be returning." The simple words had the dignity of an epitaph.

There was a snort from Morag. "And I canna' say that he will be sorely missed by the folk round here. Though it's glad I am to hear that he died like a hero, for he lived like a villain."

"Let us speak no ill of the dead," said the Laird, turning a reproachful gaze on Morag. "Sandy had his faults and I'll not deny it. But he was a brave man and he died for Scotland."

For the Stuarts at any rate, thought Maire to herself, but was too tactful to say it. She knew that to her uncle, the two concepts were synonymous.

As Allan went on with his recital of the dead names he could vouch for, Maire reached out and poured herself a glass of claret. It had been fetched hastily from the Laird's cellar to greet Allan's arrival. She noticed with annoyance that her hand was shaking as she poured. She sipped a little of the wine to steady herself. And all the time, her ears were straining and her nerves screaming inwardly, waiting for the one name which would end her hopes. And it never came.

Finally, Allan finished telling of the Macdonald clansmen whom he knew would never return. It was up to the Laird now as chief, to carry the sad news to their families.

Maire became aware that Allan had turned to her at last. Why had he waited so long? Was the news that he had to impart so terrible? At first she could hardly understand what was being said to her and then the meaning began to filter through. Alasdair was not dead. That, at least, she could rejoice at. But he was not going to return to her either, for according to Allan, he had been taken prisoner. The worst news of all was that Alasdair had been wounded.

"Not badly," Allan hastened to tell her, "but he can only walk with a limp. His leg was hurt by grapeshot. Luckily, the wound was not deep. I bandaged it as best I could. I think the men in his party have been sent to the Canongate prison in Edinburgh. I – I heard the soldiers talking about the destination of the prison hulk which rode out at anchor in the Moray Firth. Would that I had better news for you, Mistress Maire!"

She knew that he meant it too. She also knew that if Allan could have done anything to save Alasdair, he would have. "I am grateful to you for this much," Maire told him. "There is at least some hope."

Once more, as she looked into his honest brown eyes, Maire had the feeling that not all had been told. Allan was holding something back. But what?

She was to find out that very evening, in a way she did not expect. The company had all eaten and Morag was looking for her son in order to return home. Dolina, strangely, did not know where he was, and so Maire and a few of the others went in search of him.

As she passed by the quiet, empty stables, a low sound of sobbing reached Maire. It was unmistakably the noise of human grief and it seemed to come from a man, rather than a woman. Maire went into the dark stable without fear, and rustled her way through the straw to the figure sitting on a bale of hay. She knew who it was, before a stray patch of moonlight showed up his

176

haggard face. Somehow, she had known it was Allan. But she could not begin to guess what was tearing him apart like this.

"Allan," she whispered, putting a hand on his arm. "Do not distress yourself. Is it the loss of your friends?"

She was appalled at the angry, ravaged countenance he turned on her, though she had no illusion that the anger was meant for her. It was obviously directed savagely against himself.

"Aye, it is the loss of my friends" – he spat out the words – "and it is because I too should have fallen there, on Culloden field. Would to God that I had!"

"But what good would that serve?" Maire was sure it was guilt that was torturing Allan; guilt that he was alive when others were dead. She was right but not for the reasons she thought.

Suddenly, it all came tumbling out of the tormented clansman, and as Maire listened to his story, she felt she was transported from the stable at Loch Mhor to the icy bleakness of Culloden on that terrible 16th day of April.

"I saw Captain Alasdair fall near me, his leg grazed by the grapeshot and bleeding sore. There was smoke all round us and I couldna see – I couldna see! But when the smoke cleared I was hardly able to believe what I saw. There were bodies all round me – some our men, some of other clans. There was blood everywhere and we were ankle-deep in mud. It was like those nightmares you have as a bairn when you try to run and you cannot lift your feet because they feel rooted to the ground."

Yes, Maire thought, I know that feeling, and not just in dreams either.

"Then," Allan continued dully, "there was the shouting. Yelling English voices and screams in Gaelic from our Highlanders as they were cut down. I didna ken where to go but I knew we had to leave that place. So I pulled Alasdair free of the mud and hoisted him on my shoulders. Somehow – I don't know how – I found my way through the bodies and the smoke and managed to reach a wee hut. I thought we could find shelter there. But it was full of wounded men already. I learned later that it was one of the places the Redcoats burned down."

He stopped and swallowed hard. Somehow Maire knew that the hardest part of his story was to come. The part he did not

177

want to tell.

"When I could walk no more, I put Captain Alasdair down on a grass bank by the side of the road. I wanted a wee rest to get my breath back. We were no' the only ones. There were groups of men, mostly wounded, scattered all the way up the road to Inverness. And then the Redcoats came. I heard them coming but I couldna' move – not if the Devil himself was after me! They were on horses, these ones, and they had swords in their hands. I wasna' afraid then. I was prepared to die and I was too tired to care. They stopped at a man who lay near me. He was groaning and badly wounded. I heard every word. 'Charlie?' they shouted at him. 'Charlie – did you fight for the Prince?' The Highlander nodded his head and they plunged a sword into him. And it was then that I realised."

"Realised what, Allan?" Maire's lips were dry and she had to moisten them in order to speak.

Allan looked at her and his eyes were dark tunnels of pain.

"That I didna' have to die like a dog in yon ditch. The soldiers couldna tell which side we had fought on because there were clans on Cumberland's side as well. There was no sure way to tell except one – the white cockade we all wore in our bonnets. And do you ken something, Mistress Maire?" Allan smiled but it was a terrible smile with no mirth in it.

"Our cockades were so dirty with mud and dirt that they were white no longer. They were just like the black cockades of the Duke's army. And that was when I knew that I was going to lie. I knew it in the few seconds it took them to reach me and Captain Alasdair. He was unconscious from weakness, so there was no-one to gainsay me. They asked me the same question. Had I fought for Prince Charlie, and I shook my head. But that wisna the end o' it. Oh no! A Highlander who was with them stepped forward and asked me my name in Gaelic. And I heard my voice telling them that I was Allan Campbell from Argyll and I fought against the Jacobites. I who have never told a lie in my life! And when they pointed to Alasdair, I said he was my brother. And so they passed on and left us. All I felt at the time was relief that we were still alive. But now my soul is filled with shame and I wish I had died with the rest on the battlefield. I am not worthy of my name, lassie. I am no longer a Macdonald!"

178

Maire was aghast at this story but not because she despised Allan for his lie. She was appalled at the cruel savagery which had driven him to it. She comforted him as best she could and told him truthfully that if it had not been for him, Alasdair would certainly be dead.

"There is no disgrace in what you did, Allan," she said. "You are one of the most honourable men I know and I am proud to call you my friend. Thank you for saving Alasdair's life. But how did he come to be captured?"

It appeared that Allan had gone to seek for water at a nearby stream as Alasdair had a fever and a raging thirst. On his return, he found that another party of soldiers had arrived to collect Rebel prisoners. More merciful than the last, they loaded them onto wagons and took them to the coast. Allan, distraught, had followed them, keeping out of sight until he found their destination. The hulk was to leave for Edinburgh.

Maire did not know exactly when she decided on her plan. All she knew was that by the time Allan had finished his story, she had made up her mind. She would go to Edinburgh. She would rescue Alasdair from prison. How, she did not as yet know.

Even the journey to Edinburgh was a precarious enough prospect at the present time. Bands of Redcoats were roving around the Highlands, crushing "rebellion" wherever they found it, sometimes with the paltriest of excuses. Cumberland was determined that this was the last time the chiefs would raise their clans for the Stuarts, and turned a blind eye to any savage brutality his orders had unleashed. Spurred on by the mistaken belief that the Jacobite army before Culloden received orders to give no quarter to prisoners, should it be victorious, the Government soldiers saw no reason why they should not mete out the same treatment. In fact, no such order was ever given; it was a cunning forgery in order to sharpen the edge of the soldiers' fury.

Maire did not know these details, but she had no illusions about how dangerous it would be for her to travel alone. So she fretted silently about how she could reach Edinburgh. Another worry nagged her also. She knew the family relied on her support in many ways, especially in Janet's absence. Who would take her place if she left? Dolina was willing enough but needed guidance in running the household. All in all, her dream of reaching Alasdair, let alone managing his rescue from prison, seemed impossible.

Chapter Twenty Six

"Sir! See down there! It looks as it our men have flushed out another Rebel."

The captain in the uniform of the Royal Scots, sighed inwardly as he took in the scene in the glen below. He had seen too many sights like this in the last few weeks and, unlike many of the men around him, he had no more stomach for them. A Lowlander himself, he had never before visited the Central Highlands but he knew that the policy of fire and sword being so assiduously carried out, was turning the place into a wasteland. Enough, he thought to himself with disgust, was enough. These people after all were fellow-Scots, his own countrymen. He realised however that these were not thoughts it would be wise to speak aloud in King George's army.

That awful business two days ago – the captain felt a wave of sickness rise in his gorge and swallowed hard to dispel the bitter taste of bile in his mouth. He could still see in his mind, the man they had hanged from a beam in his own byre; the face purple and convulsed, with tongue lolling out, made him look like some grotesque marionette. And for what crime? Because he bore the same name as one of the clans who had fought at Culloden for the Young Pretender.

The captain hadn't asked to be involved in the murder. He had come upon the soldiers unexpectedly while riding alone back to camp. It was an ugly little scene, but typical of these dark days of vengeance. A small party of Redcoats from another regiment had looted the farmhouse and tied up a woman, whose clothes were torn and face bore the marks of bruises from several fists. From the ribald remarks and coarse laughter, it was clear to the officer what plans they had for her. He was about to intervene when the whole situation changed and got out of control so fast that it resembled a dream sequence. Or rather a nightmare.

The farmer arrived suddenly, his sheep dog already growling defiance at the intruders. A bone crunching kick tossed it into the air and sent it yelping into the heather. The soldiers, led by a pockmarked sergeant with eyes of blue marble, accused the man of being a Rebel, despite his denials.

"There were plenty of your clan at Culloden Field," one of them spat out viciously. "We learned your name from your wife. Jacobite rats, all of you Frasers. Vermin to be put down. But we'll do her a favour before she follows you into eternity. She'll know what it is to have real men inside her, instead of a cursed cripple. Who goes first, lads?"

It all happened very quickly. The farmer, outraged at the threat to his wife, reached down instinctively to his stocking and drew his *scean dhu*, the tiny black-handled knife carried by all Highlanders. He drew back his hand, ready to throw, but was at once overcome by the soldiers. They hustled him towards the byre, the sergeant, a man called Rogers, walking behind, carefully knotting a hempen rope into a noose. He did it with callous enjoyment.

"Bearing arms is a hanging matter," said the sergeant with smug malice. "To say nothing of attacking His Majesty's troops. Eh, sir?" He squinted up at the officer with a suggestive leer. "You can have her first, sir. But I'm next, in order of rank. This little business won't take a moment. Lucky he has a byre to be hanged in. Yesterday, we had to use a tree for another of the dogs."

The captain had watched it all with horrified fascination, with a dry mouth, his heart thudding a tattoo inside him. He had seen death in battle, of course – that was different. But this careless snuffing out of a man's life for no reason except that he bore the wrong name – God in heaven, he reasoned to himself, the man was probably innocent! And what husband would not draw a weapon in defence of his wife? However, in spite of his private misgivings, he had said not a word. The man unluckily called Fraser had died while he himself had uttered nothing. Why? He still wondered. Perhaps he was ashamed of his own squeamishness, unwilling to appear weak before these cruel, war-hardened soldiers who had no such qualms. That sergeant was a criminal type if ever he'd seen one. The officer was, he had to admit, a little afraid of him. Looking into those hard eyes was like gazing at opaque blue glass with nothing beyond.

At least, he had saved the woman from further harm. A swift slash of his knife at the cords which bound her and a curt order to flee – that was the one honourable action he had performed that day. She had hesitated for a moment, her dark eyes large and filled with agonised indecision. The others were still at their murdering work in the byre. The officer clearly saw her anguish as she realised there was nothing she could do, and that she would certainly be next. Leaping on to a sturdy little pony which came to her call, the woman fled towards the hills. The sound that came from her as she galloped away, had haunted his waking moments ever since. It was a kind of wailing sob, the mournful Highland lament called keening, which was the most melancholy sound he had ever heard.

He'd left the place quickly, after outfacing the thwarted fury of the men who had been baulked of their prey. Asserting his rank at last, he curtly ordered the men to proceed back to their regiments with all speed.

"You have done enough work for the Government here today," he said with biting irony. "And these hills are still full of Jacobite sympathisers. It is best you make yourselves scarce before any of Fraser's friends chance to pass this way. Our uniform is not exactly loved in these parts."

They had gone, sullenly enough, but with no real argument. From the baleful look of the sergeant's pale blue eyes, however, it was clear that he would cheerfully have slit the captain's throat.

Though it happened two days ago, he had not been able to rid his mind of the incident. At times, he even found himself wondering what had become of the Fraser woman. Not that it was any of his concern. He must watch that tendency to softness in himself or he would be thought womanish. He imagined the jibe behind his back at camp – "not officer material".

So today his stomach muscles contracted in a spasm of nervous revulsion when he looked down at yet another scene of violent arrest. It seemed to be the same scenario, he observed bleakly. A man struggling in the grip of two Redcoats, a woman shouting imprecations in Gaelic as she fought with another soldier.

"Shall we approach, sir? We may be able to help." The soldier by his side was eager to do so, that was evident. Help with what, thought the captain sourly. Another summary execution? He'd be damned if he'd be involved in another such incident. But he had to go down into the glen and investigate. It would be considered strange if he simply rode past. He was after all, an officer of the Crown and his duty was clear. Weren't they scouring the Highlands? He nodded with reluctance and spurred his horse forward down the hill.

The little group heard the chink of his horse's harness and turned to watch his approach. The three Redcoats grinned to see further support arrive while the young man's struggles quietened down as if he now lost all hope. His head sank down on his chest. He looked the very image of a condemned man. The captain now saw that the woman was older than he had thought – probably the prisoner's mother. She was muttering in her own tongue between clenched teeth and rolling her eyes heavenwards as if she expected some help to appear from the skies. Perhaps she was praying.

"He's a Rebel, sir, no doubt about it." A young, fresh-faced soldier of about eighteen proudly held up the proof of guilt for the officer to see. This was the kind of thing, the youth gloated mentally, that got one noticed, perhaps even mentioned in dispatches. He wanted to be an officer one day, like the one sitting on his horse looking at him with an expression which, the young man noted with disappointment, could have been more delighted. The English lad wondered what was going through the officer's mind. Then he noted the insignia of the Royal Scots. A dour lot, these Scots. One never knew where one was with them.

"No-one can quarrel with this, sir," he said somewhat aggressively. It's proof positive, good enough for a court of law. A newly sharpened claymore, been in recent use, I should say. I was the one who found it in the roof thatch. Typical hiding-place with these Highlanders, sir. They never learn." The young soldier couldn't manage to keep the complacent note out of his voice. This was his big moment and he was savouring it.

"How can you be sure it's seen service recently? Are there bloodstains on it?" The officer's voice was cold, discouraging. He didn't, the young Redcoat realised with chagrin, seem to be at all impressed by their cleverness in trapping one of His Majesty's enemies. The three Redcoats eyed one another uncertainly, before the young one spoke up again. He seemed to have appointed himself the voice of the group.

"Well no, sir, there aren't any bloodstains on it. But there wouldn't be, by now. The blade would be wiped clean before it was hidden. It's certain he's a Rebel sir. This is Jacobite country. And," he ended on a triumphant note, "he belongs to the Macdonald Clan!"

"We all know how many Macdonalds fought at Culloden," one of the other soldiers growled impatiently. "What are we standing here, arguing about? Let's put a sword through him and be done with it. We'd have finished him by now if you hadn't interrupted us." He shot a reproachful look, bordering on insolence, at the officer who had spoiled their fun. "Sir," he added as an afterthought, managing to make it sound like an insult.

The officer was beginning to feel hopelessly trapped in a repeat performance of his previous nightmare. He knew he was seconds away from having more blood on his head. More innocent blood? He looked curiously at the prisoner who was now gazing into the distance as if this whole scene had nothing to do with him. The officer doubted if he was guiltless. He knew in his heart that the hidden weapon was strong evidence of recent rebellion, even if not iron-hard proof of it. He hesitated and the Redcoats saw his wavering and their opportunity. The elder soldier spoke again and this time his insolence was more brazen.

"Let's waste no more time! The only good Highlander is a dead one. That's a safe rule of thumb for any man. And we're all men here, I take it?" His contemptuous look flicked in the officer's direction, though without meeting his eyes. "And that hellcat of a woman should die, too. She almost scratched the skin off my face. There's a good length of strong rope lying over there. It ought to serve for both of them." He pointed towards a hillock. "And there's a tree fit for our purpose! It may be that the captain would prefer not to see blood before he takes his dinner. Well, I'm sure we can oblige him and still see justice done."

It was all happening as before. The officer felt like a puppet actor in a drama which was already written and in which he had no part to play. Cold sweat prickled on his neck. He tried to think of some way to stop this horror but could find none. The victims were already being dragged towards their place of execution, a gnarled old tree with winter-bare branches stark against the sky.

"Stop!" The call was so unexpected and authoritative that the three Redcoats froze immediately. Someone was riding towards them. It was, the captain saw with amazement, a young woman. A pretty one, too, in spite of the expression on her face, hard, angry and resolute. There was something familiar about her. As she drew closer, memories stirred within him of another time in his life – of balls, and dancing and gay soirées in Edinburgh before all the ugliness of this war came to Scotland. It seemed now a long time ago.

He looked at the girl as she reached them, sitting tall and seemingly fearless on a grey mount. He knew her now. He'd have known that copper hair anywhere and the straight, unnerving way she had of looking at you directly with her dark blue eyes. He remembered them as laughing eyes, full of fun. They weren't laughing now.

To the soldiers' surprise, she spoke not in Gaelic but in perfect English, though with a Lowland Scots accent.

"What kind of devil's work do you think you are up to? Have you not done enough to these people? The reputation of your army stinks through the entire Highlands. Let them go, at once! They have done nothing for which to be punished. Furthermore, they are our tenants and under our protection. Let them go, I say!"

The Redcoats, whose mouths had dropped open with astonishment, looked towards the officer with amused disbelief. He would surely make short shrift of this foolhardy wench who dared to interfere with His Majesty's army about its lawful duty. With incredulity, they heard him address the hussy with something approaching respect.

"Miss Maire Drummond, is it not? By all that's wonderful! Do ye not ken me, Maire? I surely havena' changed that much." He swept off his hat and bowed in the saddle with an attempt at gallantry he was aware was somewhat out of keeping, given the present circumstances. "Captain Neil Ferguson, at your service."

The blue eyes widened and lost a little of their frostiness. "Neil – can it be you? I saw only the uniform. So you are a captain now!" Quickly, Maire rallied from her surprise, realising shrewdly that perhaps she could turn this situation to her advantage and that of her friends. "And is this how you spend your time, Captain Ferguson, arresting harmless crofters and hastening them to an early death? I thought better of you in the old days."

Neil Ferguson felt his courage rising within him. He no longer felt alone, caught up in a situation he was powerless to influence. Her coming had subtly changed everything and he was conscious that he would give much to win her good opinion. She was, after all, he reasoned to himself, an old acquaintance. He turned to the three Redcoats who were looking at the newcomer with undisguised hostility. It was transparent, Neil observed with satisfaction, that they were not at all sure how to react. He knew this moment must not be lost. His voice rang out with all the authority he could muster.

"This lady is Miss Maire Drummond of Cramond, near Edinburgh. She comes from a Lowland family of unimpeachable reputation and loyalty to the Crown. Her uncle, Mr. Hector Grant, is a well-known wine merchant and on friendly terms with all the important folk in the capital. A man of great influence in high places," said Neil, warming to his theme. Maire heard this bolstering up of Hector Grant's reputation with a certain wry amusement. It was, she thought, in a good cause.

"Since this lady's credentials are impeccable," Neil continued with ringing confidence, "I trust there is not one of you who would dare to question her honesty as a witness." He paused to glare at the discomfited trio, still clutching their prisoners but with less zeal. The rope lay unheeded on the ground. Neil turned to Maire.

"Can you vouch for this man's innocence? Was he out in the recent Rising or is he the simple crofter he professes to be?"

Maire thought swiftly. Though quite prepared to lie to save a man's life, she preferred not to do so, especially on oath.

"I swear," she declared firmly, "that Allan Macdonald has never taken up arms against his rightful sovereign, nor would he ever do so."

After all, she thought to herself, she spoke only the truth. It was simply that to Jacobites, the rightful sovereign was the "King-over-the water".

She prayed that there would be no further, more searching questions. But this seemed to satisfy Captain Neil Ferguson; indeed he seemed rather pleased by the prospect that there would be no hanging that day. The same could not be said for the disappointed soldiers, who slunk away to rejoin their regiments and hope for better pickings tomorrow. The captain dismissed his foot soldier and ordered him to return to camp.

"I shall continue alone to Inverness," he said. "I am to take ship for the south," he told Maire, as he prepared to take his leave. "I carry letters from the Lord President, Mr. Duncan Forbes, and they must be delivered safely."

"Do you go a long way?" asked Maire idly, more out of politeness than genuine curiosity but the reply galvanised her into sharp attention.

"Not far, Maire. Before long, I shall see the lums of Auld Reekie again and glad I'll be to see them. The ship I take is bound for Edinburgh."

Chapter Twenty Seven

Isobel Macdonald twisted her hands nervously as she watched her husband stride up and down the hall in a rare outburst of anger. What could Maire be thinking of, asking a captain from the Royal Scots to supper that very evening? She had known that her niece was not so strongly committed to the Stuart cause as they were; that was due to her Lowland upbringing, no doubt. But she must surely know that a Government uniform was anathema to this Macdonald household! It wasn't like Maire to be so insensitive. She must, her aunt decided, have a good reason. She looked at the girl standing her ground before her uncle's tirade. Pale though she was, there was a purposeful determination in her which did not escape her aunt.

Maire waited till the Laird had had his say. She wasn't surprised at his reaction on being told that his own niece had invited the enemy to dinner. She couldn't blame him. It was essential to her plans however, that she kept Neil Ferguson from continuing his journey just yet, for when he did leave by sea from Inverness, Maire intended to accompany him. A safe and fairly quick method of transport to Edinburgh – it was the answer to her prayers. Captain Ferguson had mentioned three to five days, depending on the weather. The fact that her passage would be provided courtesy of His Majesty, King George, did not trouble her in the least. In fact, the situation had a certain sardonic humour, especially considering the reason she had for making the journey.

It took all her powers of persuasion to bring Uncle Ewan to an acceptance of the unwanted guest at his table. Only when Maire pointed out that it would be an excellent way of learning how the Jacobite leaders had fared since Culloden, did the Laird stop protesting. News was scanty and unreliable. He dearly longed to know who had escaped after Cumberland's victory, and in particular, if Prince Charles was still at liberty. Rumours flew around of the Prince's whereabouts but no-one knew where he was. The reward of thirty thousand pounds was still on his head. He was also mollified on learning that the captain had spared the lives of Allan and Morag that very day, though he was furious to learn of their treatment at the hands of the Redcoats.

"Lucky you chanced by that way, Maire," he said. "It's a pity I wasn't there myself."

Secretly, Maire was glad he had not been present. She knew well that it was her former connection with Neil Ferguson that had worked in her favour. In a way, what the captain had done was for something the Scots called "auld lang syne".

She decided to take both of them into her confidence about her desire to go to Edinburgh.

"Do not press me for details," she begged. "For I cannot give them to you. I just feel it is high time I went home. I have things to see to."

"Aye," said Uncle Ewan, readily. "You are a woman of property now, are you not?" Always a businessman, this was a reason he could understand for his niece's departure. Maire looked at him in surprise. With so many urgent matters on her mind, she had almost forgotten about her inheritance but if it served as a convincing reason for her to leave, she was grateful.

The evening went off better than she expected. Neil Ferguson seemed very aware of how painful a reminder his uniform might be to a Macdonald host and played down his military activities as much as possible. He obviously assumed that the Laird must have taken no part in the recent Rising, since it was clear his life lay in farming and running the estate. No-one mentioned that the clan had been "out" in the Forty-Five.

A bookish man, Uncle Ewan discovered to his unexpected pleasure, that his guest also read widely and the conversation became at times quite erudite. This did not entirely suit Maire. She was anxious to obtain some information about the Jacobites but was unsure how to bring the subject up. Any little detail could prove useful, she thought. The guarding and transport of prisoners, for example. Even – she jibbed a little at this thought – the punishments meted out to them.

She finally decided to use the direct approach. Neil was obviously keeping off army matters deliberately, and she couldn't help liking him for it.

"Tell me, Captain Ferguson," she asked as she refilled the wine decanter with more of Uncle Ewan's now dwindling supply of claret, "what happened to the Jacobite leaders after Culloden? Were many of them captured?"

She sensed, rather than saw, Uncle Ewan and Aunt Isobel stiffen slightly as they listened intently for the answer. Neil Ferguson looked startled at the question; it was not a subject he had planned to discuss tonight in case of giving offence. Still, if he was asked, it must be because this family had nothing to do with rebellion. Certainly, not all the Macdonalds had fought for the Stuarts – he knew that. Sitting back in his chair, tilting his wine so it caught the ruby glow of the fire, the captain felt more relaxed now than he had the whole evening. Any little doubt he had entertained about the loyalty of these relatives of Maire's, was quite dispelled.

"A good many of the ringleaders have escaped," he said. "Lochiel, chief of Clan Cameron, for one, though it is said he was wounded in both legs. His clansmen carried him off the field. Others, too, have evaded capture. Lord George Murray, for example, seems to have vanished."

"And what of the Pr – I mean, the Pretender?" asked Maire, anxious to keep Neil's thoughts flowing along these lines in the hope that he would drop some useful information.

The room went unnaturally quiet as the two hosts hardly dared to breathe.

"Still at liberty. Some say he has fled to the west, some even mention the Islands. But no-one knows for sure. He seems to have the devil's own luck in evading his pursuers, in spite of the reward on his head." Neil did not seem sorry to tell them this. Perhaps in his heart, he secretly hoped the Prince would escape, rather than face the axe on Tower Hill.

"I do not think," said Ewan Macdonald with great seriousness, "that the man would live long to spend his reward money. Not in the Highlands, at any rate."

Neil Ferguson shot him a quick glance. "You may be right, sir. You know these parts better than I. And certainly it is clear how greatly Charles Stuart was loved by his supporters. Not all of them fighting men, either. For the ladies of Jacobite persuasion, he will always be 'Bonnie Prince Charlie'. Lady Anne Mackintosh was one of his most ardent followers, and now she is a prisoner in the Guard Room at Inverness. I met her there and took tea with her. A very pretty woman, but I had the feeling that she had no regrets about raising the clan for the Pretender. If she had the chance, she'd do the same again."

I have no doubt of it, thought Maire, and set her glass down in case her hand trembled and she spilt her wine. She was upset to hear what had happened to Colonel Anne and hoped nothing worse would befall her.

"They say," went on Captain Ferguson, mistaking her silence for interest, "that she was preparing for a grand ball to celebrate a Jacobite victory on the very evening of Culloden. Only the guests who arrived were not the ones she expected. It must have been quite a shock!" He laughed merrily and at that moment, Maire felt she hated him. She had a swift mental vision of the scene at Moy Hall: Anne dressed in her shimmering tartan ball gown, the table laid ready and waiting, and then the arrival of the Redcoats, flushed and swaggering with victory, fresh from the day's slaughter. Maire shuddered and Neil Ferguson saw it.

"Have you taken cold, Miss Drummond? It is chilly in these parts in the evenings, is it not? At least, for us Edinburgh folk!"

The words immediately struck a chord in Maire and recalled her to her present purpose. It was no good brooding about the past, or even the present. She could do nothing about Lady Anne's predicament. She still had her own problem to solve.

There was no light conversation after this. The captain had been reminded of his role as an army officer in hostile territory and the temporary feeling of truce, even of warmth, between himself and the Macdonalds, seemed to evaporate. He took his leave shortly afterwards, and Maire saw him to his horse. She was now desperate to achieve the object of the evening. Quick-witted as ever, she saw a chance to use the slight coolness which had ended the dinner party.

"Oh, Neil!" she breathed, looking up at him as he sat in the saddle. "How I wish you would take me with you! I would give anything to go back home. I get so – so – homesick for Edinburgh!"

192

Neil was taken aback to see her bury her head against the sleek hide of his horse and sob heartbrokenly with a distress he had not even suspected. He was quite at a loss what to do but he felt something was expected of him. She was an old friend and besides, he admitted freely, a remarkably attractive woman into the bargain. He found himself wishing that he could indeed sweep her up on to his horse and gallop away with her. And what then? Life, he reminded himself sternly, was not a fairytale. More's the pity, he thought.

"If there was anything I could do –" he began and was startled to hear her response, so vehement, so eager, so difficult to refuse.

"Oh, but you *can*, Neil! There is a way you can help me to reach home. Listen –"

He didn't seem able to do much else. She had an answer to every objection he raised, and by the time Captain Neil Ferguson rode off that evening towards Inverness, he had promised somehow and with all the means at his disposal, to arrange a berth for Maire on one of His Majesty's ships.

Neither of them saw a figure arrive in the twilight and shrink against the wall, so it blended into the shadows. Only when the captain had left, did the figure detach itself and stumble wearily towards the door which Maire had recently entered. A soft tap brought the girl to the door again and suddenly Maire found herself staring with disbelief at yet another former acquaintance. This one, however, brought back very different memories that were vividly recent.

"Kirsty! Can it be? What brings you so far from home and how did you get here? Oh never mind – come in, come in! For whatever reason, you are welcome."

Kirsty Fraser sank gratefully into a kitchen chair and looked at her young friend with unmistakable reproach.

"I did not think to see you so friendly with our country's enemies, Maire. That was a Government soldier, was it not? I recognised the uniform even in the gloaming. I think I have heard his voice before, too. It was two days ago – the day a party of Redcoats hanged my husband because his name was Fraser."

These words struck Maire with the harsh force of stones. She felt all the muscles in her body clench with horror. Such

193

things could not be, surely? Duncan had not even been a Jacobite! Far from it. It made his death all the more bitterly unfair, incredible even. And that Neil Ferguson should have been a party to it – that was the worst of all! She felt sick at heart that a man she had regarded as a friend, could have been so brutal.

Kirsty's next words, however, brought a small measure of comfort.

"Nevertheless, I owe my life to that officer, whoever he is. For a reason I couldna' fathom he cut my bonds and let me escape while – while – they were murdering Duncan in the byre."

Kirsty broke down a little at this, and then went on. "I didna' want to go and leave him. But what else could I do? I knew it was what Duncan would have wished. Ye see, lassie, it wisna' only my life I was saving." She smiled at Maire's wondering gaze, and the smile had some secret source of joy behind the terrible sadness. "You weren't long gone, Maire, when I found that I was to bear a child. Imagine! At my age! I couldna' believe it. It was like a new beginning for Duncan and me. We were so happy – before the soldiers came."

"Before the soldiers came," repeated Maire dully. How many families throughout the Highlands were ruing that day?

She went and put her arms round Kirsty Fraser and held her close. There were no words to express what she felt at such a calamity, so Maire wisely did not use any. Kirsty had given her refuge and she had dearly wanted to repay her. Now it seemed she had her chance. She could easily arrange for Kirsty to become part of the household for she was so practical that she would be an asset rather than a burden. She could stay until the child was born, helping with the running of the house. It would be good for Kirsty too, to be kept busy.

Something clicked in Maire's head. Here was the answer to her second insurmountable problem! She need have no fears now about leaving the family. And her first problem of transport had already been solved. There was nothing now to prevent her leaving. Her departure was imminent.

For an instant, the flagstoned kitchen at Loch Mhor receded before her eyes and dissolved into the scene which awaited her a few days hence at the coast.

A wooden merchantman lay at anchor, moving uneasily on the grey, restless waters of the Moray Firth, and beyond, foamed the awesome breakers of the North Sea.

PART III

EDINBURGH: MAY 1746

Chapter Twenty Eight

The stench of the prison assailed Iain's nostrils as soon as he turned into the Canongate. He loathed his visits there; it was little enough he could do to alleviate the hardship of the inmates crammed in under impossible conditions. Many of the prisons in Scotland, and some in England, were overflowing with Jacobite prisoners awaiting trial.

This morning, there seemed to be a flurry of activity at the prison gates. Iain quickened his step, wondering what was happening. An escape perhaps, he thought hopefully, but on seeing the man talking earnestly to the jailer, his spirits fell again. It was that human vulture, Ned Sharpe – a man he detested and knew well by sight from his days as a medical student. Sharpe, well-named because of his pointed weasel-like features, was part of the Edinburgh underworld from which he emerged from time to time to ply his trade. And a grisly trade it was, Iain thought with disgust, for Ned trafficked in dead bodies among other commodities. He was a regular, if illegal, visitor to the surgeons with his toadying manner and his frequent offers of raw material for their studies in anatomy. Such middlemen were no doubt necessary, for it was not always easy to obtain a body for research purposes. But Ned Sharpe had always revolted Iain, as he smacked his lips with unctuous hypocrisy over the latest corpse. As if, Iain thought with a shudder, it were a meal!

"A good, fresh body, sir, just ripe for the surgeon's knife! All the organs complete and ready to be extracted and put into yon wee bottles –"

Iain wondered at times where Sharpe obtained his supplies. No doubt from the many unfortunate beggars who starved round the Edinburgh streets. Since the disaster of Culloden, their number had been swollen by homeless Highlanders, desperate for bread, many of them merely children.

It was just as Iain expected. Ned Sharpe had a wooden cart

with him and the jailer, a stupid but sly man known to locals as "The Jiley", already had his hand out to receive the chink of money. The objects of this exchange lay stretched out just inside the door of the jail. Iain looked down at the two prisoners who had not lasted the night. They were not men he knew, and he felt a momentary relief of which he was immediately ashamed. Macdonalds or other clansmen – what did it matter? They all suffered alike. Lack of food, filth and disease carried many of them off before ever they saw a court of law. It could be said, Iain thought grimly as he looked at the two wretched bodies, that these were the lucky ones. Certainly, the survivors had little to look forward to. The best sentence they could hope for was transportation to the American colonies and a life of virtual slavery. The worst and most severe penalty was execution. Those of noble blood were destined for the axe on Tower Hill. That was at least a quick death. Iain reserved his compassion for the ordinary officers and men unlucky enough to face the ghastly fate of being hanged, drawn and quartered. This barbaric but time-honoured death for traitors still provided exciting entertainment for a bored populace.

Still, these two would not endure such a dreadful end. They had, in a way, escaped. Iain decided that it was probably a mixture of starvation and jail fever which had killed them. He hoped it would not mean the outbreak of an epidemic in prison. His eyes met those of the Jiley, studying him watchfully, his palm no longer outstretched, but no doubt still itching. His weasely-faced friend had melted into the shadow of the jail, out of the May sunshine.

"Burn the straw these men were lying on – and much of the bedding around them, as well. It is high time the cells were cleared out – this place is overrun with vermin." Iain's voice was curt, authoritative. The Jiley nodded meekly, his eyes shifting uneasily from the flinty grey ones which seemed to bore into him. He always agreed to carry out instructions. It was easier that way. Then he would do what he liked as soon as that interfering doctor's back was turned.

"I'm a poor man, sir," he whined ingratiatingly. "I dinna get much pay for this filthy job o' mine. And I've a wife and bairns to keep. It isna' easy to keep the place clean. But," he added hastily as he saw an impatient gleam in Iain's eye, "I'll do my best. There'll be fresh straw the nicht." The Jiley felt it only right that he should skim a little for himself out of the money for the upkeep of the prison. And if the prisoners went short of food or fresh bedding, who was to know? No-one cared about the welfare of prisoners in an Edinburgh which had suddenly become loyal to King George again – least of all Rebel prisoners.

In the whole city, there was suddenly not a Jacobite to be found! All those citizens who had cheered the Prince from their balconies as he rode in triumphantly last September or queued at Holyrood to catch a glimpse of him, seemed to have vanished, or put on their Whig clothes again. To a certain extent, Iain admitted, he had done the same thing. He had never been known as a Stuart supporter in this city and no-one knew of his brief involvement as an army surgeon before Culloden. When news of that fateful battle reached him, Iain delivered the last of his wounded men to their homes and then made his way south to Edinburgh. He knew many of the prisoners were being taken there and hoped at least to care for the wounded among them. Though in his heart he had never agreed with the Stuart cause, he felt appalled at the way the clansmen were being treated. Abominably, in his opinion, like the vermin that infected their disease-ridden cells. It occurred to him that these bodies also had better be disposed of as safely as possible.

"See that these two corpses are removed and buried as quickly as you can arrange it. Or even better, see if they can be burned. We don't want the fever to spread. So if you had other plans for the bodies, you had best forget about it, or I may report you to the authorities. I will return tomorrow to see if you have replaced the bedding. Remember – fresh straw!"

Iain turned on his heel without waiting for a reply, but he could feel the look of pure hate and frustrated greed that followed him up the Canongate. He walked quickly, glad to get away from the stench of death, and those two carrion crows that fed on it.

In the High Street, near the fashionable shops and the Luckenbooths, he was startled by a voice saying his name.

"Why, father, if it isn't Iain Macdonald! Or should I call you Doctor Macdonald now?" A girl's laughing face, full of life and with none of the shadows and tragedy that seemed to stalk him nowadays, appeared in front of him. Iain found himself smiling in return. She had just alighted from a carriage, one of the few to brave the narrow Edinburgh streets, and her father was following her out, rather more stiffly.

Iain was delighted to see them. Dr Galbraith had been one of his favourite teachers and mentors, and a constant source of encouragement to him as a struggling, young student. Dr Galbraith dismissed the carriage and turned to his young friend with a warm beam.

"The very man I wished to see, young Macdonald," he said. "You'll not have heard yet?"

"What?" Iain asked wonderingly.

"Why, you have been recognised by the Edinburgh Corporation of Surgeons and Barbers as a fully qualified doctor. So no-one dare call you a quack now – if ever anyone dared to do so, which I doubt, for I cannot think of a more honourable addition to our profession. Well done, laddie!"

"And let me also add my congratulations," said his daughter with great sincerity and, Iain imagined, with open admiration. She was a pretty girl in a buxom sort of way, with very rosy cheeks and bright hazel eyes. Everything about Jean Galbraith was healthy and shining. Her skin shone as if it had been scrubbed and her teeth gleamed white against her very pink lips when she smiled. She was smiling a lot at the moment. She was a pleasant sight on that May morning, and Iain found it difficult to take his eyes off her. She was such a salutary reminder of life. After the morning he had spent, he found it welcome.

"We were on our way to your lodgings to leave a message for you," said Dr Galbraith, noticing shrewdly the way the young people were gazing at each other. "I wished to be the first to inform you of your success and to invite you to sup with us this evening. If you are free, it would give us great pleasure."

Iain's social engagements being very few, he was of course free and delighted to accept. It was with a lighter heart that he continued his work that day, visiting some sick people he was caring for and obtaining supplies of medicine from an apothecary he trusted. His duties finished, he decided to retire early to his modest lodgings in the Cowgate and dress for the evening's engagement. It was good to have something to look forward to. Not that he had much in the way of finery to wear. His jacket was somewhat threadbare. He had the feeling however that it did not matter in that household. Dr Galbraith was no snob.

Smiling and humming a tune, he turned down one of the dark, narrow wynds that led to the Cowgate. Perhaps it was the fact that he looked relaxed and like a young man about town instead of the serious doctor he actually was, that he attracted the young prostitute's attention.

"Is it company you are wanting, kind sir? I can tell you, you will not be regretting it at all, at all."

The Gaelic accent was unmistakable. Iain peered at the slight figure in the gloom and saw that she was, if not exactly pretty, certainly young and in some way striking. There was a fey quality about her, as if she were not quite mortal. It might have been the slanting green eyes, which shone luminously in the pale face. They stirred a memory in him which he could not fathom. It was almost as if he had met her before. Then the moment passed and the feeling of unease and vague menace with it. He was mistaken. He had never seen this girl before. She must be one of the many displaced Highlanders who had come to Edinburgh to avoid starvation. This apparently was the only way she could make a living. Pity moved him to reach in his pocket for a few coins which he could ill spare, especially since he had a carriage or a sedan chair to pay for this evening. The Galbraiths lived right out of the city.

He gave her the coins and dropped into his native tongue, to her obvious surprise.

"This is all I can spare but you are welcome to it. I am sorry to see someone from my own part of Scotland come to this sorry state. Did you lose your man in the Rising or were you driven out by the soldiers?"

She started back as if he had struck her. Pulling a tattered shawl round her head and shoulders, she vanished into the recesses of the wynd, her bare feet making no noise. He stared after her, wondering what had scared her so. Perhaps she was so used to ill treatment, that she could not recognise sympathy when she found it. It saddened him and once more, he had that strange feeling of half-recognition, of a shadow from the past.

He managed to shrug it off however, while he dressed for dinner. His last pennies obtained him a ride in a carriage towards Duddingston. Looking out at the darkening mass of Arthur's Seat and the Salisbury Crags, Iain wondered why his thoughts had turned inexplicably to Maire. Not that she was ever far from his mind, he reflected ruefully. But he had to face facts. The truth was that the man she loved was languishing in the Canongate. Iain had done his best for his wounded leg and it was now healing well, though what Alasdair's future would be, heaven alone knew. As one of the leaders of the Rising, it looked very bleak. For Maire's sake however, Iain had to admit that he had a momentary feeling of relief when he saw that Alasdair was not one of the dead brought out that morning.

Oh! What was the matter with him tonight? He was going out for a pleasant, celebratory evening with good friends, including, he would hazard a guess, a pretty young woman with no complications who was more than a little interested in him. If Iain read her character correctly, and he was a fair judge of people, young Jean Galbraith was ready to fall in love very easily with the right man. And he had to admit that the match would be a good one from his own point of view. Dr Galbraith was a very eminent and influential doctor. Yes, he could do a lot worse for himself than that good-natured, easygoing, pliable young woman.

The coach swayed and rocked on the uneven road out of Edinburgh. Iain would soon be at his destination, and among friends. With such an enjoyable evening before him, with his career suddenly taking an upward surge, he wondered why there was this aching emptiness in his heart.

Chapter Twenty Nine

Next day, the sun struggled to rise in a sky full of rain clouds. Edinburgh woke to a chilly dawn and the faint sound of drums borne on the breeze from the army camp outside the city.

Two men were due to be hanged that morning. The execution was to take place at 8 o'clock on the pair of gallows left behind by General "Hangman" Hawley, during his time in Edinburgh. He had built another pair in the Grassmarket, but these ones stood between Edinburgh and the port of Leith, at which young Tom's regiment had recently disembarked.

The drummer-boy still felt a bit unsteady on his feet, but at least the ground wasn't coming up to meet him any more. Sergeant Robert Wilkins, whose advice he had come to rely on, advised him to eat some dry bread and put something in his stomach. Tom wondered for a moment if Wilkins remembered the hunk of stale bread he had once thrown to him when he was a fugitive. Somehow, he doubted it. Wilkins was very much a man who lived for today and even if he did remember the act of kindness, he'd hate to be reminded of it. Probably earn me a cuff round the ear, thought Tom, and smiled to himself as he dutifully chewed. He had to admit, he was feeling more like himself now.

Then his stomach lurched again as it dawned on him what was to happen today. He was detailed to turn out as part of the Picquet on duty to lead the prisoners to their executions. The drummers were to form a square about the gallows, a military pattern known as the "dead-man's guard". Their steady, continuous drum roll would accompany the hanging.

Tom had not done this duty before and he wasn't looking forward to it. He had no choice, though. He knew that well enough, and he was in no hurry to invite further punishment from King George's army.

The salty air which blew in from the sea refreshed the boy and helped him overcome his nausea. He checked his uniform and tightened his drum. It was time to report to the officer in charge of the Picquet. To be late was a serious offence. Tom told himself that this was, after all, just another job to be done. It wasn't as if he knew the unfortunate men who were to be hanged. That helped a little.

The prisoners were duly collected from the tent, which served as a temporary guard-house and escorted towards the waiting gibbet. It was a dull, sullen day with that fine drizzle which resembled a morning mist. The arms of the gallows stretched upwards into the grey sky like a sinister warning. Tom shivered as he looked at them. Even on a sunny day, they would be grim reminders of violent death. He remembered being told by other soldiers that General Hawley had left the bodies of his deserters hanging for days to encourage the others to stay loyal: "One deserter left hanging saves six in the ranks."

In spite of himself, Tom began to wonder what these two men had done. Were they deserters too? He had deliberately kept his eyes to the front up till now and since the men were marching behind him in the dead man's guard, he had not even seen their faces. The prisoners were being escorted now to the steps of the gallows and out of the corner of his eye, Tom saw that each wore pinned to his breast, a white placard bearing his name and the offence for which he was condemned. Curiosity gripped Tom, and he swivelled his eyes to read the notices as the two soldiers passed him, close enough to touch.

One man passed too quickly for him to focus his eyes in time but he managed to read the other's card. "Will Rogers – desertion – also looting the property of a Government supporter." He didn't manage to read which regiment Rogers belonged to, for by then Tom's gaze had shifted to the face above the notice.

It was as well for the drummer-boy that his hands could carry on automatically tapping out the chattering rhythm expected of them. His mouth almost fell open with shock and horror as his eyes rested on a face he had seen before, a face which had lurked in his dreams and haunted some of his waking moments too, since he had seen it last. A cruel face, scarred by pockmarks, it had the chilliest blue eyes Tom had ever seen. It was the man in the cave – the one who had raped his friend

Maire, and had been about to kill her. Since then, Tom had dreaded meeting this soldier, afraid that he might perhaps recognise the boy who had felled him with a stone. In vain he had told himself that it was unlikely the man had seen his face. He still lived in fear.

Now the drummer found it in his heart to be sorry for the man who faced death in a few moments. Tom wouldn't wish such a fate on anyone. And yet, with the essential honesty that was central to his character, he had to admit to a certain relief flooding through him. A great terror was being removed, a bogeyman put to rest. That face would no longer pursue him in nightmares.

Looking rigidly ahead as he drummed, Tom deliberately blotted out the barbaric ritual that was taking place before him by switching his thoughts to something pleasant. It was a device for dealing with life's ugliness, which he had perfected, and it kept him sane. He had learned already in his young life, that there was always a tomorrow. Fiercely now, he concentrated on his favourite dream, which was to be back home. With practised ease, he selected his most precious memories and savoured them one by one. He could almost smell the scent of the newly picked hops and feel the sun of a late English summer on his face.

Tomorrow, his regiment was moving on towards Carlisle. It was to help with the guarding of Jacobites, who were choking the prisons. Carlisle, Tom remembered with exultation, was across the Border. As soon as they crossed the River Esk they would be in England, and every step he marched southwards, Tom told himself, would take him nearer to his beloved Kent.

Chapter Thirty

Two days after Tom's regiment marched south, another ship put in at Leith harbour. It was a merchantman from the Moray Firth, making a brief stop here on its way to Tilbury Docks.

Maire had been taken aback to discover that below decks, her ship contained a large number of prisoners from the jail at Inverness, which could no longer contain them all. Fugitives were still being rounded up throughout the Highlands and numbers were beginning to be a problem. This consignment of poor wretches was destined for the *Pamela*, a prison hulk on the Thames. Those that would survive the journey, at any rate. Many had already succumbed to the intolerable conditions, especially those who were wounded.

Maire was revolted by the cruelty of some of the sailors to their charges. She had actually witnessed the careless drowning of one prisoner whom she saw a few of the crew haul on board by a rope from the sea. The man was dead and it appeared that the sailors had made a wager about killing the lice that infested the prisoner's body without actually drowning him as well. When the sailors discovered that their victim had expired, they showed no distress. They simply tied a stone to his feet and threw him overboard again. Maire fled back to her tiny cabin, speechless with outrage and horror. She tried to intercede on the prisoners' behalf by telling Neil Ferguson what she had seen, and begging him to have a word with the captain.

"It will do no good, Maire," Neil said, frowning. "The men would simply deny it. A lot of cruel actions happen in war, that would not be tolerated at other times. And, after all, these men were Rebels!"

Maire knew then that it was no good hoping that Neil would interfere with the behaviour of His Majesty's navy. He was not a man to invite trouble. Neil always backed away if possible, from any conflict situations. But the incident only made her the more determined to rescue Alasdair from the prison in Edinburgh.

Now the smell of Leith harbour reached her on deck and curled round her nostrils, a mixture of salt, seaweed and rotting fish. Maire sniffed it ecstatically. It smelt as sweet to her as the orrisroot powder she had worn at Moy Hall. That was because she longed to be on dry land again. For part of the voyage, Maire had experienced the dreaded *mal de mer*. It was worse than anything she had ever known, but did have one advantage. It made her troubles recede into the far distance and seem unimportant. A solution to her problems seemed suddenly very clear to her, as to all similar sufferers of seasickness. She simply wanted to die!

The little boat which carried her to the shore soon scraped against the jetty. A wiry sailor helped her out on to dry land. Maire could have fallen on her knees and kissed it. All of a sudden, she felt wonderfully confident.

Now she was on her own home ground, near Edinburgh and friends who might possibly help her to achieve her aim. The first person she intended to see was her lawyer and old friend, Mr. Ramsay. He had seen that she inherited what was rightfully hers but more importantly, he had strong Jacobite sympathies. He would surely assist her in her task. Maire was sure of it.

She soon found out how wrong she was. This was a different John Ramsay and a different Edinburgh. The gay capital which she had last seen awash with tartan sashes, white cockades and Jacobite sentiment, had become a cautious Whig stronghold again. "The Young Chevalier" had turned into the Young Pretender and Charlie was no longer their darling. Mr. Ramsay was scared. Maire could almost smell his fear in the dusty office in the Lawnmarket where he entertained her by pouring her a glass of Madeira with a hand that was none too steady.

"I hope I have not understood you aright, Maire," he said, his voice as shaky as his hand. "And I wish to hear no more of such madness. The Lord Provost of Edinburgh himself has been arrested on suspicion of Jacobite sympathies! And that is only because it was felt he let the town fall too easily to the Jacobite army last autumn. There is talk of terrible reprisals against the Rebels. Many are bound to be executed – far more than after the failure of the '15. Do ye know the penalty for treason, Maire?"

She could hear the barely suppressed note of hysteria as his voice rose higher and higher, in spite of his valiant efforts at self-control. It was hard not to feel afraid herself. Fear was contagious.

"First they hang a man, but they cut him down after a few minutes before he is dead." Maire wanted to shut her ears but his voice continued, as if determined to torture her with ghoulish details she didn't want to hear.

"Then he is disembowelled and his entrails are burned before his eyes. Only then is he granted the privilege of dying by the axe. His body is quartered and his head displayed in a public place for the mob to jeer at. That is the way the state deals with traitors, my dear. Believe me, this Government will show little mercy. Put any thought of trying to aid a Jacobite prisoner out of your mind."

Well, thought Maire, at least I know where I stand.

She hurriedly changed the subject and they spoke of happier, everyday matters. The house in Cramond was ready for her to occupy it. There was no problem in evicting Hector Grant. He had changed sides once too often and his trade connections with the Jacobites becoming known, he had fled abroad.

"What of that dreadful woman he kept as a housekeeper?" Maire asked with interest. "Though I am positive she was his mistress as well. How she used to bully me when I was young! I hated her."

"Have no fears, Maire, my dear." Ramsay was smiling now, quite like his old self. "I finally got rid of her myself, on your behalf. I told Miss Wilhelmina Burt for the last time to pack her bags and go. You were the new mistress now and you would not be requiring her services." He chuckled at the memory.

"She wasn't pleased. I would not care to repeat some of the things she called me. Even more vicious than last time. Anyway, she will not be bothering you again."

They parted very amicably, with John Ramsay wishing her a happy return to Edinburgh with all his heart.

"You have all life before you, my dear," he said in his fatherly way. "Live it in the sunlight. Don't let the shadows we spoke of earlier, come near you. I've dwelt under them for a great part of *my* life. Don't you make the same mistake!"

It was good advice. Maire knew that. She also knew that she had no intention of taking it.

Chapter Thirty One

The smile of recognition froze on Maire's face. She couldn't believe her eyes. It was with delight that she had seen the neat, sober-suited lawyer, Mr. Ferguson, approaching her and was ready to greet him with the same warmth she had expected to receive from that old friend. There was no doubt that he had seen her too. She saw him stop, his steps faltered and his eyes fell uneasily to the cobblestones; then, incredibly, he deliberately turned away to cross to the other side of the High Street. He had refused to recognise her!

Maire stood transfixed for a moment, wondering why she deserved such treatment. Then, with a slight lift of the heart, she saw her old school-friend, Sheena, hurrying towards her and looking about for her father. Surely Sheena was still the same.

The smile of welcome on her friend's face for a moment reassured Maire. Sheena's words, however, did not. A spark of anger began to glow inside as she listened.

"Maire, my dear. How good it is to see you! I knew you were back in Edinburgh, for Neil has told us. He accompanied you, I believe? I must tell you, Maire, do not be distressed by my father's behaviour to you. He is not the man he was. He is nervous of meeting anyone who knew of his past foolishness and does not wish to be reminded of the time when he – when he –" Sheena stopped and swallowed as if the words were choking her.

Maire was not in a mood to be kind.

"When he supported Bonnie Prince Charlie? When he was one of the first to pay court to him at Holyrood? Oh, it is changed days indeed!"

Sheena went pale and looked around her quickly to see if they were being overheard.

"Sssh! Maire! I beg of you! Do not speak of that time. It is not safe. Father has gone through a lot and is suffering still. He has his business to think of. It would not do if folks thought him a –" Her voice fell to a whisper, "a Jacobite sympathiser."

Maire thought of the old days in the Ferguson household. She thought of the white cockades being sewn and the Jacobite songs Sheena had sung. If she needed any further proof that the Stuart cause was finished, she had it now.

The girls parted with mutual embarrassment and false promises to meet soon. As Maire continued on her way up the High Street towards the castle, she felt sorrow and a slowly mounting despair.

Near the Luckenbooths, she paused and listened. A girl was singing words Maire found familiar. She used to sing that song herself. The voice was like a bell and the bittersweet melody cascaded out of the upper window and filled the street below:

Then shall neither coif come on my head nor comb come in my hair;
Then shall neither coal nor candlelight shine in my bower mair;
Nor will I love another one until the day I die,
Since the Lowlands o' Holland have parted my love and I.

The last line reverberated mournfully in Maire's mind. The song was old but the pain of lost love was perhaps always the same, she thought sadly. The words struck a weird chill inside her in her present mood. She felt more depressed than ever. She had longed to return to Edinburgh. Now she found herself in a friendless city, with the sole exception of John Ramsay. There was no-one to help her in her self-appointed task. Things looked dark indeed.

They were worse even than she knew. As she walked up the street, a pair of green eyes followed her, strange eyes with an odd light in them. Just now they were gleaming with malevolence. A slim girl, shabbily dressed, shrank back into a doorway as Maire passed by. The eyes almost bored a hole in her back, causing Maire to stop with some sixth sense and look around. She saw no-one, and continued on her way, busy with her own thoughts and a growing feeling of hopelessness.

Fiona stood for a few moments looking at Maire's retreating figure. Her head throbbed with feelings of hate, whirled with plans for revenge. Of all the people she expected to meet on the

Edinburgh streets, Maire Drummond was the last. Seeing her aroused a fever in Fiona which she had thought was past. It brought back painful memories, which had been buried. Like any wounded animal, she made her way home. Down the Cowgate, through the Grassmarket she walked in a daze, not seeing the tall storeyed tenements that pressed in on either side, nor hearing the shrill street cries of the herring-women with full creels on their heads. Edinburgh for her ceased to exist; it was the purple mountains and shining water of Loch Mhor that Fiona saw. The memory pierced her like a sword.

She arrived at the tavern, which doubled up as a bawdyhouse at night, without knowing how she got there. Her green eyes glittered in a pale face, blank and empty as a sleepwalker's. Big Ina, who ran the establishment, took one look at her and wondered what had got into her latest protégée. She'd always been a strange lass but Ina put that down to her being from the Highlands. They were weird folk up there, as all Lowlanders knew. Barely civilised.

The only reason she bothered with the girl at all was that she seemed to possess some strange magnetic quality of attraction for certain men. She was certainly no beauty, but there was something about her. Perhaps it was those eyes, green as a cat's and just as inscrutable.

"What ails ye, hen?" asked Ina, worried not about the girl's health but her ability to earn a few bawbees. She couldn't give the girl accommodation if she wasn't able to pay for her keep. Big Ina did not believe in charity; she was strictly a business woman.

"Ned Sharpe was round here, asking for ye," said Ina in a meaningful tone. "So ye'd better be all richt by tonight. He pays well, does Ned."

The girl shuddered. "I am not liking him," she said with revulsion. "He always has the smell of death about him. Why do I have to go with him?"

"Because he has money and for some reason, you seem to please him," retorted Ina. "I canna think why, for ye're a skinny wee thing. But there's nae accounting for taste. Anyway, beggars canna be choosers." She looked curiously at the girl. "What is it? Ye look as if ye've seen a ghost!"

Fiona's thin lips tightened. "Aye, that I have," she said. "Someone I've hated since I left home, the girl who ruined my life and caused the death of my lover, that's who I've seen. There she walked, proud as a peacock in her fine clothes as if she was owning the High Street – Maire Drummond! I am hating her more than –"

Big Ina did not want to hear the measure of Fiona's hate. At the mention of a name she also detested, her mouth, slack at the best of times, fell completely open, showing several missing teeth. "Weesht, lass," she hissed between the gaps. "Ye dinna mean to tell me that yon wee bitch is back in Edinburgh? You say *you* hate her! You canna wish her all the harm I do, for she is the cause of my coming down in the world. I used to live in a grand house, ye ken, over Cramond way. It belonged to Hector Grant and me. We were going to be married. But it never came to pass, thanks to yon wee limmer! She plotted and schemed until she managed to get the hoose in her name. And I was turned out of doors, without a penny to bless myself with except," Ina added, with an unbecoming air of virtue, "some money I had managed to save out of the housekeeping. This was the best place I could get and a poor hovel it is. Do ye think I like living so close to the Nor' Loch with its smells and its foul mists coming off the water? Every summer I live in fear of catching the ague. Pass me that brandy bottle, hen. Maybe I should have a wee dram now to keep away the chill."

Fiona obligingly passed the bottle which was a frequent solace to her employer. In a moment of rare generosity, Big Ina poured some in a rather dirty glass for her young companion. They had something in common now – a shared hatred. She felt quite warm towards the girl.

"Doon wi' the wee bitch!" cried Ina, sucking greedily from the bottle. Fiona looked at her, a speculative expression coming into her emerald eyes. She was not a stupid girl. It occurred to her that it was a tremendous stroke of luck, finding someone else who had a score to settle with the Drummond wench. On her own, she could do little against Maire. She had no money, no power, no contacts. But Big Ina was a different matter. Most of the Edinburgh underworld frequented her tavern. If she played her cards right, Fiona decided, she could achieve what she now desired most in all the world – to bring about the end of that girl who had turned her out of doors and brought her to this miserable existence. Like a lot of people, Fiona believed her own version of past events. In it, she was completely innocent and Maire was to blame for everything.

The brandy warmed her like an inner fire. Suddenly, Fiona began to feel that perhaps life had something to offer after all.

Chapter Thirty Two

"Mistress Maire, I hope we're doing the richt thing. It was maybe no' such a good idea, you dressin' up as a laddie." The caddie saw his friend's crestfallen look and went on hastily, "But maybe that's because I ken ye. Yon Jiley is a stupid dunder-heid, anyway. I doubt if we'll hae much trouble wi' him."

Maire hoped sincerely that Colly was right. She didn't relish being exposed as an impostor at the prison and she dreaded even more bringing trouble on the little caddie. He had agreed to help her for "auld lang syne" and she simply had no-one else. She had to enter the prison somehow and alert Alasdair to the prospect of escape; he must be ready. The other part of her plan was to obtain a wax impression of the main door key, and have a duplicate made. She had obtained the wax from an apothecary and Colly numbered among his many contacts, a locksmith who would ask no questions.

Maire had pondered deeply over the problem of entering the Canongate Jail without incurring the normal vigilance that would accompany a visitor. The last thing she wanted to do was ask for an interview with a prisoner called Alasdair Macdonald, and declare her interest so openly. That would simply draw attention to herself and him – and the chance of her obtaining a wax copy of the key was non-existent. Two days of steady, furtive watching the comings and goings at the Canongate Prison brought her reward at last.

It was late afternoon when two young lads arrived carrying a basket between them. Maire had a quick look at the contents and saw that the basket contained various, not very appetising, scraps of food. They were all jumbled together and looked as if they were destined for some kind of animal. Hens, perhaps. She was about to turn and make her way home at the end of another fruitless day, when she stopped abruptly. The two youths were ringing the bell at the main gate of the prison! The food, Maire realised with a shudder, must be destined for the men inside. It brought home to her how hungry they must be if they could eat that disgusting mess.

When she saw how easily the boys were admitted with their basket, the germ of an idea began to form in her mind. The next moment, she realised that one of the lads, known only as Colly, for he never had a second name, was an old acquaintance! Sheer joy filled her as a plan leapt into her brain. Except for a few details, Maire now knew exactly what she was going to do. All that remained was to enlist Colly on her side. It wasn't difficult. For one thing, the caddie well remembered how Maire had saved him from a savage beating a year ago. He'd adored her ever since, and was convinced she was the bonniest lass in Edinburgh. He was furthermore a high-spirited youth and the temptation to cheat the Jiley was too good to resist. It would, Colly thought, be a great adventure and he joined in Maire's plan, with great eagerness.

Now however, he had to confess to a few misgivings as the two of them walked boldly down the High Street towards the Canongate. They had collected the basket from the usual tavern where the Jiley had an arrangement. For a small sum, he could supplement the prisoners' diet, save on the food money, and pocket the difference. It was one of the perks of his job.

Colly sneaked a look at his companion over the basket slung between them. She'd pinned up her hair and pulled on a shapeless bonnet Colly had lent her. The trouble was, curly wisps kept escaping from under the hat and framed her face in a becoming but very unmasculine way. Her figure was slim and neat enough to pass for a boy, he had to admit. But there was something wrong with the way she walked. He couldn't quite decide what.

"Take bigger strides, Davie," hissed Colly, uncomfortably aware that even that would not rectify everything. "Davie" immediately obeyed and soon they were at the gates of the prison. Maire could feel her heart beginning to flutter inside her like an entrapped pigeon. The die was cast now. God help them if she had made a mistake. The responsibility was all hers.

The heavy door creaked open on its rusty hinges and the unprepossessing face of the Jiley came into view. He looked,

Maire thought with relief, even more stupid than from a distance. His small, greedy eyes flicked over the two of them, resting for a moment, on the expected basket. Then his gaze returned to Maire and she was puzzled to see an odd, muscular spasm struggling with his usual expression of sheer avarice. He looked as if he was in pain, and then she realised with amazement, that he was, in fact, attempting to smile. It did not come easily to the Jiley. He was very out of practice, but he did his best. Still smirking, he cleared his throat.

"Who," he asked Colly with an ingratiating leer, "is yer wee friend? I havena' seen him before."

Colly looked at the Jiley, gazing enthralled at his companion and cursed himself for forgetting one vital fact. The man was well known for his predilection for good looking young males. How could he have forgotten? This was very awkward.

"It's my cousin, Davie," said Colly in a businesslike tone. "He's just up from the country and he wanted to see the inside of a jail. You dinna' mind, I hope?"

The Jiley burst into a cackle of laughter that shook his corpulent frame. Maire looked at him with disgust. *He* certainly wasn't on short rations, she thought bitterly.

"Go in, the two of ye," said their host munificently. "Go in and throw the scraps to yon scarecrows, if it amuses ye. Ye can see them fight over a few crusts. I'll see ye when ye've had your fun. Then we can have some fun ourselves maybe – eh?" He winked lecherously at Maire and dismissed them with a further oily simper.

The interior of the prison was so fetid and gloomy that it took Maire a few minutes to find her bearings. Foul smelling straw lay at her feet and the odour that rose up as she shuffled through it, made her brain reel. Men lay in corners on the soiled bedding and she heard the moans of those who were wounded or feverish. Colly went round distributing scraps of food as fairly as he could, and gave Maire an urgent nod to do what she had come for. His eyes sent her a very clear message that she had better be quick.

Maire looked round her wildly. Her eyes began to get accustomed to the dim light and she could see better now. But where was Alasdair? She only had a few seconds left to find him. She dare not call his name. What if he were locked in one of the cells?

Her gaze fell on a man sitting with his back to the damp wall, very straight and still. He was completely in shadow but a ray of sunlight crept in through the tiny window and fell on him. Something about the way he sat with that straight military back made her go over to him. It was Alasdair! He looked up at her unseeingly as if his mind was far away. He doesn't recognise me, thought Maire, hurt for a moment till she remembered her disguise.

Colly was beckoning her to go and she could hear the rattle of keys as the Jiley approached. She only had a moment. Leaning over Alasdair, she whispered swiftly in French so she would not be understood by others. "*Ne perds pas l'espoir. Sois prêt!*" His face turned upwards and a change took place in that dull despair that tore at her heart. She would have given anything to be able to stay! But she knew that everything would be jeopardised if she did. She had not come this far to throw away all chance of success.

Maire collected the empty basket and left with Colly. The Jiley was waiting for them, a grin of anticipation spread across his face. Maire didn't like that grin. Something told her it was directed mainly at her. She looked at Colly uncertainly. He was no help; merely shrugged as if it was nothing to do with him. Maire could have hit him. Didn't Colly know how serious this could be for her – for both of them? They had better get out of the Canongate prison as fast as possible. Away from that unsavoury creature who was licking his lips with lascivious relish and eyeing her as if she was a dainty morsel for dinner.

Gripping the basket firmly, Maire tried to push past the Jiley to reach the main gate. She wasn't sure what happened but Colly must have released his handle suddenly and Maire found herself staggering into the arms of the very man she was anxious to avoid. Pinioned against the stone wall, she felt the plump hands begin to rove over her body, starting to undo her jerkin and slipping inside to fondle her chest. His eyes moist with desire, the Jiley snuggled into Maire's neck, uttering endearments which would have afforded her a certain wry amusement if the situation had been less grave.

"Whit a bonny wee laddie ye are, to be sure! I'll wager

there's no razor has touched this cheek yet." He rubbed a plump finger tenderly on her chin.

You never spoke a truer word, thought Maire, torn between exasperation and revulsion. There was, she decided, something faintly ridiculous about this particular predicament. She was used to repelling advances of varying kinds from men but this was a novelty she had not experienced. It was disconcerting to say the least. It was also fraught with danger. Discovery that she was a woman would soon lead to the conclusion that she was a Jacobite spy trying to help prisoners to escape.

Desperately, Maire wriggled away from the inquisitive hands and could now glimpse Colly, doing a frenetic kind of jig round the Jiley. He kept tugging at the older man's clothes as if to distract his attention away from the girl, but so far ineffectually.

"Leave young Davie alone," shrieked Colly at last. "Or I'll call the City Guard and tell them what an auld villain you are. Leave him alone!"

The hands withdrew reluctantly. Just in time, thought Maire thankfully. Another minute and her sex would have been in no doubt! Colly certainly had taken his time to intervene. Still, he had managed it in the end; she mustn't be ungrateful. The two made a hasty exit, almost forgetting the basket in their hurry to leave that stinking hole.

Up the Canongate they ran, tripping over the cobblestones till they reached the Nether Bow Port and entered the High Street. They took refuge for a few minutes in one of the many narrow closes. This one was called the Fleshmarket. The sun did not penetrate into this cool haven and Maire laid her feverish cheek against the cold stone of a doorway. She looked reproachfully at Colly.

"Why did you let that loathsome creature paw me like that?" she said with uncharacteristic petulance. "I thought you were going to leave me to my fate for a moment."

Colly just smiled – a little smugly, Maire thought with annoyance. Then he carefully took out of his pocket the slab of wax and held it up jubilantly for her to see. There was a perfect impression of the jail key deeply embedded and clear in every detail!

"I'm sorry I had to ignore you for a few minutes, lassie," said Colly, not sounding in the least sorry. "But I knew it was our big chance and I couldna' risk finding another. He was so taken with you – ye must mak' a better laddie than I thocht!" Maire gave him a withering look, but could not help smiling herself at their success. Everything was coming right at last! She felt a sudden surge of elation. She had gone a long way to achieving her ambition and she was sure now that she would succeed. The best part of all was that she had set eyes on Alasdair and now knew he was safe and well. The nagging worry about his welfare was laid to rest.

The two conspirators were so deep in self-congratulation and plans that they did not notice the frowsy middle aged woman who staggered out of a tavern just beyond them. She belched loudly and leant against the wall of the close, blinking in the light which seemed bright to her after the dim interior of the dive behind. Stowing the habitual bottle carefully away in the voluminous folds of her skirt, she belched yet again and prepared for her homeward lurch. Then her eyes hazily focused on the two young lads in front of her and suddenly they cleared and sharpened to needlepoints. Step by step, she moved slowly along by the wall until she was able to catch the tail-end of the conversation before the two young people moved on out of the close. The words she caught were few, but enough to bring a smile of satisfaction to her coarse features. It was a smug, nasty smile, which boded ill for someone. Her lips moved in rhythm with her steps as she determinedly repeated the information she had gleaned by her eavesdropping. The two plotters had arranged a rendezvous for tomorrow with an exact place and time. Blackfriars Wynd – the High Street end – three o'clock. It was all she needed. Big Ina felt happier than she had done for a long time.

Blissfully unaware that a net was beginning to close round Maire, the shabbily dressed pair emerged again into the High Street, but had hardly gone a few steps when they were rudely stopped. A hand gripped each of their collars and hauled them around. Maire's jaw fell open with surprise. Iain Macdonald was glaring at them, especially her, with an exasperated fury he could scarcely contain.

"What in the name of all that's holy –" he began but continued in a lower voice as if aware that it would be as well not to draw attention to them. "What," he hissed angrily at Maire, "do you think you are doing? Dressed in these clothes? No doubt it's some harebrained scheme or other. You usually have some reason for wandering round Scotland on your own, inviting danger. And if you think you pass for a boy, let me tell you, Miss Maire Drummond, that I would have known you anywhere! What is it all about?"

Now furious herself, Maire was speechless. How dare he interfere in this way! And so rudely! She shot him a frosty glance and did not deign to answer but Colly who obviously trusted Iain, told him the whole story. The only detail not mentioned was the name of the prisoner they planned to rescue. Iain did not seem to find it necessary to ask.

"Do you have any idea, the two of you," he said in a softer tone, "just what could happen if your plan is discovered? There is still a pair of Hawley's gallows in the Grassmarket, and I would hate to see you both dangling there. Think again, I beg you! Your plan has little chance of success. Which of you addle-pated dunderheads thought of it?" He spoke to both of them but he was looking at Maire.

She felt she was being patronised and resented what she saw as his arrogant, authoritarian manner. Iain Macdonald, she reminded herself, had never been the soul of graciousness. His curt, abrupt way of dealing with anyone or anything he did not agree with, must lose him many friends. He had certainly lost her friendship!

With a few cold words, Maire brought the interview to an end and said good-bye to Colly until next day. It was high time she returned to Cramond. These boy's clothes were beginning to irritate her in any case, being of rougher material than she was used to. She felt thoroughly out of sorts suddenly, and was sure it was all the fault of Iain Macdonald.

Chapter Thirty Three

Maire heard a town clock strike the quarter hour as she hurried along the Cowgate to keep her appointment with Colly. She'd taken a carriage from Cramond and was completing the rest of the journey on foot. It was impossible to gain access to these narrow streets any other way. There were always delays and holdups with carriages, even on the High Street.

Her pace slackened now as she heard the chimes announcing a quarter to three. She would easily be in time to meet Colly. They were going to see the locksmith about having a duplicate key made. The boy knew where he was to be found; Maire would pay for the job, and handsomely too, as the price had to guarantee the man's silence. As she climbed up the steep slope of Blackfriars Wynd, her thoughts were busy. Once more dressed in her own clothes, she was careful to keep her wide skirt from brushing against the filthy stone walls. Edinburgh smelt every bit as bad as she remembered, especially in the warm weather.

Maire did not know exactly when she first felt uneasy in the dark lane. There was nothing and no-one to be seen as she looked behind her in a moment of sudden caution. The arc of sunlight at the Cowgate end was unbroken and when she looked upwards, there was nothing to justify the prickle of fear on the back of her neck. With a shrug of impatience, she continued climbing up towards the High Street.

There was nothing to prepare her for the ambush. A furtive movement seen out of the corner of her eye, was the only moment of warning and that came too late. A heavy piece of material – probably a sack – was thrown over her head, blotting out the daylight and nearly stifling her. At the same time, her arms were pinioned behind her with cord and she was half dragged, half carried down the wynd. She knew she was going downwards because she could feel the slope.

After the initial shock, Maire tried to rally her thoughts and put up a struggle. But it was useless because she had lost the use of her arms and her enemy was invisible. One thing however, she was certain of – there were two of them.

They must have reached the bottom of the wynd. She sensed it because they seemed to change direction. Then, just as Maire managed to kick one of her assailants, raising an oath from him, she felt herself lifted bodily and thrown on to a pile of straw. The scrape and clatter of hooves and a jerky forward movement told her that she was in some kind of cart. Where were they taking her? And who? If these were ordinary footpads, why had they not simply snatched her purse and made off? There must be some reason and Maire was afraid to think what it might be. Perhaps the authorities had been watching her and had discovered her plot to rescue a Jacobite from jail? And yet, she could not believe that either. The City Guard or the soldiers would simply arrest her if that were the case. There was more behind this, and she felt intuitively that it was something sinister.

The cart at last creaked to a halt. Rough hands picked her up like a sack of oats, set her on her feet and pushed and pummelled her forward. She could hear other voices now. Women's voices and strangely, they seemed to Maire in her dazed state to be in some way familiar. She had heard them before, but being so completely disorientated, she could not for the life of her, place them. One was coarse and strident, the other soft and feline, almost purring, with some unknown cause of satisfaction. There was also an accent to the second voice which was well known to her – surely a Highland accent? The two voices seemed to have no connection in her mind.

It was as well that she could not hear the plans which were already being laid and were to be carried out in a few hours' time. A last discussion was now taking place and the plump cheeks of Big Ina were flushed with triumph as well as wine. With unwonted generosity, she passed the bottle around, not even grudging a share to Ned Sharpe and his crony who had after all achieved for her, her dearest ambition. Now she could get even with that little slut who had cheated her out of what was rightfully hers. Revenge, Big Ina decided, was sweet. She smacked her lips as they left the bottle and turned to the girl who had proposed the whole scheme but so cleverly that Big Ina was under the illusion that the plot was her own.

"Come on, hen," she said shoving the brandy bottle under Fiona's nose. "Have a sook o' this. It'll do ye good. Put colour in yer cheeks."

Fiona shuddered. The smell of the drink turned her stomach. Couldn't this stupid, drunken harlot see that she had no need of that kind of stimulant? Let them guzzle the bottle like the beasts they were. She had a fire now lit inside her that could not be quenched. For the past year, she had been living in a shadow world of misery and painful memories, only half alive. Now at last, she felt free again – free and happy, now that Gavin's murderer was to pay for his death.

In Fiona's tortured brain, details of the past had become confused. She only knew that her life was ruined by losing Gavin and that someone should pay for it. She didn't particularly mind who, as long as it was a member of the Laird's hated family. Besides, she had always been jealous of Maire. A smile curved the corners of her mouth, making her for a moment, almost pretty. Ned Sharpe's eyes dwelt on her, avid with lust. He couldn't say what it was about the little witch that entranced him so. She was a skinny little thing; not much better than a bag of bones. But she had got into his blood and ran there like a fever. He couldn't have enough of her and was putting more money in Big Ina's coffers than he had for years. She'd put the price up too, damn her greedy eyes. It hadn't taken that shrewd bitch long to spot his passion for the wee Highland wench with the strange eyes. There was a fey, unearthly quality in them as if she came from a far-off land to which she still belonged. It reminded Ned Sharpe of that story about the man who fell under the spell of the fairies and vanished – Thomas the Rhymer. The thought astonished him. It was unlike him to think of ballads or fairy tales. That lass Fiona must have bewitched him right enough! He basked in her temporary approval and enjoyed the rare smiles she sent him.

Big Ina put the bottle away and got down to business. "Ye'll do it the nicht," she ordered Sharpe. "After it's dark. Ye havena' far to go to the Nor' Loch. I'll give ye a sack to carry the body and then it'll be goodbye to Mistress High-and-Mighty." In a mood of jubilation, she fished out the brandy bottle once more.

Ned Sharpe accepted the proffered drink and passed the bottle round. He said nothing about the night's planned activities. If Big Ina was happy to leave the business to him, then surely it was up to him how he arranged it? And to carry out her orders to the letter, Ned reasoned, would be a terrible waste of a good, fresh body. They were hard enough to come by these days, especially one not riddled by disease or starvation. He would easily find a customer for that kind of corpse; he had no doubt of it. Still, there was no need to inform Big Ina of all the details. She might get angry and worry about the murder being traced back to her. Best to keep his business to himself.

He certainly had a use for the money. With a last hungry look at the girl who so inflamed his senses, Sharpe smiled secretively and took his leave.

Chapter Thirty Four

Iain Macdonald was not in the best of tempers. A frustrating day, trying to obtain certain drugs which he needed for his patients gave him a long fruitless search round the streets of Edinburgh. At 4 o'clock outside one of the apothecary's shops, he met Dr Galbraith who was delighted to see him and chided him for not visiting them recently.

"Young Jean is always asking after you," he said with a cryptic smile. Iain tried to return his smile as heartily as it was given. How could he explain that his world had been turned topsy-turvy since yesterday? One meeting with that obstinate, maddening, headstrong girl had brought all his most cherished and secret dreams flooding back. His sense of equilibrium had been shattered and he felt edgy and irritable with the whole world.

He noticed Dr Galbraith looking at him with concern and made an effort to pull himself together. He must not be abrupt with this kind old man who had been such a good friend. In a mollified mood, Iain was glad to agree to accompany him to the house of Dr Munro, a surgeon whom Iain greatly respected. It would take his mind off things at any rate, he reflected, and that could do no harm.

They took a carriage to the Grassmarket and alighted. If Iain had been alone he would have walked because it was no great distance, but Dr Galbraith was beginning to feel his age. He mopped his brow with a handkerchief as they walked up the steep, cobbled West Bow to Dr Munro's house. Before they arrived, they heard voices, one angry and the other whining and placatory. It was the doctor who was shouting and he seemed to be packing someone off with a flea in his ear.

"Get awa' with ye, man! Ye should ken better than to come and ply yer foul trade here. Get off my property before I set the dog on ye!"

A small weedy man backed hastily away down the path uttering various apologies with such oily insincerity that Iain stood stock still. He knew that voice. He had last heard it at the Canongate Tolbooth. Ned Sharpe surely! And up to his old tricks by the sound of it.

A brief glimpse of the pointed, rodent-like features confirmed Iain's suspicions. Dr Munro, who was a most honourable man, but had a very testy nature, turned towards them. His face was mottled red with anger.

"Why man," exclaimed Galbraith, "what has got you into this state?"

"Och, I'll not waste your time with it." Dr Munro then proceeded to tell them exactly why he was so incensed.

"I canna' stand these human scavengers," he exploded. "Just because we need to have a constant supply of material for dissection if we anatomists are ever to make progress, Sharpe and his like turn it into a filthy trade. I've told him before that I refuse to stoop to do business with him. How do I know where he gets his bodies from? This time he offered me a young woman. 'A good, clean corpse – no disease about it.' Not long dead either, according to him. I couldna' help wondering if the poor young creature, whoever she was, had actually breathed her last, yet. I tell you I wouldn't put it past that blackguard to give someone who was dying a shove into the next world!"

"Neither would I," said Iain with an odd chill. "It's a pity Sharpe and his kind have things all their own way. Can nothing be done about them?"

Dr Galbraith frowned thoughtfully. "It's no easy matter, my young friend. The problem is one of scarcity. Doctors have never really had the wholehearted approval of church or state to lay claim to any bodies for research purposes – even those that are unclaimed by relatives or friends. The whole business is regarded with revulsion by the public. And so we have the hole-and-corner operators like Sharpe, who dig up bodies freshly buried, or acquire them by even more doubtful methods. One day, we shall have a gigantic scandal about the whole thing, you mark my words!"

Iain had never thought of it in that way before. "It may not be a bad thing if we do," he said. "For then, the authorities would have to solve the situation. Perhaps they could pass an Anatomy Act to legalise our position. That would put Sharpe and his cronies out of business."

"In the meantime," said Dr Munro heavily, "he is making a good living out of other folk's deaths. And though I sent him on his way with no comfort, he will not find it difficult to sell the body of that poor nameless lass. Dinna' you fear: there's many an unscrupulous quack who will be glad to take it off his hands."

It was a depressing thought but Iain knew it was probably true. The whole business was very ugly. Best not to dwell on it. He brightened up when they entered the house and took tea with Dr Munro who was doing some fascinating work on the lymphatic system and talked at length about his experiments. The afternoon seemed to fly and Iain was sorry when it came time to go. His mind had become quite settled in the last hour and a half. Iain loved his work and could always find consolation in it. Galbraith and he walked carefully down the West Bow and Iain saw the old man into a sedan chair, which would take him to the outskirts of the town. There he could pick up a carriage. The kindly face under its grey wig peered out through the curtains as the chairmen picked up their carrying poles.

"Dinna' forget, Iain! We're aye glad to see you at Duddingston. Especially – och, no matter!" He leaned back in his seat and the chairmen loped away with their tireless step. Iain looked after the chair, wondering what Galbraith had been about to say but not wondering for long. "Especially Jean" were the words he had kept back, no doubt out of tact. He was a good old man and they were a warm-hearted, generous family. He was lucky to be so well thought of by them all.

For some reason, though, his restlessness had returned and Iain decided to walk for a bit before returning to his lonely room. There was always something to see in Edinburgh. His stroll took him to the High Street and it was there he noticed a forlorn, little figure huddled in a doorway. He was about to pass by when he realised he knew this lad.

"What's wrong, Colly? Have ye lost an important letter? You look as if you had tragedy sitting on your shoulder. It canna be that bad, surely."

The tearstained face turned up to his and Iain's cheerful

smile of sympathy faded. He'd never seen that look on Colly's face before and the haunted despair in the boy's eyes caused a hard knot to tighten in the muscles of Iain's stomach. He guessed there was something very wrong; his heart told him that it concerned Maire.

"Tell me!" The words were curt, peremptory, but they cut through the glazed hopelessness which had sent Colly into a trancelike state. He began to talk, numbly at first, then faster and faster until the words tumbled out of him.

Iain listened and became more and more worried. Maire had not kept her appointment with Colly at 3 o'clock. He had waited with slowly mounting anxiety, hearing the bells of St Giles striking the passage of time like a knell. He wandered up and down the Canongate and then the High Street searching for her. He hoped that perhaps she had mistaken the opening so he searched them all before he went back to Blackfriars. That took him a long time as there were dozens of closes and wynds. There was no sign of Maire. She had completely disappeared.

"It's no' like Mistress Maire," Colly sniffed, wiping his nose with his sleeve. "She would never let a body down if she could help it. Something must have happened to her."

Iain agreed with this. Maire had her faults – impetuosity was one of them – but she was nothing if not reliable. She had been carrying money, certainly. Colly had told him about the proposed visit to the locksmith. Had she been kidnapped and if so, by whom? If she had been waylaid by footpads, then surely they would simply have snatched her purse and run? Unless – Iain swallowed hard – she had been knocked unconscious or worse and left lying in some back street or yard. They had better search for her again, and this time, he would help Colly so they could cover more ground. Iain stifled a voice which whispered to him that he could not search the whole of Edinburgh. He could have a damned good try, couldn't he?

During the course of the next hour, while Colly and he walked up more streets, closes, wynds, yards and back alleys than he had ever known existed, the inner voice became louder and louder. In the end, it was like a deafening scream in Iain's head. He felt a slight touch of hysteria which was totally unlike him. Some instinct deep inside him was hammering out the message that Maire was in danger. But if he had no idea who her enemies were, how could he have a chance of finding her? It was a hopeless quest.

Iain licked lips that were as dry as paper, and realised that he had a scorching thirst suddenly. He looked at the downcast figure of the caddie and saw how pale and weary he looked. We must have some refreshment, Iain thought. We can't go on indefinitely searching all these closes and wynds.

There was a tavern in the close in which they now found themselves. It happened to be the same Fleshmarket close that Colly and Maire had visited yesterday, and it smelt just as bad today. Still, Iain longed to have a drink and decided that though this was not the cleanest alehouse in Edinburgh, it would serve the purpose. He took Colly by the arm and led him in.

The darkness inside almost blinded him for a few seconds. Then, as he became accustomed to the gloom, he could make out chairs and tables with people he could tell at once belonged to the Edinburgh underworld. It was obviously a gambling den among other things. Iain decided it was a meeting-place for all the ruffians and riff-raff of the town. He and Colly would not stay long in this low dive. They would drink their ale and continue what Iain was beginning to fear was a useless search. If only, he thought with fervent longing, they had some clue, however small, to guide their steps.

They sat at a rickety table near the only window in the place, but it was so grimy and cobwebbed that very little daylight managed to struggle through. A slovenly woman served them two tins of ale, banging them down on the table so that it rocked and caused their drinks to spill over on to the stained wood. What a disgusting place! Nevertheless, they drank deeply and gratefully and found the ale quite palatable.

It took Iain a few minutes to notice the couple over in the darkest corner. It was the sibilant whispers and giggles from the girl which caused him to look over. They were totally engrossed in each other; at least the man was clearly besotted with his companion. He hung over her like a bird of prey waiting to devour her. Like a vulture, Iain thought and in that moment, he realised who the man was. It was Ned Sharpe: either drowning his sorrows or more likely celebrating a successful business arrangement. No doubt, Iain thought sourly, he has found a buyer for his grisly merchandise. The idea revolted him and he wanted to leave the place as soon as possible. He finished his ale in a last gulp.

Colly and he stood up, ready to leave and it was then that Iain saw the girl's face properly for the first time. She had tossed her head back and was laughing, her pale face animated and her eyes – strange, slanting eyes – gleamed green as emeralds in the dim light.

In that second, Iain recognised her. It was as if a door had been unlocked in his mind and the memory came surging back. She was the girl from Loch Mhor. The servant who had poisoned the Laird. The one person he could think of in all the world who must hate Maire! – Maire who had uncovered her crime; Maire who had turned her out and sent her away.

Iain slumped down in his chair again, to the surprise of Colly. He motioned to the boy to sit down again, ignoring his questioning look. He wished his heart would stop racing so quickly but thoughts were flashing through his head even faster. The answer to Maire's disappearance was here somewhere, if only he could find it. Iain knew it deep in his soul. He strained with every ounce of his deductive reasoning to make sense of it all. Colly, sensitive to Iain's change of mood, sat quiet as a mouse and let him think.

Then it was if some secret compartment clicked in Iain's brain. This was no accidental meeting between these two people. They had conspiracy written all over them. There was no doubt in Iain's mind that Fiona wished Maire ill. He remembered hearing that she had cursed the entire family. She wanted Maire dead. He did not want to follow through his thoughts but his relentless logic made him do so. The body Sharpe was offering to the medical profession. The body of a young woman who had no relatives to miss her. The coincidence was too strong not to be significant. Iain could have groaned aloud. He was sure now that the body Sharpe was offering was Maire's.

Chapter Thirty Five

Outside, the daylight was fading fast. It seemed to Iain in that ghastly moment as if the whole world had tipped into darkness. A world without Maire – it was unthinkable. Unbearable. It could not, must not be true! Perhaps it wasn't – at least, not yet. It was possible that Maire was still alive though in great peril. Iain with his doctor's mind forced himself to do a quick calculation of the number of hours needed before a body would become respectably cold, and therefore saleable. Even an unscrupulous quack would surely jib at a body that was still warm! These were morbid thoughts and they brought out beads of agonised sweat on the young doctor's brow. However, the answer to his tortured question was comforting as far as it went. There were still plenty of hours before tomorrow morning. The deed may well not yet be done.

All at once, Iain found himself praying. Please God, he asked silently, let Maire still be alive – and well – and I promise that I'll do anything in my power to procure her happiness. Anything.

He found himself wishing with all his heart that he had been more sympathetic to her the day before. Why was it that they always seemed to argue when they met? Iain felt that it was partly his fault that Maire had fallen among enemies. He should have looked after her better. He hoped he could make up for it now.

As soon as Sharpe got up to leave with his companion, Iain put a warning hand on Colly's sleeve. The two lurched past them towards the door, Fiona steadying the man with an arm round his waist. He had obviously drunk copiously for an hour or so and was the worse for it. Iain kept his head down as they passed out, then whispered urgently to Colly. "Prepare to follow them. I think they may lead us to Maire. Don't ask questions. Just do as I say."

The boy was only too ready to follow Iain's suggestion.

During the last few hours his heart felt as if had been wrapped in lead. Any hope of finding Miss Maire was enough to lighten this terrible heaviness that weighed down his spirits.

As soon as they came out of the door, Iain's hand pulled Colly back into the shadows. The lad could guess why. The pair in front had not moved far yet owing to Sharpe's sudden succumbing to the effect of the open air. He was leaning against the stone wall and filled the echoing close with the harsh sound of his retching. The girl stood apart, pulling her shawl round herself as if she was cold. Her rigid posture successfully conveyed her disgust. Sharpe wiped the vomit from his mouth and belched loudly.

"That's better," he said cheerfully. "Sorry about that, lass, but I couldna' keep it in. Now let's get to Ina's. I've work to do the nicht, and the auld bitch is paying me well for it."

This last statement seemed to alter the girl's attitude to him. She took his arm and hung on it as they made their way, more steadily now, up Fleshmarket Close. Iain and Colly followed cautiously, taking cover where they could in the darkened doorways until they reached the High Street. Then they threaded their way through the narrow streets of the city. At last they reached the maze of back alleys and courtyards below the Castle rock. This was the rough part of Edinburgh, a haunt of pickpockets and murderers where no-one asked too many questions if a well-dressed body ended up in the gutter with a knife in it and all valuables taken. A man should have had more sense than to walk there at night. That was the attitude of most respectable citizens. Iain sniffed. They must be near the Nor' Loch. The dank smell of its unhealthy vapours rising off the water hung heavy on the warm evening air. They were, as Iain well knew, the cause of much of that shivering misery in summer which people called "the ague". The only answer would be to drain the foul water and clean out the stinking hole. Iain hated to think of Maire in a place like this.

The couple before them stopped before a door and knocked on it with what was clearly a signal. One hard rap, three light ones, followed again by a hard one. The door was opened and Iain saw in the lamplight a big, coarse-faced woman who struck a familiar chord within him. As Sharpe and Fiona entered and the door closed behind them, Iain frowned in an effort to recall where he had seen her. This was not a part of Edinburgh he frequented. Colly gave him his answer.

"Big Ina," he whispered to Iain. "She runs a tavern and the most notorious bawdy-house in the toon. She used to work as a housekeeper for yon rascal Hector Grant until she got thrown out to make room for Mistress Maire when she inherited the big house in Cramond. It was a' the talk of Edinburgh at the time. She's a right old miser, Big Ina. She'd sell her granny for a few bawbees."

Colly was nothing if not well-informed. You could always rely on a caddie to know all the town gossip. Iain knew that and was thankful for it. He felt almost light-headed with the sudden certainty that he was right about Maire's whereabouts. There was no doubt at all in his mind now. A house which contained not one enemy but two – that clinched the matter as far as he was concerned. Gaining entrance now was the next problem. Since it was clearly a den of thieves, Big Ina would be cautious about whom she admitted. Iain remembered the special knock well enough but he feared their clothes might betray them immediately as interlopers. What they needed was an instant disguise. His eyes fell on two seamen sitting on the ground and leaning together against the tavern wall. They were snoring gently and had clearly been recent patrons of Big Ina's tavern. Iain knew they were not likely to wake up.

Gently, he relieved them of their sea-caps and then, with Colly's deft-fingered help, their jackets. It wasn't a wonderful disguise but it might serve. Iain hoped that their visit to the brothel would be brief enough to allow them not to be recognised. It was the shifty, restless eyes of Ned Sharpe he had to fear.

Carefully, Iain knocked, hoping he had got the signal right. Loud, three soft, then loud again. Heavy footsteps were heard and the door creaked open. It was the proprietress herself who stood peering at them uncertainly in the lamp light spilling into the dark alley.

"Do I ken ye?"

"Och aye, woman!" blustered Iain roughly. "We aye visit ye when oor ship docks at Leith. Noo let us in for God's sake for

I've a thirst on me that could drink a well dry. And," Iain added coarsely with a suggestive laugh, "that's no' the only kind o' need I want to satisfy. My pocket's jingling wi' siller for we've just been paid."

The clink of coin against coin had a magical effect on his hostess. Clearly, it was music to her ears. A smile puckered her plump cheeks and her eyes, hard as pebbles, shone with the soft light of avarice.

"Sit ye doon," she said hospitably, "and I'll fetch ye a cup of ale." Her eyes fell on Colly and she frowned. "He's no sailor! A wee shrimp like him?" Iain thought frantically.

"Cabin boy!" he pronounced. "I thocht it was time he learned what it was to be a man. Ye follow my meaning?"

Big Ina, it appeared, did. Directing Iain to a door leading to the back of the tavern and giving him definite instructions which room to go to, she kept a proprietorial eye on an increasingly uneasy Colly. He hoped sincerely that Big Ina had not taken a fancy to him. The woman revolted him. He was beginning to wish that they had never come here. He felt like a fly caught in a particularly nasty web.

Leaving Colly to cope with his own problems, Iain hurried to the door and on opening it, found himself in a corridor of about seven or eight rooms. He had been given specific instructions to enter the second on the left. He carefully avoided doing so and prowled up the passage like a caged animal, his ears strained for any sound, and using only the balls of his feet to avoid being heard. This was a ticklish situation. He had only to walk into the wrong room and Big Ina would suspect he was there for some other purpose. He could hardly search the entire brothel. If only there was some method of ascertaining where Maire lay! Even if she were tied up, she might manage to make some noise to alert him as to her whereabouts. But how to communicate with her without arousing the entire household of whores, to say nothing of their customers?

Iain started to whistle softly but tunefully as he moved slowly along the dark passage. It sounded casual – the noise any man with nothing much on his mind, might make. Except that the tune was carefully chosen. It was a few bars from *Flowers of the Forest*, the song Maire had sung at Loch Mhor, and which he

237

knew was her favourite. It was a long shot but Iain could think of nothing else. Inside him, a feeling of panic was beginning to grow. What if he was wrong? What if Maire wasn't there at all? What if – he stifled that last question. It was too dark even to contemplate.

It was as he was near the end of the corridor that he heard the tapping. Not so much a tap, but a thud, regular and deliberate, as if someone was thumping weakly and insistently on the wall. Then his heart quickened its pace. There was a further door he had not seen, hidden behind a thick curtain and invisible up to now.

It was the work of a moment to slip behind the musty hanging, mouldy with dust and mildew. A small door faced him, like the door to a back cellar. The thumping was still there but fainter now as if the person was growing tired.

Frantically Iain tried the iron handle. Locked! The door would not budge. Sweat broke out on his brow. They were finished now. How could he possibly obtain a key? Then he thought of some other reason why the door could be fast. Feeling with his fingers, he found a heavy bolt shot across the top. Tugging desperately, Iain succeeded in scraping it back with a protesting squeal. The door gave way at last.

In a second, he had Maire in his arms, cradling her and trying to undo the cruel gag on her mouth and the twine which cut into her ankles and wrists. Luckily, he had his *scean dhu* and the sharp little blade cut through the bonds like butter. He rubbed her ankles and tried to get the blood moving so she could walk. Neither of them spoke much. They both knew that while they were in that place, silence was their only hope of escape.

"Come!" Iain's urgent whisper cut through her confused state and obediently, Maire allowed herself to be led along the passage. Agonising pins and needles shot up her legs as she moved but she bore the pain gladly. In fact, it helped her to recover from the torpor into which she had sunk. She only hoped that this rescue was not just a happy dream.

They paused outside the door into the main tavern. Iain knew that from now on secrecy was out of the question. Speed and surprise were their main weapons now. A quick dash to the door and heaven help anyone, Iain swore, who got in his way. A cold anger had seized him when he saw what they had done to her. He knew too that he had only just been in time.

Throwing the door open, Iain ran quickly across the room, supporting Maire with one arm. His other hand still held the *scean dhu.* Startled faces looked at him, cups raised halfway to lips as if the clients of the tavern had become suddenly petrified. No-one made a move to stop him. Iain weaved his way to the outer door and pulled it open.

The unnatural silence alerted Big Ina who had been laughing heartily at some huge joke over at the counter. The joke, which was also being enjoyed by her cronies, involved a red-faced and highly embarrassed Colly who seemed somehow to have lost his breeches. It transpired from the crude remarks that Ina had wanted to check on the wee lad's "equipment" before allowing him to partake of the riches of her establishment. She was still wiping away tears of merriment when her eyes fell blearily on Iain and Maire. Her expression suddenly became baleful.

"Whit the devil –! Stop them!" she screeched wildly. "Thieves – murderers – get after them! Sharpe! Fiona! Where are ye?"

Iain waited to hear no more. With one cry to Colly to follow them, he was out of the door and into the blessed fresh air – at least, it seemed fresh after that smoky, stinking hovel. Up the alley he pounded, half carrying, half supporting Maire and in a few moments, his anxious ears heard the light patter of Colly's nimble feet following them. The lad was trouserless but safe!

A great exultation filled Iain. That afternoon had been one of the worst of his life. Never had he realised how much Maire meant to him until he thought she might be dead. He felt now that nothing in his life could ever be so bad again.

The bells of St Giles were striking 10 o'clock as they came on to the High Street. It was the hour for "Gardy-loo" and all the windows of the city high above were opened and the various refuse of the last twenty-four hours thrown out on to the heads of any unwary passers-by. Usually, the warning cry was in time; sometimes however, it was not and the filthy contents splattered their way unerringly and noisomely on to the three somewhat weary night travellers.

Cheerfully, Iain removed a herring skeleton from his shoulder. Life had worse to offer than this, after all. Nothing could mar his happiness tonight. He had found Maire and she was safe. The noise of pursuit had long since died away.

Tomorrow no doubt would bring its own problems. Iain did not want to think about tomorrow. For the moment, it could look after itself.

Chapter Thirty Six

The sounds of a new day woke Maire. Birds singing outside, feet on distant cobblestones, the neighing whinny of a horse. Familiar noises. And yet lately, unfamiliar. She stretched luxuriously in the clean, lavender–scented sheets and wondered for a moment if she was still dreaming of being back safe, in her own bed. In that miserable cellar, she had heard none of these sounds. They were the noises of home.

Sleepily, she opened her eyes and looked around her, almost afraid of what she might see. All was well. A wave of gladness swept over her as she found that she was indeed safe back home in Cramond. She lay for a few moments savouring the unbelievable comfort, and remembering.

She had been kidnapped in that dark close, thrown into a cell-like room and kept there for what seemed an eternity. The worst part of it all for Maire was not knowing why, or who had done this to her. She only had one clue and that was when the door was opened and a dish of food was placed on the floor along with a mug of ale. The slim figure of the girl who brought it had quickly disappeared but not before Maire, watching from under the fringes of her lashes as she feigned sleep, had recognised her. Fiona! What was she doing here? Maire didn't know the answer to that, but one thing was certain. Nothing would persuade her to eat or drink anything *that* girl had provided. Maire preserved very clear and terrible memories of the poisoned mushrooms Fiona had given to the Laird. And she had no illusions about the former servant's feelings towards herself. Fiona had every reason to hate her and wish her dead.

From that moment, Maire knew the cold chill of real fear. Up to then, she had cherished the hope that perhaps these people were only holding her to obtain a ransom. As the minutes and then the hours crawled by, she could not comfort herself any longer with that forlorn hope. Maire tried to prepare herself for the worst.

It had been a mistake not to get rid of the food and drink, however. Maire realised that too late. She ought to have thrown it away in a corner of the room for as soon as it was found that she had not touched it, she was bound again and this time gagged. She knew then that the food was tampered with. Maire struggled to think constructively. If she had to be silenced, there must be a reason. Perhaps people were expected to arrive at this place. What was it? A tavern? She thought it was, because of the overpowering smell of ale mixed with urine, which turned her stomach.

She fought against the nausea, aware of the danger of choking on her own vomit with the gag in her mouth.

Just when she was losing all hope, a sound cut through her fading consciousness. It was a tune she knew well. Someone nearby was whistling it and it aroused memories which jerked her back to life again. Complex, intertwined memories of her childhood with Janet, of Alasdair and the night she first met him, of the clansmen who had fallen for Bonnie Prince Charlie. *Flowers of the Forest* – a song she had always loved because it captured everything she felt about her homeland. It was for her the very essence of Scotland.

Some instinct forced her to crawl over to the door with her last remaining strength. It was her bound feet drumming on the wood as a desperate call for help that brought Iain to her.

Maire had only a hazy recollection of what happened after that. She recalled a mad rush through the back streets, the sudden appearance of her friend Colly, who for some reason was half-naked, and then the carriage journey to Cramond, paid for by some coins which Iain found in the sailors' pockets. It all had the disjointed and unreal quality of a dream.

Maire realised suddenly that she was starving. She hadn't eaten since midday yesterday and then very little. She rang the bell for Jinty, her servant who ran the house for her while she was away. The plump, pleasant-faced girl came bouncing in immediately, obviously delighted to see Maire awake. Her round eyes were wide with curiosity as to why her mistress had been brought back last night by that nice doctor, Iain Macdonald and in such a state that she had to be almost carried in. Jinty had tried to ascertain exactly what had happened but her questions were parried skilfully by Iain, who ordered her tactfully not to bother Maire but to put her to bed at once.

"And see that no-one disturbs her," he said to Jinty, and then added with a charming smile, "I know I can rely on you." She'd carried out his orders gladly, but now she would give a good deal to know just what had happened yesterday. Her mistress however seemed to have no intention of telling her. She only requested that Jinty bring her a hearty breakfast of bread, cheese, meat and hot chocolate, which she proceeded to devour with a voracious appetite.

Then Jinty helped her to get ready for the day, carefully brushing an inordinate amount of tangles out of the copper curls. She even had to pluck out fragments of *straw!* Jinty regarded these with disapproval before getting rid of them. What on earth had her mistress been up to? She decided to probe before she died of curiosity.

"Young Doctor Macdonald is well known in Edinburgh, ye ken," said Jinty, carefully pouring warm water into a basin for Maire to wash. "They say he's one of the best doctors in the town. He has new ways o' curing folk and he disna' believe in bloodletting or leeches."

"Oh?" said Maire with interest. She did not know that Iain was so successful but she was glad of it. He deserved it. The next statement from Jinty however took the wind out of her sails for a moment.

"He's a great friend of old Doctor Galbraith. They say he's practically engaged to marry his daughter, Jean. Do you know her, Mistress Maire?"

Yes, thought Maire, indeed I do. We went to school together at Miss Morrison's Academy for Young Ladies. She always had an eye for the boys, Jean. Quite a bonny girl in a plump, pink way – if you liked that sort of prettiness. Apparently, according to Jinty, Iain Macdonald did.

Ah well! Why shouldn't Iain have found a girl he loved, after all? It was none of her business. And Maire could see why it was a very suitable match because of the medical connection. It could only help Iain in his future career. Thus Maire reasoned internally, and was cross with herself for feeling unaccountably betrayed. It was ridiculous!

"Stop tugging, Jinty!" she snapped edgily. "You'll have all my hair out by the roots. I'll finish brushing it myself."

Later that day, Iain came to visit her at Cramond. By then, Maire felt fully recovered from her experience, the only physical reminders were red marks on her wrists. Iain inspected them silently and professionally. "Good!" he said. "The skin is unbroken. The redness will soon fade. How are you feeling now?"

His voice was solicitous. But then, Maire thought, it would be about any of his patients. It did not mean that she was special to him. It annoyed her to think she cared. However, she reassured him that she was now quite herself again.

"Who were those people, Iain?" There was a slight tremor in her voice which she tried to control. Iain detected it at once and kept his voice very calm as he answered her.

"You need have no fear of them any more. I can assure you of that! They were simply a gang of criminals who got together, egged on by two women who wanted you out of the way."

"I know who one of them was – Fiona from Loch Mhor," said Maire, but was amazed to learn who the other enemy had been. That dreadful woman who had lorded it over her at Cramond when she was too young and vulnerable to stand up for herself.

"Wilhelmina Burt – a common prostitute!" she said with incredulity.

"More than that," said Iain dryly. "She was the Madam who ran the bawdy-house. But not for much longer, I fancy."

He had no intention of telling Maire all the details. Certainly not about the fate which had been planned for her by Ned Sharpe, the body snatcher. Iain still shook with fury when he thought of what might have happened. He had spent a very busy morning, however. A visit to an influential friend or two, some remarks dropped about a "health hazard" to the Edinburgh public, a thieves' den where no citizen was safe, a hint about possible disease spreading from a certain tavern near the Nor' Loch – Iain smiled a grim but satisfied smile. He was certain that before the sun set that day, Edinburgh would be cleansed of at least one nest of vipers.

Today, he had special business to discuss with Maire. He wasn't sure how best to approach it. Certainly, he must do so with great care, and with no display of feeling. It was his only chance of success. He wished that Maire did not look so attractive in a gown of green silk which set off her gleaming hair to perfection. It made his job harder.

Iain's manner now became much more brisk and businesslike. The caring, almost tender look vanished from his eyes. He looked at her steadily and without any sign of emotion. Maire wondered what was coming. She sensed that something was.

"I am glad you are well again," he said, "because you will have need of every ounce of strength. I intend that we rescue Alasdair Macdonald from the Canongate prison before the week is out."

Maire was flabbergasted. What did he mean – "we"? What did her plans have to do with him? He had shown no sympathy at all with her scheme – when was it – two days ago? It seemed like a million years after all that had happened.

She could hardly find the breath to answer him. "This is a change in you, Iain. What has decided you to help me free Alasdair?"

He did not answer that. He had no intention of answering it. How could he explain to Maire the promise he had made to himself when he was desperately searching Edinburgh for her? He would die rather than tell her. She loved another man; he had grown to accept that. The last thing Iain Macdonald wanted was to place Maire under a feeling of false obligation to him, just because he had saved her life. She must never, he decided with iron determination, know of his real feelings. Pride alone, as well as his love for her, made it incumbent on him to treat her as coolly as possible. There was a task he had set himself to perform; let them therefore proceed with it sensibly and cautiously.

"Your plan is too risky, Maire," he began. "The use of a duplicate key is fraught with danger, and has all kinds of drawbacks. I have evolved a better idea, I think. It is simple but many of the best escape plots have been simple. That is why they have worked."

245

His voice was calm, assured, authoritative. Maire did not feel she could argue. She just listened. Iain's plan was to go into the prison on one of his visits, change places with Alasdair and after the latter was free, call the jailer and claim that he had been overpowered.

"The substitution ploy has led many to freedom in the past," Iain claimed. "Remember Lord Nithsdale. He escaped from the Tower of London the very night before his execution, dressed as one of his lady's maids."

Maire knew that story. It was one of the great tales of the '15 Rebellion. It also had the merit of being true. There was a lot in what Iain said about the simplest plan having the best chance of success. She could see one possible snag however. What if no-one believed Iain? If he were thought to be lying, his life would be forfeit. Why was he risking everything in this way? Her heart told her that it was for her sake, and yet she could find no sign of tenderness in his face.

With calm seriousness, the doctor explained his plan in all its details. He had obviously given it a great deal of thought. Colly was to create a small diversion at the moment of Alasdair's exit from prison. Maire was to wait in a carriage at a prearranged spot nearby but out of sight. She was also given the responsibility of arranging passage to France or failing that, the Low Countries. Iain gave her the name of a man in Leith whom he was sure would help her to contact the right sea captain.

"He seems to feel he owes me a favour," he said briefly. "Just because I was lucky enough to save his father's life when he had a septic wound that threatened to turn to gangrene. I was sure the leg would have to be amputated but I tried Janet's remedy and it worked – a mouldy bread poultice slapped on the wound drew out the poison. It's really Janet who should be thanked."

His face became animated for a second as he remembered how pleased he was at saving a life he thought was lost. Then the businesslike expression returned.

"In any case, if I give you a note with my signature, he is certain to aid you in any way he can. You must have a boat ready and waiting to sail on the evening tide out of Leith. I leave it to you, Maire. Then I can arrange to time my visit to the prison to fit in with the time of sailing."

Iain stood up and picked up his hat, ready to go.

"I will leave you now. I am sure you have much to see to. You will have your own packing to do and preparations to make for departure."

"Departure?" echoed Maire faintly.

Iain raised an eyebrow. "Naturally, I assume that you will be leaving with Alasdair. I know how things are between you. And certainly, Alasdair will assume it. In view of all you are doing to save him, he would have every right to expect it."

With a few words of farewell, he was gone, leaving Maire's feelings in turmoil.

Chapter Thirty Seven

She sat down and tried to think clearly. Events were moving too fast suddenly. Her own reactions disturbed her and she found it hard to make sense of them. Certainly, Iain had taken her completely by surprise. The last thing she would ever have expected was his wholehearted commitment to the rescue of Alasdair from prison. Why was he doing it?

His last words chimed a melancholy echo in her ears. "I assume you will be leaving – he will have every right to expect it." He had said it so coldly, so rationally. Iain was nothing if not reasonable. It was one of the qualities she admired in him, being impulsive herself. She had to face the truth. Iain wanted her to go. It was perhaps the best answer for him, to clear her out of his life and prepare to marry that – that pink doll, Jean Galbraith! This flash of bitchiness was uncharacteristic of Maire and she was ashamed of it the next moment. She had no right to grudge Iain his right to happiness. After all, what if he *had* loved her once? She had been in love with Alasdair all along, hadn't she? It was with him that her future lay. It was simply that she had not planned to leave Scotland so soon. But what difference would it make? She would have joined her lover in France soon in any case.

Maire sighed. One of her faults was rushing into action without always thinking it through. All she had seen in front of her was the enormous task of breaking Alasdair out of the Tolbooth and spiriting him to safety. She had simply not considered all the implications of her plan. Well, she could see them now. Thanks to that clear-sighted observer, Iain Macdonald.

It was a pity she had to leave her house in Cramond so soon after inheriting it. However, it could not be helped. Also, she could not tell Jinty and the other servants why she was going. She could not even say goodbye to them. A letter to be opened after her departure would have to suffice. The thought saddened Maire. What would Janet think about it all? Maire couldn't help wishing she was there to discuss her problems with, as she had done when she was younger.

There was another cause for regret too. Janet was about to return to Edinburgh since the death of the sick relative she'd been nursing. She was to become Maire's new housekeeper. Together, they would transform the house where both had been so unhappy, into a real home. Now that was not to be. Maire sighed and bit her lip. She hoped her old friend would understand her reasons for leaving. After all, she was a grown woman now and must make her own decisions. She pulled herself together with sudden resolve. This brooding was doing no-one any good, least of all Alasdair. He was relying on her. She had made him a promise and she was determined to keep it. He must not stay in that stinking Canongate prison one more moment than was necessary.

Maire felt much better now that she could concentrate on action. There was plenty for her to do if Alasdair was to be free by the end of the week. Iain had entrusted her with the booking of the sea passage, the carriage and horses that must be waiting in Leith Wynd, and she had much to see to in her own personal affairs before she left.

It was as if a lump of granite had fallen from her shoulders. Maire was sure now what she had to do.

***

The creak of the rusty gate being swung open was not louder than Iain's thudding heart. He wondered why no-one but himself could hear it. Outwardly, he was the calm, professional doctor; inwardly, he was filled with trepidation. Now that the actual moment had arrived, he was prey to all kinds of doubts and misgivings. It was one thing to plan an escape in a comfortable living room; quite another to take part in the reality. He was uncomfortably aware that it would only require a stroke of bad luck, a fault in timing and he would be exposed. And what then? Iain had no illusions. Alasdair Macdonald would not go alone to his execution. He forced such morbid thoughts out of his head and greeted the Jiley with his usual steady gaze. The grey eyes did not waver.

"I've come to check on the prisoners' bedding," he said curtly. "There's a fear of disease in the city and we must take all precautions. A rat-hole like this could constitute a danger if it is not kept clean."

"It's a wee bit late," whined the Jiley who was just settling down to his evening tipple.

"No matter. I'll not be long," said Iain, hoping sincerely that he spoke the truth. The door clanged behind him with a sound like the knell of doom. He followed the Jiley to the cells.

"Just leave me here and go back to your work. I've no doubt interrupted you," said Iain with unusual courtesy. The Jiley saw nothing suspicious in this, however. Never very quick on the uptake, he was only too glad to return to his cosy corner and his drink. As Iain turned to the cells to search for Alasdair, he heard the door knocker again. That, he knew, would be Colly. He now only had a few minutes. Their plan's success depended on speed. At no time must the Jiley get a good look at the departing "doctor".

Alasdair leapt to his feet as soon as Iain entered. He seemed to have a premonition that this visit was special. He had been waiting for an unusual happening since Maire's whispered message – "*Sois prêt!*" – "Be ready!" He realised afterwards that it was Maire, though the boy's clothes fooled him for a minute. Every day since then, Alasdair had remained alert, hoping that he would soon be out of this fetid hole. The surgeon did not usually come at this time of day; it was enough to set the prisoner on edge with excited anticipation.

To Alasdair's surprise, Iain motioned him to absolute silence and quickly stripped off his own coat and waistcoat. An urgent whisper to Alasdair galvanised him into the same activity. It did not take long to divest himself of his shabby clothing. He'd worn it since Culloden. The two men changed garments and looked at one another with a silence more significant than any words. Alasdair with a questioning gratitude; Iain with a crooked little smile as if he was amused at finding himself in this unlikely position. They clasped hands for a moment and then Alasdair was gone.

The worst moment was still to come. How to pass out of the prison without being noticed by the Jiley? Alasdair did not know but, trusting his friends, he walked boldly out to the courtyard with the tricorne hat pulled low down over his brow. He stared at the cobblestones as if deep in thought and prayed no-one would force him to speak. A voice was something he could not imitate.

He need not have worried. Colly was coping manfully with his part. Alternately teasing and flirting with the Jiley, he moved steadily towards the door and Alasdair did the same. The big key was produced and waved aloft. Colly and Alasdair looked at it, their eyes glistening with secret longing. That was their passport to safety. Alasdair had to restrain an overwhelming desire to snatch it.

The Jiley inserted the key in the lock. "But will ye just tell me where Davie is?" he whinged to Colly. "I took a real fancy to the lad. Bring him wi' ye next time ye come."

Lying in his teeth, Colly promised vehemently that next time he would certainly bring his cousin. He was rewarded by an unctuous smirk and – best of all – by the scrape of the key in the lock. The best sound they had ever heard.

"After you, doctor," said Colly politely and next moment they were in the Canongate. Alasdair would have been lost but for the boy. He guided him through closes and finally to the coach, which was waiting with Maire inside. As soon as Alasdair arrived, the coachman was ordered to drive to Leith as fast as possible. The horses clattered their way down Leith Wynd as the two lovers were reunited.

She was in his arms in a moment. It was just as she had once known it would be. How could she ever have doubted? Maire looked with concern at his face, showing the prison pallor. He had lost weight as well, which was not surprising. But at least he was safe at last! And the hazel eyes glowed as warmly as ever. There was a light dancing in them which Maire read correctly: Alasdair was *enjoying* this adventure. It was exactly the kind of excitement that appealed to him.

He told her briefly about his escape and while he spoke, Maire's eyes dwelt on him tenderly, her thoughts already turning to how she would look after him, how she would feed him properly till he regained his strength, how they would be everything to each other. The physical longing she used to feel for him in the long, lonely days at Loch Mhor, when the ache in her loins was a sharp, wanting pain, was in abeyance. Her feelings had changed; Maire told herself they were more mature.

Alasdair did not need to ask whether she was accompanying him to France. He took it for granted that she was. So Iain was right, Maire thought with a moment's vexation. Why did he always have to be? She looked down at the valise she had packed with her most precious possessions and thought ruefully of all the anguish it had cost her to reach her decision. So much for heart-searching; her lover did not – would never – have any idea. Alasdair was not a person who ever stretched himself on the rack of self-doubt or indecision. She knew him well enough to know that.

The thud of the hooves on the rough track told her that they were between Edinburgh and Leith. The road was full of potholes, which made the coach sway dangerously at times. Alasdair's hand reached out to steady her as the jolting nearly sent Maire out of her seat. He leaned forward to kiss her cheek and murmur in her ear.

"Soon, sweetheart, we will be in France. I shall introduce you to everyone at court – including 'King James' himself. You'll see – you will love it there."

Will I? thought Maire. She found it strange to imagine a royal court across the water with all the panoply of courtiers and servants and titles – yet largely unrecognised by the rest of the world. It seemed to her like living in a world of shadows. She preferred to live openly in the sunlight. However, she said nothing.

A sudden thought struck Alasdair. "The Prince?" he asked Maire urgently. "Is there news of him? Pray God he has not been taken."

"Prince Charles is safe and in hiding," Maire reassured him. "No-one knows where."

"*Grâce à Dieu*," murmured Alasdair, already beginning to think in French. Gloomy memories seemed to descend on him now and he sat, staring into space for a time. Maire was silent, realising that he was reliving the past and, sensitive to his feelings, she did not interrupt his thoughts. When he raised his chin and spoke finally, it was as if he issued a challenge to some ghostly adversary.

"It is not over yet," he said in a harsh whisper. "When Prince Charles returns, we will band together again and try once more. And next time, if God wills it, we will do to them what this time they have done so terribly to us."

Next time! The words filled Maire with horror and dread. He could not mean it, surely. No-one could ask Scotland to endure again what it had suffered, what it was still suffering. Of course, she thought desperately, clutching wildly at straws, Alasdair could know little about all the vengeance taken since Culloden. He'd been incarcerated since the battle. When she told him what the ordinary Highlanders, many of them guiltless, had gone through during Cumberland's policy of fire and sword, he would surely change his mind.

Maire told him all she knew as clearly and vividly as possible. Men hanged because they bore the wrong name, women and children roaming the hills, starving because their homes were burnt, crops destroyed, the clans broken and scattered – even the tartan was forbidden to be worn. At times, her voice trembled but she spared him – and herself – no detail. It was important that Alasdair knew all this.

He listened, his finely-chiselled features becoming harder and more resolute by the minute. "They shall be made to pay!" was all he said.

Maire saw that her account was having the opposite effect to the one she intended. She fell into silence. There was nothing more to say.

The coach thundered on through the Lowland countryside. Maire looked out at the evening sky, at the purple, massing clouds rolling inland, gilded by the orange rays of the setting sun. They must be near the sea by now. Soon their journey would be over.

The rhythmic thud of hooves lulled Maire like a rough lullaby. Fragments of some melody sifted through her disjointed thoughts, dissolving and elusive at first but finally forming a recognisable tune:

Oh waly, waly, but love be bonny,
A little time while it is new!
But when 'tis auld, it waxeth cauld,
And fades away like morning dew –

Maire stopped abruptly, stilling the voice in her head, which sang the lament of the woman deserted and betrayed by her lover. Why should she remember that song? It was a sad, old ballad; a song about the death of love. Very beautiful and haunting, but it belonged to the past. It had nothing to do with her present and certainly not her future. Her lover had not betrayed her; he was devoted as ever. Maire decided she would be glad when they reached the coast; this journey was beginning to unnerve her for some reason.

She had her wish in a few moments for the unmistakable salty odours of a sea port filled the carriage. They were in Leith. The two of them stepped out and Maire sent the carriage on its way; to save time, the driver was already paid.

They walked to the jetty and looked out at the harbour. The boat for the Low Countries had to sail on the evening tide. The captain had warned her he could not wait. He was being well paid – half already and half when the passengers went aboard. Maire had the money ready. Thank goodness they had not been delayed; they ought to be in time. She peered out anxiously, trying to make out the shape of a boat. It was already quite dark. There was no sound but the gentle lapping of the water.

A lone seagull screeched somewhere far above her head. It was a mournful sound, like the cry of a lost child. She remembered the Gaelic superstition that such birds were really the souls of dead sailors. At that moment, she could almost believe it.

Maire felt strangely numb as she stood on the shore of her native land. She could not believe that she might never see Scotland – her beloved Scotland – again. It was difficult to take it in.

A soft whistle came from the water, and a bobbing lantern informed them that the rowing boat was ready to take them out. At the oars was the man who had helped Maire arrange the passage. As soon as he'd learned that it was to oblige the young doctor, nothing had been too much trouble.

Stiffly, because of his bad leg, Alasdair clambered into the boat and turned to hand Maire down. The black mood of depression that had affected him on the journey, passed away. Now that the journey was starting and a new life lay ahead of them, he felt ebullient and full of hope. His old resilience had returned and his hazel eyes glowed warm with love for her.

Maire only hesitated for a moment. She picked up her bag and stepped aboard. She had made her decision. She would do whatever she had to.

***

Iain rode like a man possessed along the Leith road that night. He could not have said what was driving him so; he felt like a man with the Devil on his tail. He only knew he must reach the docks before the boat sailed; he had to see Maire for one last time, if possible.

This night ride had not been planned. He had intended that, should he be fortunate enough to talk his way out of the prison, he would go home and celebrate his release with a stoup of wine with Colly. In the event, the whole episode was easier than he imagined. The Jiley, who was by that time somewhat inebriated, accepted Iain's version of the escape without demur. He looked at the doctor rubbing his brow and knew a moment's panic when he thought of what the authorities would say. He might be blamed for carelessness.

"Ye'll speak up for me, sir, will ye no? Ye'll tell them it wisna' my fault?"

Iain heard the ingratiating whine with secret pleasure. A man on the defensive would hardly be in a position to attack. His story as a doctor was obviously above suspicion. It took Iain five minutes to effect his exit, and he could not believe how quick it was.

That was when he realised that the two fugitives could not be that far ahead of him. They might only be halfway to Leith. An ungovernable impulse drove Iain to seek out a livery stable he knew near Holyrood and hire a horse. He had swung into the saddle and galloped out before he was even sure why he was going. He knew it was completely out of character. But then, Iain smiled ironically as he swayed in the saddle, a lot of his actions seemed to be untypical these days. He concentrated only on the journey then, and he had need to: a stumble on the uneven road could lead to a bad accident.

He made the journey in record time and pulled his horse up by the jetty. Eagerly, he scanned the shoreline for the two familiar figures, especially Maire's. The shore was empty. Iain's heart sank. He was too late. They had gone. Disappointment surged up inside him like bile. Unseeing, he looked out at the Firth of Forth, as empty and desolate as his future life seemed at that moment.

***

The plash of the oars was soothing to Maire. There was something so regular, so rhythmic about them that helped to distance the agonising moments she had just experienced. She thought this must be one of the worst times of her life. To hurt anyone was difficult, to inflict pain deliberately was even harder, but to lacerate someone you loved who also loved you, that must rank as torment, and Maire was in great distress.

She did what she had to do – what in the boat, she gradually came to realise was the only solution. She said goodbye to the man she loved. The pain was like a physical wound; Maire had not known that parting could hurt so keenly. Now she was back in the boat, being rowed to the shore, glad that the dark night cloaked her silent tears. The dream she had cherished was broken.

There was no way she could envisage a future for herself and Alasdair. She had tried. God! How she had tried! It was in vain. He was a Jacobite to the root of his being. Maire knew that she was not and she was too honest to pretend it did not matter. The distance between them was too great; it could only increase with time.

At last, the little boat reached the jetty. She scrambled out clumsily, tears still blinding her. A dark shape emerged from the night, calling forth an involuntary cry from Maire. Then she saw arms reach out to her and realised as she was drawn close to him that it was Iain. He had been on the point of leaving in despair when he saw the boat return with a passenger.

Maire laid her head on his chest and wept unrestrainedly. Somehow she knew that from now on there would no longer be any pretence between them, nor any misunderstanding.

"I – I couldn't go with him. I couldn't leave Scotland." These were the only words she managed to say.

There was no need for words with Iain. He held her to him and, cupping her face in his hands, he kissed her, tenderly at first, then with increasing passion. His heart, dumb for so long, suddenly began to sing. Then he ceased to kiss away her tears and nestled her against his shoulder. It was enough for the moment; he was content. Maire was not his yet but he didn't care. He would wait for her, no matter how long it took.

It was warm and safe in his arms: like finding a haven after all the storms that had tossed her around for so long. She felt strangely secure and it was a good feeling. Moreover, there was a slowly dawning realisation that was wholly unexpected. Through and beyond the anguish which still tore her, Maire became aware of a deep conviction that she had truly come home at last.

AUTHOR'S NOTE

Loch Mhor is a real location but the Macdonald Clan who lives there, is imaginary.

The reader may like to know more details of the historical characters and events in this novel.

CHARLES EDWARD STUART: After Culloden, he spent four months evading Government forces determined to capture him. This part of his life earned him the title of "the Prince in the heather" and he had many hair's breadth escapes. The most famous of these is the one where he cheated the Redcoats by passing as a somewhat clumsy maid-servant of Flora MacDonald, "Betty Burke". This adventure is commemorated in the *Skye Boat Song*:

> *Carry the lad that's born to be King,*
> *Over the sea to Skye.*

At last, a French ship rescued him with some companions from the very coast he had landed on with such high hopes just over a year before. He was destined never to set foot in Scotland again. His legend, however, lives on; he will always be "Bonnie Prince Charlie", "King of the Highland Hearts", "The Young Chevalier" etc., because of the one episode in his life when he came close to altering history. The romantic tale of his doomed Rebellion is the theme of many Scottish songs, such as the jaunty "*Charlie is my Darling*" and the yearning "*Will ye No' Come Back Again?*"

LORD GEORGE MURRAY: One of the last to leave the field after Culloden, his bravery was beyond question. Tact, however, was never his strong point and he had many arguments with the Prince during the campaign. He wrote a letter to Charles immediately after the battle, blaming him for a great deal of the misfortunes that befell the army, including lack of provisions, choice of battlefield, etc. It was a very bitter letter and Charles never forgave him for it. The two men never spoke again.

LOCHIEL: Rescued with Charles in September and sailed to France. He was given a commission in the French army and was thus well provided for, but he never got over the disaster that he had brought on his Clan. He died two years after Culloden, some felt of a broken heart.

LADY ANNE MACINTOSH: Imprisoned for six weeks, for her support of the Jacobites. It was General Hawley's ambition to provide her with a "mahogany gallows and a silken cord" but he was not granted his wish. She was released unharmed.

THE DUKE OF CUMBERLAND: After a fruitless search for the Young Pretender, he returned to London to a hero's welcome. He was called "the martial boy" (though Culloden was his first and only victory) and met with adulation on all sides. Handel wrote *Hail, the Conquering Hero Comes* to celebrate his return. A grateful country increased his personal allowance from £15,000 to £40,000. A fragrant flower, Sweet William, was named after him; in Scotland they named a foul weed "Stinking Billy".

It is an interesting fact that no British regiment now has Culloden among its battle honours.

THE ANATOMY ACT: Passed, at last, in 1832, after public outcry at the notorious murders of Burke and Hare, the Edinburgh body-snatchers, who between 1828 and 1829, killed at least 15 people.